LIGHTHOUSE BAY

# CHRISTMAS LANE

AMY AISLIN

Beta read by LesCourt Author Services
Edited by Meroda UK Editing
Copy editing by Labyrinth Bound Edits
Proofread by Between the Lines Editing
Cover art by Jay Aheer at Simply Defined Art
Interior design and formatting by Champagne Book Design

*To everyone who loves Christmas as much as I do.*

# CHAPTER ONE

*22 days until the parade*

THERE WAS A BUTT STICKING OUT FROM UNDERNEATH the sink in Tiny's Panini. It was a nice butt. Round. Firm. Encased in faded denim.

Zach Greenfeld would know that butt anywhere.

He stopped mid-step on his way into the café from the kitchen and swallowed back drool. Someone bumped into him from behind, making him fumble his box of tea bags. A few of them fell off the top, scattering across the floor.

"Move, Zach."

His older sister, Alana, brushed past him. She turned to that Grade A butt but didn't seem as enamored with it as Zach.

"How's it going, Mr. Stone?"

The butt backed out from underneath the sink, revealing a strong torso, solid shoulders, and corded arms in a white, V-neck, long-sleeved T-shirt, and a narrow face with a slightly pointed chin, long nose, and high forehead. The chin and jaw were unshaven and covered in dark brown scruff liberally peppered with gray, matching the hair on his head that stood up in careless spikes.

Holland Stone could've doubled as a piece of art.

He stood to his full six-foot-two height and dropped a wrench and a flashlight into the toolbox at his feet. "Should be fixed now," he told Alana. Turning the knob on the sink, he let the water run for a few seconds before shutting it off again. "If you have any more problems, let me know."

Alana blew out a relieved breath. "Thank you so much, and I apologize again for bothering you on a Friday evening. I feel like we've called you in here to fix something at least once a week for the past few months."

Holland shrugged. "That's what I'm here for." Crouching, he threw a few more tools back into his toolbox, then snapped it closed. "Call me if you need anything else." He stood, toolbox in hand, making the muscles in his upper arms strain against his shirt. "You guys have a good night." He gave a two-fingered salute and was gone a second later, having grabbed his winter jacket off the coat rack next to the café's front door on his way out.

Zach's shoulders drooped and he almost dropped his box. "He's never going to notice me."

"Who?" Alana looked from him, to the front door where Zach was still gazing morosely, back to Zach, back to the front door, her light brown eyes—identical to Zach's—widening with each head swing. "*Mr. Stone*? You're talking about *Mr. Stone*?"

Zach winced. "Why do you say his name like he's a professor or something?"

"He was your third-grade teacher!"

"Yeah. A million years ago." He placed his box on the counter.

"You're twenty-four," Alana pointed out, her voice at a register that made his ears hurt. "Third grade really wasn't that long ago. But, seriously." Her head swung back to the front door, but Holland was long gone down the dark street.

"*Mr. Stone*? You have a crush on *Mr. Stone*?"

"Shhhh." Zach glanced wildly at the dozen or so seated patrons. All he needed was for small-town gossip about his ill-advised crush to reach Holland's ears. He'd never be able to face the man again. "Will you relax? Nothing's ever going to happen. He only knows me as the guy who keeps calling him over to fix stuff that's broken."

"But...but...it's *Mr. Stone*."

"Can you stop saying his name like that?" Zach picked his wayward tea bags off the floor and threw them into the garbage.

"He's twice your age!"

"Actually, he's only fifteen years older than me."

"*Only*?"

"Oh my god, will you stop screeching? What's the matter with you?"

"It's *Mr.*—"

"Yoo-hoo!" A knock on the countertop. "Alana, darling."

Alana's back tensed and her eyes screamed *Help me!* at Zach.

"Alana? I know you can hear me. You're only two feet away."

Zach choked on a laugh.

Alana pasted an imitation of a smile on her face and turned. "Mrs. Shoemacker. How lovely to see you."

"Mm-hmm." Mrs. Shoemacker's wrinkly lips pressed into a disapproving line. "It's twenty-five days until Christmas, Alana, and I notice you still haven't put up the Christmas lights on the awning outside or any decorations in the front window." She glanced around the café as though a decoration might appear as if by Christmas magic.

Rustic wooden tables and chairs, barn lighting, and local artwork gave Tiny's Panini a homey feel, but there was nary a holiday decoration to be seen.

Alana's fists clenched. "As I told you yesterday, and the day before, and the day before *that,* I'm currently short staffed and haven't had time to decorate. It's on my to-do list. I don't need you to remind me every day."

Mrs. Shoemacker harrumphed. Zach filched a cookie out of the cookie jar and watched in fascination as his sister went toe-to-toe with the head of Lighthouse Bay's Business Improvement Association.

"Well, it seems that I do indeed need to remind you, since the deadline to have the decorations up was the day after Thanksgiving." She paused dramatically, pale gray eyebrows rising up her forehead. "And that was over a week ago."

Zach swallowed the last of his cookie and wiped his hands on his apron. "I'll have them up by the end of the day tomorrow, Mrs. Shoemacker."

"See that you do." She speared Zach with her steely-eyed gaze, then turned back to Alana. "I don't want to have to fine Tiny's Panini for failing to follow the rules. You knew your obligations when you took over running the café from your parents." By *obligations,* she meant the one-hundred-page document that outlined proper business ownership in Lighthouse Bay's downtown area. "We all need to do our part to ensure Christmas Lane is a success."

With that parting shot, she left.

"Christmas Lane." Alana scoffed. "I still think it's stupid."

"I like it," Zach said. Christmas Lane was what the locals referred to Main Street as from Thanksgiving until New Year's Day. All the businesses put up lights and decorations, a Christmas tree stand popped up on the corner of Main and Regent Streets, carolers serenaded pedestrians every weekend in December, and the clock tower at the end of the street lit up red and green every night.

Alana rolled her eyes. "You would. You're obsessed with Christmas."

"*Obsessed* is a harsh word."

"And you can't put up the decorations tomorrow," Alana spoke over him. "You have a job interview."

"It's not going to take all day. I'll put them up in the afternoon, after my interview."

"And who's going to help me here tomorrow afternoon, then?"

"Okay, I'll put them up in the morning."

Alana threw her hands in the air. "Then who's going to help me prep the food?"

Zach took a breath and bit his tongue. Alana knew how to run a business and had kept their parents' café afloat despite the rundown equipment, yet she couldn't seem to find part-time help to save her life. Applicants were either too young, too old, lacked experience, had too much experience, or weren't available the days she needed them. But in a town the size of Lighthouse Bay, Maine, where people tended to move out more frequently than they moved in, she really needed to get over her misgivings because, at this point, she'd never find anyone and Zach would be stuck working for the family business for the rest of his life.

Hurray.

Not that there was anything wrong with working in a café. It just wasn't what he wanted to do with the rest of his life. But it wasn't like jobs in event planning were aplenty, and ones for recent college graduates were even more scarce. Especially since he lacked the coveted experience.

But how was he supposed to get experience if nobody would hire him?

The conundrum of every recent college graduate everywhere.

Even with the holidays upon them, and parties happening everywhere, he *still* couldn't find anything.

The pay at Tiny's Panini wasn't awful, but most of it was going to his student loans. The sooner he found a job in his field, the sooner he could pay them off. He had his side job/ hobby as a calligrapher too, and while the orders coming through his Etsy store weren't huge, they were enough that he could set a little bit of money aside for himself.

To someone else, calligraphy might not appear to be the most interesting of hobbies. But for Zach, it was soothing. In a world that was messy and unorganized, calligraphy was precise yet artistic. A break from the busyness of life. Working his way through a project—invitations, notecards, placeholders, event signage—was almost therapeutic.

"Why don't we just put the decorations up after we close tonight?" he said.

"Because I've been here since six a.m., and I'm tired."

"I'll call Zari. See if she can take my shift tomorrow afternoon, and I can put the decorations up then."

"Okay, thanks." Alana's smile was relieved as she pulled a box of coffee cups from under the counter and replenished their supply next to the coffee maker. "Where's your interview tomorrow again?"

"The Gold Stone hotel chain—"

"Right," Alana interrupted. "In Florida, right?"

"No, their corporate office is in Orlando, but the job I applied for is at their hotel in Portland." Which was only forty minutes away.

"Can you pass me the box of sugar packets?"

Zach sighed and rooted in the cupboard for the box while keeping half an eye on the front door.

In case Holland came back. Which, of course, he didn't.

# CHAPTER TWO

HOLLAND WALKED UNDERNEATH THE AWNING OF Tiny's Panixni, leaving light footprints in last night's dusting of snow, and got a string of Christmas lights in the face for his troubles. Cursing from above had him glancing up to where Zach Greenfeld perched precariously near the top of a rickety ladder, staple gun in one hand, string of lights in the other. One good gust of wind off the Atlantic Ocean and the ladder would topple over like it was made of feathers.

Sure enough, a cold burst of wind swept down Christmas Lane, setting the American flag on top of the souvenir shop across the street flapping furiously. The wooden sign hanging outside the pub swung on its hinges. A stray newspaper went cartwheeling down the sidewalk. The A-frame specials board outside Tiny's Panini fell over. A couple of customers struggled to open the door of Dev's Bakery next door. Wind chimes tinkled from where they hung outside the flower shop two doors down.

And Zach's ladder almost met the ground, taking Zach with it.

"Whoa!" Holland jumped to the rescue and steadied

the ladder before it could fall, bringing him eye level with Zach's feet. He followed the line of Zach's long legs up to his tight butt, framed in skinny jeans that hugged him just right. On anybody else, Holland would've taken a second look at that behind, but on someone Zach's age, it was kind of pervy. And maybe a little bit desperate. Ripping his eyes away, he focused on Zach's purple Converse instead.

"Thanks, kind stranger," Zach called from above, voice thin in the wind, his upper torso hidden by the awning.

Holland snorted a laugh. In a town the size of Lighthouse Bay, very rarely was anybody a stranger.

"Tell me you're not using staples on a fabric awning," Holland said, finally putting two and two together and coming up with one giant mistake.

"What else am I supposed to use?" Zach's voice was tight, as if he'd been at this for a while and was frustrated by the whole process. "I tried clothes pins, but the wind ripped them away."

"What about binder clips? Or better yet, leave the lights off the awning and put them around the windows and door instead. Anything you use on an awning risks getting blown away, especially in winds like this."

Zach's feet shifted. "But the Business Improvement Association's Downtown Business Etiquette Handbook says we have to have lights outside our business to ensure a successful Christmas Lane."

It sounded like he was quoting direct from the hand-book. Which he probably was. Holland tightened his grip on the ladder as wind continued to pummel the street. "Yeah, it says they have to be set up, but it doesn't specify *where* outside."

"It…" A pause as Zach seemed to ponder that. "Holy crap, you're right! Screw this, then." He climbed down, staple gun and lights clutched to his chest, and the other hand steadying himself against the ladder. A trim waist was revealed, then a lithe chest, skinny shoulders, and a flawless visage: satiny, light gold skin, and a rectangular face with a broad forehead; rosebud lips; a strong nose; straight, dark blond eyebrows; honey-colored, hooded eyes; and messy dark blond hair. He was very cute in an eager puppy kind of way.

"Damn Mrs. Shoemacker and her 'the lights need to go on the awning, Zach,'" Zach muttered, doing a fine imitation of Mrs. Shoemacker, who was the head of the BIA and a dozen or so other town committees. Zach's feet hit cement and he looked up at Holland. "Thanks for—Oh! Um, hi. Holland."

"Hi," Holland said.

Zach's cheeks pinked.

"You okay?"

"Uh-huh. Yup!" Zach nodded manically. "I'm great!"

Holland smiled. Eager puppy, indeed.

Zach's cheeks pinked further.

"Can I help you string the lights?"

"Oh no, I'm okay. I'll just—" Zach cut himself off, blinking at Holland. "Actually, yes! Yes, I could use your help." His smile revealed the small dimple in his left cheek.

Holland couldn't help but smile back at him. There was something about Zach, something about the constant smile on his face when they spoke and the way he focused so completely on Holland that always made Holland's stomach flip, like no one else existed for Zach except him. It was a ridiculous notion. Zach probably looked at Holland and saw nothing but an old, nearly completely white-haired guy who used to be his third-grade teacher—and not a very good one at that.

There'd been a time when Holland looked at Zach and saw the amiable yet serious kid he'd once taught. But ever since Zach had come home from college in May—tall, strong, confident, and, most interestingly, gay and out—Holland got a little flutter in his belly every time Zach smiled at him. He was no longer a too-quiet nine-year-old kid, but a thoughtful and motivated twenty-four-year-old hottie ready to take on the world.

"Got anything other than a staple gun to hang these up with?" Holland asked.

They crouched to sort through a box underneath the window. Lights, lights, more lights. Almost as though the Greenfelds were afraid the town would run out of stock. A second staple gun. Tinsel. Garlands. Plastic ornaments. Yet more lights. And there at the bottom: suction cups.

Holland took them out. "Let's use these. See here? We can stick the sucker to the window and thread the wire through this opening." He showed Zach the thin slit on the front they could thread the lights' wire into. "Zach?" He glanced up to find Zach staring at his hands. He bumped their shoulders together. "Zach?"

"Huh? What? Yup, I'm listening."

"Are you sure you're okay?"

"Why wouldn't I be?" Zach stood. "I'll do this side, you do that side?"

"Sure."

Zach dropped his share of the suction cups no less than four times, swearing under his breath each time and sneaking peeks at Holland as if hoping Holland hadn't noticed. The man hadn't been this spacey as a kid when he'd been in Holland's classroom, but then people changed as they grew up.

Teaching had been a mistake of epic proportions.

Hovering parents, demanding children, a school administration living in the dark ages. It might be different now, but fifteen years ago, it had spelled his doom.

Okay, he was being dramatic. It hadn't spelled his doom so much as the realization that he wasn't fit to teach. Or, rather, that he didn't *want* to teach. And he didn't want to manage a bar either, which was what he'd done for almost ten years after his three years of teaching. And bookkeeping? Also not for him. But it was while doing the books for Bud, and watching Bud build beautiful birdhouses from scraps of metal and wood, that he'd realized he wanted to build things too. Somehow, that had turned into being the town handyman, but he didn't mind. He liked fixing things. But building items from scratch was where his passion was.

Which was why he needed to win the annual Lighthouse Bay Christmas Parade Float Competition. He wasn't after the money that was part of the grand prize. What he wanted was the article that'd appear in every newspaper between here and Portland—including Portland. He couldn't ask for better advertising for his two-year-old business if he tried.

He finished sticking the suction cups to the right side of the window and started on the top, meeting Zach in the middle. Zach's fingers brushed his, and the man jumped, sputtering nonsensical apologies. He blushed and retreated to his corner of the window.

Seriously, what was wrong with him?

A couple came out of Tiny's Panini, bringing warm air and the sound of Christmas carols before the door closed behind them.

"How are your parents?" Holland asked as he started stringing the lights through the suction cups. "They like living in the Keys?"

Zach's parents had moved to Key West a few years ago,

after Zach had moved to Portland to attend the University of Southern Maine. He'd started two years late, opting instead to stay home for a couple of years right after high school graduation to help take care of Tiny's Panini when his mom—the Tiny for which the café was named—was diagnosed with breast cancer. She'd beaten it, but it had taken its toll, and she and her husband had retired to Florida, leaving the café in Alana's hands.

"Yeah." Zach grinned. "They keep wondering why they waited so long to move there. Beautiful weather year-round, the beach just steps away, no snow."

"They traded snow for the threat of hurricanes, though. You couldn't ask me to do that." Not that Maine didn't see its share of hurricanes, but the state wasn't as prone to them as Florida.

"Me neither." Zach threaded the lights on his side of the window. "I like snow. Snow means snowboarding. Not that I'll get to do much of it since I'm always here."

"Alana hasn't found a new part-timer yet?"

"Nope." Zach reached up to hang the lights along the top of the window. "The last teenager she interviewed came in smelling like pot."

The wind sent their box skittering down the sidewalk.

"Shit!" Zach chased after it, catching it before it got wedged into a snowbank. He trudged back, hair flapping in the wind, box tucked under one arm. "I could do without this wind, though."

"I vaguely remember you refusing to go out for recess if it was too windy when you were in my class."

"I hate wind. Clothes get wrinkled, things go flying, you have to yell to be heard, hair gets messed up."

"God forbid your hairdo gets ruined."

"Hey." Grinning, Zach waved a string of lights at him.

CHRISTMAS JANE | 13

"When you have hair as awesome as mine, you don't want anything to mess it up."

Zach's dark blond hair was shorn close to his head on the sides but was longer on top. Usually styled so that it swept up his forehead, today the wind teased it, throwing it into charming disarray.

"It is pretty great hair," Holland acknowledged.

Zach seemed to choke on nothing.

"Hey, Holls."

Holland turned at the greeting and smiled at his best friend and once-upon-a-time lover, Clark. "Hey, man."

The same height as Holland, Clark's dark, Italian good looks had charmed the underwear off men and women alike—Holland included, although they hadn't worked out as a couple for reasons that had to do with both of them being tops. Even though he was the same age as Holland, unlike Holland, the lucky son of a bitch didn't have a single gray hair in his shoulder-length, inky black hair, or in the scruff on his face.

"I was just at the hardware store," Clark said. "Marcella says your order came in."

"Yeah, I was on my way there but got sidetracked."

Behind him, Zach gurgled.

Clark leaned around Holland to wave at Zach. "Hey, Zach."

Zach's face had fallen, and the glare he leveled at Clark was so at odds with his normally affable attitude, it had Holland doing a double take. What had Clark done to piss him off?

"Hi," Zach muttered. He shot Holland a pained glance Holland didn't understand and went back to putting up the lights.

Clark raised an eyebrow at Holland.

Holland raised one back. How the hell was he supposed to know?

"Yoo-hoo!"

"Oh god." Zach stiffened. "Tell me she's not headed over here."

From a dozen feet down the sidewalk, Mrs. Shoemacker waved a wrinkled hand in their direction. "Yoo-hoo!"

"Sorry," Holland said to Zach.

"Goddamn it, I'm putting the damn lights up, just like I told her I would this morning. And yesterday. What more does she want?"

"What crawled up your butt and died?" Clark asked him.

It was a valid question.

Zach just scowled at him.

"Yoo-hoo, Zach."

"Yes, Mrs. Shoemacker." Zach turned to face her, a game smile on his face. "As you can see, I'm putting up the lights, as I said I would—"

"I can see that, darling, but that's not why I'm here." She thrust an overflowing binder at Zach. "We need someone to organize the annual Christmas parade."

"Uh, what?" Zach staggered slightly under the weight of the binder.

"What happened to Mr. Barry?" Holland asked.

Mr. Barry had organized the Christmas parade for the past ten years, and he usually started months ahead of time. In February, if Holland wasn't mistaken.

"His poor mother had a fall, the dear," Mrs. Shoemacker said. "Broke her hip. Mr. Barry's currently on his way to Detroit and he won't be back for several weeks. So." She turned to Zach. "We need someone to take over where Mr. Barry left off. You've got a degree or a minor or something in event management, do you not?"

"Actually, it's in hospitality and tourism, and I took all the event management courses available, but—"

"Fantastic! Then it's settled."

Zach's eyes practically bugged out of his head. "You want me to organize a parade that's scheduled for three weeks from now?" Holland read the look on his face clearly: *Lady, are you freakin' crazy*? But Zach opted for diplomacy as he said, "Mrs. Shoemacker, I'd love to help, but I just don't see how that's possible."

Mrs. Shoemacker waved an imperial hand. "You'll do fine. Most of the work is already done. You just need to see it through to its conclusion." She patted the binder in Zach's hands. "Everything you need is in here."

"But—"

"And you'll help, won't you?"

Holland swung his attention off Zach's stupefied face and onto Mrs. Shoemacker, who was staring at him with beady eyes. The calculation on her face didn't bode well. "I'm sorry, what?"

"You've been involved since the beginning, haven't you?"

"Not really. I've just been building my own float."

"In headquarters, yes?"

By *headquarters*, she meant the huge empty warehouse that was used as a staging area for the parade every year.

"Yes, but—"

"Then you'll help Zach out. Introduce him to who's doing what. Show him the ropes."

Zach was frowning. "I don't need help."

Mrs. Shoemacker pounced on that. "So you'll do it?"

"That's not what I—"

"Lovely." She patted his arm. "I look forward to your

status report in three days' time." She took off down the sidewalk, boot heels clicking with each step, giant purse hanging off the crook of her elbow.

"But I didn't say yes," Zach shouted after her. He turned to Holland. "What the hell just happened?"

Clark—who Holland had forgotten stood right next to him—smirked at them. "Seems like you guys got roped into organizing the rest of the parade."

Zach's glare was back, and it landed on the arm Clark draped around Holland's shoulders. The smile he shot Holland was tight-lipped. "Thanks for your help with the lights." He dropped the binder into the box, then picked the box up. "I'm going to help Al with the afternoon coffee rush and finish up later."

"You sure?" Holland narrowed his eyes on Zach. Why was he being weird? "Want me to come back later and help?"

Zach's eyes went to Clark for a second. Back to Holland. "Thanks, but I got it."

"Bye, Zach," Clark said.

Zach turned and went into the café.

Clark smiled at Holland, all teeth and mischievousness. "He has a crush on you."

Holland shrugged out from beneath Clark's arm and headed toward Marcella's Tools & More. "You're delusional."

"And you're blind," Clark called back.

Ignoring him, Holland waved over his shoulder and kept walking.

Zach? A crush on *him*? Beautiful, flawless-skinned, shiny-teethed, likable, perfect Zach had a crush on a guy pushing forty who'd only recently discovered what he wanted to be when he grew up?

Holland snorted as he walked into Marcella's, the bells

on the door ringing.

*You wish.*

At least the binder was organized.

Zach read through Mr. Barry's list of volunteers and tried to commit all the names and roles to memory. There were volunteers helping build the town-sponsored floats. Others would hand out reindeer noses to kids on the day of the parade. Still others were in charge of ensuring each float left the queue at the right time. And yet more would be driving the floats along the parade route.

On top of the parade, it seemed Zach was now in charge of running the Christmas fair too, which was always scheduled to start right after the parade ended. Everyone congregated at the park at the end of town for food, games, and last-minute holiday shopping. But since it started right after the parade, and Zach couldn't be everywhere at once, it meant there were also volunteers to help set up tents and stalls at the park the day before, to help decorate, to put out wares and set up the food the morning of, and to help take everything down the next morning.

Zach's head hurt just thinking about it, but at least Mrs. Shoemacker had one thing right—Mr. Barry had already organized everything and Zach just needed to see it through to completion. He'd spent the last two summers interning in the corporate events department of the Boston Convention and Exhibition Center, but he'd been a lackey, never given much responsibility beyond keeping track of lists and confirming details.

This parade and the Christmas fair were bigger than

anything he'd ever organized.

Whatever. He could totally do this. He might not have the experience, but he had the knowledge. This was what he'd studied, and if he did a good job, maybe it'd convince the Gold Stone hotel chain to hire him for the position in Portland.

He flopped back on the bed, groaning. His lower back hurt from sorting through the boxes in the basement of Tiny's Panini, looking for the Christmas decorations. His shoulders hurt from having his arms suspended, stringing up lights. And his feet hurt. They always hurt. Since Alana couldn't find a new part-timer to save her life, he was stuck picking up the slack, which meant he had a shift every day. Most days. Every day? When had he last had a day off? August? Not since one of Alana's part-timers had moved to Connecticut for college. He was getting tired of the sore feet and of constantly coming home smelling like coffee.

He didn't even like coffee. Just the smell made his nose itch. And never mind getting food on his hands. If there was anything nastier, he didn't know what it was. The plastic gloves he wore for food prep made things only marginally better—he could still feel the sliminess of certain foods.

Like avocado. Ew.

His phone buzzed on the nightstand, and he reached for it blindly. The text was from Alana.

How'd the interview for the Florida job go?

It's not in Florida, it's in Portland he started to type, then erased it and started over. She wouldn't remember anyway. Good. Really good, I think. It's for a junior role, and they said my internships in Boston were exactly the kind of experience they're looking for, so... They still have more candidates to interview. I'll know either way in a few weeks.

Man, he wanted that job. *Needed* it. Otherwise, his feet

might fall off.

His phone buzzed again. An alarm this time, reminding him to get up and get ready for his date. A date he wasn't in the mood for, but the dating app had given them an eighty-seven percent compatibility match, so how could he not go?

Two hours later, he was regretting every decision he'd ever made, especially the one that had had him giving up on ever finding someone special organically and resorting to online dating.

He'd heard the horror stories, yet he'd caved and created a profile anyway. A very *specific* profile that outlined *exactly* what he was looking for. He'd even added a disclaimer to the end of the "What I'm Looking For" section: *I'm looking for a relationship, not a fuck buddy. If you're looking for someone to put out on the first date, look elsewhere.*

That should've been enough of a deterrent for people looking for hookups, but he was proven wrong when, midway through dessert, his date—who was a little too suave, a little too slick, a little too fake for Zach's tastes—said, "So, your place or mine?"

Zach swallowed a resigned sigh. "Did you even read my profile?"

"Sure. I mean, I skimmed it. Most of it." His date, Don, aka Donster1993, removed an invisible piece of lint from his suit jacket. "Okay, I mostly drooled over your profile picture." His smarmy smile was probably supposed to look playful.

Ugh. Zach contained a shudder. He should've known it'd never work out between him and someone with the childish username Donster1993, regardless of that eighty-seven percent compatibility match.

He snagged their waitress's attention. "Can we have the

check, please?"

"Your place then?" Don ran a finger over the back of Zach's hand.

Ick. "Sorry to disappoint," Zach said, reclaiming his hand and fisting it in his lap. "But had you read my profile, you'd know that I'm looking for a relationship, not a fling."

"So?" Don shrugged. "Doesn't mean you can't have a thing on the side with the Donster while you look for The One. A friends-with-benefits kind of thing," he added, as if Zach didn't get it.

"No, thanks," Zach said, as politely as he could when he really just wanted to run from *the Donster*, oh my god. "I don't do that anymore."

Trying-too-hard Don morphed into annoyed-with-a-side-of-disgust. He huffed and slumped in his chair. "You're paying for dinner."

Zach sighed.

Ten minutes later, he was in his ancient car on his way back home from Biddeford, which was about halfway between Lighthouse Bay and Portland, where Don lived. The restaurant had been beautiful, the food delicious, the service top notch. The company?

Disappointing.

Thirteen first dates with thirteen different guys he'd met through his dating app. Conclusion? Online dating was for fools.

Hence, he was a fool.

No wonder he was still single. Who wanted to date a fool?

Back in Lighthouse Bay, his car chugged its way into the parking lot of the Christmas parade's headquarters. Armed with Mr. Barry's binder, he double-checked the sheet tucked into the inside front pocket for the code, input it into the door lock, and stepped into the huge, cavernous space. A huge, cavernous space that should've been empty at this time of night. But a light was on near the back, and the *thunk, thunk, thunk* of a hammer hitting a nail reached his ears.

He bypassed parade floats in various states of construction, tables littered with fabric, cabinets filled with tools, and bunkers piled high with wood. A thin layer of sawdust carpeted the concrete floor. It was chilly in the open space and Zach yanked his scarf up to cover his chin.

In a back corner of the warehouse, where the persistent thunking was coming from, Zach found a mostly built float that took his breath away. Made entirely of wood, it stood on an eighteen-foot-long wheeled platform. Main Street's clock tower stood tall on one end, keeping vigil over a road that bisected the street. On one side of the street: the church, the tallest peak of which was level with the clock tower; Lighthouse Bay Souvenirs; Molly's Fashions; Stefano's Italian Restaurant; Namaste Yoga; Scoop's Ice Cream; Martine's Daycare; Evie's Toy Store. On the other side: the Genealogy Center run by the Historical Society; Pipit's Candy; Dev's Bakery, which supplied its pastries and cakes to Tiny's Panini next door; Flowers by Daisy; The General Store; Rent-A-Bike; Annie's Irish Pub; Marcella's Tools & More. And on the other end of the street from the clock tower: the park, set up with tents and stalls like it was every year for the Christmas fair.

"It's Main Street!"

The thunking stopped, and a graying head popped up from the other side of the float.

"Holland?"

"Zach? What are you doing here?"

Zach waved at the float. "It's Main Street!"

Holland came around to Zach's side, his huge shoulders making Zach feel puny in comparison, even though he was only a couple inches shorter. Hands on his hips, Holland surveyed his own work. "You like it?"

"It's awesome! You've even got The General Store painted just the right shade of brown."

"Yeah, it's not too shabby." Holland rubbed his chin.

"'Not too shabby?' You've got the wooden sign outside Annie's, the flowerpots outside Daisy's. The flag atop the souvenir shop. And look at this—the café has an awning! You even have the white and red columns outside the candy store." He leaned closer to get a better look at the details on the window of Tiny's Panini. It even said *Tiny's Panini* in gold script, an exact replica of the real thing. "This is so cool."

Zach would've sworn Holland's chest puffed out. "Thanks. I'll be putting up the lights next."

"Lights?"

"Christmas lights on all the businesses. It's meant to be Christmas Lane. The clock tower will have a working clock too if it arrives in time."

"Wow," Zach breathed. "This thing's going to be epic. Can I help?"

"Thanks, but…" Holland nodded at the binder in Zach's arms. "I think you'll be plenty busy without the added work."

"Yeah, I guess."

Holland eyed him up and down, and his jaw clenched, eyes darkening. Zach glanced down at himself. Was there something wrong with his outfit? Black boots, dark skinny jeans, purple shirt tucked into his pants. He'd thought the leather jacket—rather than a blazer—would make him look badass. Not that he had any badassery in him, but first

impressions were everything. Not that it had made a difference tonight.

Or maybe it had worked too well.

"You look…nice," Holland finally uttered. "Hot date or
something?"

"Or something." Zach slumped onto a wooden bench
placed against the wall next to Holland's float. "I don't think
I'm made for the dating scene."

Holland's shoulders loosened. "Why do you say that?"

"I just don't understand it. What happened to getting to
know someone before jumping into bed? I spent my entire
college career being someone's one-night stand, and I hated
it. I'm not doing it anymore. I want something solid. Real.
Someone who gets me."

There'd been times in college when Zach had hit it off
with someone at a party and ended up having sex with
them, only for that person to completely dismiss him the
next morning. He always felt used and degraded. Like his
one-night stand couldn't be bothered to give him a second
thought.

And the sex had been…not great. In fact, it was awful.
Nobody told him how awkward and messy sex was or how
much it hurt. Maybe his expectations were too high? It was
his own fault anyway, for equating sex with…not love, but
*like* at least.

Well, he'd learned his lesson. He was done with assholes who made him feel like trash.

Not to mention, he'd never been sexually attracted to
the guys he slept with, although the potential for something more had slept under his skin. Something more that
had flowed between him and his partner while they chatted
each other up prior to jumping into bed. He'd thought the
sex would lead to that *more*, but it never did.

Maybe he was asexual?

"You're looking for someone who doesn't treat you as an afterthought," Holland said, gaze distant.

"Exactly! Why are people such douchebags?"

Holland threw his head back and laughed. The long line of his neck caught Zach's attention, as did the portion of defined pectorals Zach glimpsed through the stretched V of Holland's well-worn T-shirt. Zach gulped. Talk about douchebags; here he was unloading his relationship woes on someone who likely didn't give two shits. Just because he'd been crushing on the guy for months didn't mean his feelings were reciprocated.

Besides, they weren't friends. Not really. Holland was the guy Zach called when something inevitably broke down at Tiny's Panini. Holland came; Holland fixed. The end. This morning Holland hadn't even called Zach a friend when he'd spoken to Clark. Not, "I was on my way to Marcella's, but stopped to help my friend," or even, "Stopped to help Zach." Nope. Holland got *sidetracked*. Zach was a sidetrack.

What did that even mean?

And Clark. Zach wanted to despise the guy simply for having Holland not only as a best friend but as a one-time lover, and he kind of did. Clark, with his swarthy, swoon-worthy Italian good looks, oozing charisma and sex appeal as if he'd been born with them. If that was the kind of guy Holland went for, Zach didn't stand a chance. It didn't help that they were so close and constantly seen together that small-town gossip said they were back together.

Which left Zach nowhere. Not that he'd been anywhere with Holland to begin with, but still.

He cleared his throat and stood, binder hugged to his chest like a shield. "I'll head out. I didn't mean to interrupt your work."

"I don't mind." Holland jerked a thumb over his shoulder. "Did you see Mr. Barry's workstation?"

"He's got an office?"

"I don't know if I'd go that far, but it's certainly a place for you to work."

It was a desk, a small filing cabinet, a desk lamp, and an old, uncomfortable-looking chair. Right across from Holland's float.

Score.

# CHAPTER THREE

*20 days until the parade*

HOLLAND WALKED INTO PARADE HEADQUARTERS THE next morning at eight, expecting to be the first to arrive, but he found Zach at Mr. Barry's workstation. Mr. Barry's binder was open next to him, and he was surrounded by charts, spreadsheets, invoices, and a day planner. Loreena McKennitt's "Good King Wenceslas" played from a set of portable speakers. Zach hummed along as he typed away on a laptop.

Holland's heart skipped a beat. Coming in so early on a Sunday morning wasn't all bad if he got greeted by the sight of a studious Zach.

"You're here early," Holland said.

"Hmm?" Zach glanced up and smiled at him, the dimple appearing in his left cheek. "Yeah, I wanted to get myself organized before I dove into everything."

"I can see that."

On the wall to Zach's right hung three wall calendars. One appeared to have a list of deadlines and to-do items for the parade. The second was for the Christmas fair. And the third was an amalgamation of both. Everything from confirming and re-confirming details with vendors, invoice due dates, volunteer training sessions, and following up with the businesses that'd signed up for a stall at the fair.

A persistent beeping sounded. Zach silenced the alarm on his phone and stood to put on his winter jacket over his jeans and hoodie. "Be right back," he said. Flashing Holland a smile, he was out the door a second later. The music cut out as the door closed behind Zach, so Holland connected his own phone to the speakers and cued up a holiday playlist.

*Right back* was more like forty-five minutes, but when Zach returned, he brought breakfast sandwiches from Tiny's Panini, pastries from Dev's Bakery, and a large thermos of coffee complete with disposable cups, creamers, and sugar packets. The two dozen townsfolk who'd trickled in while he'd been gone jumped to clear a space from one of the tables and helped themselves to breakfast after Zach spread everything out.

"If this is the way you're going to treat us, can you organize the parade next year too?" Holland heard someone say.

"Yeah, right on, Zach."

"Are these Dev's chocolate croissants? I'm going to get fat working for you." A pause, then, "Worth it," mumbled through a full mouth.

"There's tea too," Zach said, retaking his seat at Mr. Barry's desk. Zach's desk now.

"Huh?" Holland stared at him. Mr. Barry was great, but he'd never brought in sustenance for the workers who spent months'-worth of their weekends working on the parade floats, sometimes pulling twelve- or fourteen-hour days, especially the closer it got to Christmas. Crunch time and everybody panicked, putting in more hours. Holland wasn't immune. He'd finish with a few days to spare but was still spending every available free moment in headquarters working on his float.

"Vanilla?" Zach said.

"Vanilla what?"

Zach cocked his head at him. "Tea. You don't drink coffee, right?"

"There's vanilla tea in that second thermos?"

"Hot water. The tea bags are next to it."

"Oh. Wow, thanks, Zach."

Zach shrugged. "No biggie." He focused on something on his laptop and cleared his throat. "I don't drink coffee either. We have that in common." The top of his cheeks pinked.

"I guess so." Since Zach wasn't looking, Holland took the opportunity to study him. His hair was nicely coiffed. The navy hoodie dwarfed him yet was probably warm and cozy. His jeans were an older, looser pair, and today his Converse shoes were yellow.

How many colors did he own? And why didn't he have snow boots?

Holland dismissed the inappropriate flutter in his belly and fixed himself a vanilla tea. Then he chose a second tea bag and doctored another cup. He handed that one to Zach.

From behind the laptop, Zach blinked up at him. "For me?"

"Apple cinnamon, right? No milk, extra sugar?"

Zach's eyes went wide and a tiny, pleased smile quirked his lips.

Holland's shoulders squared, and he held Zach's gaze. *Yeah, I pay attention too.*

"Thanks." Zach took the cup.

Holland winked at him and went to work on his float.

Except he kept getting distracted by Zach's presence.

And was it his imagination or was Zach sneaking peeks at him too?

It was on the sixth such occasion, Zach smiling shyly and quickly looking away when Holland caught him staring, that Holland broke the silence between them.

"Are you feeling better?"

"Feeling better?" Zach parroted.

"You seemed kind of down last night."

"Oh." Zach snorted and rolled his eyes, presumably at himself. "Yeah, sorry for dumping my relationship challenges on you. I guess I'd reached that hopeless, nothing's-ever-gonna-change stage."

"Things don't seem so hopeless this morning?" Zach was way too good to be someone's one-night stand. He deserved someone who'd respect him, who'd cherish him, who'd encourage him and never let the light in his eyes die. Holland didn't know what he'd do if Zach's glow ever dimmed.

Their eyes met across ten feet of empty space. An electrical current supercharged Holland's veins, and his heart kicked up a notch. Sweat slicked his palms, and he almost dropped the hammer onto his foot.

"I don't know yet," Zach said over the din of construction and conversation, appearing to choose his words carefully. "There's something I thought would never happen, and it might actually be possible. But…" He stared at Holland like he was expecting a response of some sort. He swallowed hard, Adam's apple bobbing. Holland followed the motion. "But it's hard to say at this point. So maybe I'm not feeling so hopeless, but not quite hope*ful* either. Somewhere in the middle?" He raised an eyebrow, a dare challenging Holland to…reciprocate?

Holy shit, was Zach actually into Holland like Holland

was into him?

The raised eyebrow became two, and a tiny smirk lifted Zach's lips.

Well, fuck him stupid.

Holland took a step toward him. "Zach—"

"Hey, Holls."

Clark appeared at Holland's elbow, dressed in insulated hiking boots, waterproof pants, and a puffy weatherproof jacket. His hair was tied back at the nape of his neck, and a wool hat covered his head.

"Are you freakin' kidding me?" Zach muttered under his breath.

"Clark?" Holland's head took a second to reorient itself, instinct wanting to take him toward Zach, but years of friendship forcing him to greet Clark instead. "Are you taking a group hiking?"

"Yeah, I'm meeting a few guests from the B&B at the trailhead in a bit." Clark ran a hand down the side of the clock tower. "I wanted to come by and see how your float's coming along first. It's great, Holls!"

"Thanks." Holland turned to Zach, only to find the chair behind the desk empty. He sought Zach out and found him at the food table, refilling his teacup and shooting Clark dark looks in between keeping an eye on the water level in his cup.

*Are you freakin' kidding me, indeed.* If Clark had ruined the one potential shot he could've had with Zach, his best friend would never hear the end of it. Although, realistically, it was probably going to be Holland who never heard the end of the I-told-you-so's from Clark when Clark found out he'd been right about Zach's crush.

"There are a lot of great floats, though," Clark said, oblivious to Holland's distraction. "You've got some competition on your hands."

"Yeah, I know."

Zach made his way back to his desk, cup in hand, eyes pinging from Clark to Holland and back, a question written all over his face. Holland knew about the small-town gossip that claimed he and Clark were back together, but he'd never seen any reason to dissuade it.

Until now.

*They're not true!* he wanted to shout at Zach. *I haven't looked at anybody but you since you moved back from college seven months ago.*

"Hey, Zach?" Clark said when Zach retook his seat. "I noticed that in amongst these parade floats, none of them are for Santa."

"You mean the final float?" Zach blew on his tea to cool it. Holland tried not to let the image of Zach's pursed lips take over his imagination. "Nobody wanted to build it, so Mr. Barry's arranged to borrow one from…" Zach consulted something in Mr. Barry's enormous binder. "Manchester, New Hampshire. They had their parade last week." From outside came the high-pitched squeal of a large truck coming to a stop. Zach checked his watch and stood. "Actually, that should be it."

"Question," Clark muttered to Holland as they followed Zach outside. "Why wouldn't anyone want to build the most anticipated float?"

"*Because* it's the most anticipated. Would you want the job of building Santa's float? The one *all* of the kids are most looking forward to?"

"Good point."

Outside, the sky was overcast, the wind cold enough to hurt. Holland eyed Clark's winter jacket with envy.

A guy maybe a few years older than Zach, wearing a

flannel shirt underneath a puffy vest, jumped down from the cabin and met Zach halfway across the parking lot.

"Mr. Barry? I'm Todd."

"Zach Greenfeld." Zach shook Todd's hand. "I took over from Mr. Barry. Is this my float?"

"Um." Todd took the red baseball hat off his head and worried it in his hands. "About that. Maybe it's best if I just show you."

"Show me what?" Zach's tone was wary.

"Just…" Todd turned, heading for the back of the trailer, and waved at Zach to follow him.

Zach glanced at Holland over his shoulder, worry coloring his honey eyes. Holland steered him forward with a hand at his lower back and said, "Come on. Let's see what's wrong."

Inside the trailer's cargo space, Santa's sleigh tilted to the left. One of the runners was twisted and bent, the other missing entirely. The red fabric was spotted with what appeared to be mud, dirt, and random wet patches. The string of lights slung around the body of the sleigh drooped to the ground, most of its mini lights smashed and broken.

Zach's mouth dropped open. Clark whistled low and long.

"Where's the rest of it?" Holland asked. "I'm assuming the float had more than just a broken sleigh."

"Well, see, that's the thing." Todd continued to wring his hat. "We sort of had a little… accident. After our parade." He waved his hat at the sleigh. "This is all that survived."

Zach finally found his voice. "Why weren't we told?"

Todd shrugged. "I don't know, man. You'd have to ask Bob Lewis, the parade lead. I'm just the driver."

"Why would he send me a broken sleigh?"

"He thought you might be able to salvage it."

Holland climbed into the trailer and surveyed the damage to the sleigh. The remaining runner could be fixed, and a new one could be built and attached to replace the missing one. The lights were replaceable. He pressed his hand against the mysterious wet spot in the fabric. Melted snow most likely. The fabric was a goner, but if he ripped it up…

"I can fix this for you, Zach."

"Thanks, Holland, but it's one piece. I need an entire float. Where am I supposed to get one on such short notice?"

Holland took in Zach's stooped shoulders and the lines in his furrowed brow. The way he chewed his bottom lip. The circles under his eyes that hadn't been there yesterday.

And made an offer he'd never regret, even if it set him back on his own float and cost him the competition.

"I can build Santa's float for you."

Clark coughed. "In three weeks?"

"Thank you." Zach shot Holland a thin-lipped smile. "But I can't ask you to do that."

"You didn't ask." Holland hopped out of the trailer, coming face-to-face with Zach. He squeezed Zach's bicep. "I offered."

Zach's entire body softened, and he rested a hand on Holland's forearm. "Thank you, really. But you need to focus on your own float. I'll figure something out. You'll see." A game smile graced his face. "Everything'll be fine."

Everything was not fine.

Zach sat at a table in Tiny's Panini two hours after closing later that day and crossed the last town off his list. After he, Holland, and Todd had unloaded the damaged sleigh from the truck, Zach had spent all morning and a part of the afternoon before his shift at the café calling neighboring towns. And then not-so-neighboring towns. And then major cities. Every place he could think of within a two-hundred-mile radius.

But towns either didn't have a Santa float to loan him, couldn't get it to him in time, or flat out didn't want to give it to him.

Okay, that was fine. He could just purchase one online. An optimistic thought that yielded zero results. Nobody sold entire floats. Parts, yes. Those might come in handy, so he bookmarked those sites and started cold-calling construction workers, woodworkers, and carpenters. Could anybody build him a float last minute?

He got laughed at.

Out of ideas, Zach scrubbed his hands over his face. An acoustic cover of "Have Yourself a Merry Little Christmas" played from his laptop. Instant tears pricked his eyes as the guitar chords washed over and through him, and the harmonies touched his heart. No matter the version, his favorite Christmas song never failed to bring out the feels. Something about it made him ache.

He'd turned the lights off in the café, leaving only the white fairy lights he'd strung on the walls and around the front windows yesterday. Faux-pine garlands hung from the rafters, decorated with delicate ornaments hanging by red-and-green thread. A nutcracker sat atop the fireplace mantle. Each table was adorned with a white candle set in a red glass bowl. All that was missing was a Christmas tree.

Sitting alone in an empty café while, out on the street, townsfolk walked by in pairs or small groups, either heading home after work or doing some holiday shopping, Zach

CHRISTMAS JANE | 35

had never felt more alone in his life.

With a lump in his throat, Zach considered a visit with Alana, but he'd spent half the day working with her and they definitely needed a break from each other. He'd never been good at making friends in elementary or high school so didn't have any nearby ones to call on. He could call Dev from the bakery next door. They were friendly. Sort of. Or he could drive into Portland and hang out with some of his friends from college.

Before he could fall further into his pity party for one, the bells on the door jangled as the door opened. "Sorry, we're…"

"Closed," Holland finished for him, shutting the door behind him. "I know. I was on my way home and saw you. Thought I'd see how you're holding up."

Zach shook off the surprise and ignored the pitter-patter of his heart. Just the sight of Holland smiling at him caused butterflies to erupt in his stomach and his neck to break out in a nervous sweat. That Holland had sought him out at all after Zach had uncharacteristically called him out on the attraction between them this morning was a good sign. Meant he hadn't completely freaked him out.

Besides, Zach wasn't even sure the attraction went both ways. Sure, he'd thought he'd seen something in Holland's eyes today, something in the way Holland kept glancing at Zach when he thought Zach wasn't looking. Or maybe that was Holland wondering how an inexperienced kid like Zach was going to pull off this parade.

Or maybe he was easily distracted. Who the hell knew?

But the more he'd thought about it, the more Zach had convinced himself he'd been seeing things, and that brief moment of hope from earlier had turned defeatist.

Holland took a seat across from Zach at the table and

shed his winter coat, draping it over the back of the empty chair to his right. He nodded at Zach's inherited binder. "Any luck finding a Santa float?"

"Nope." Zach slammed the binder closed. "Think we could go without one this year?"

"Sure. Why not?"

Zach stared at Holland. "Wait, seriously? I was kidding. Sort of."

"Nothing says Santa's float has to be the traditional sleigh, reindeer, Santa's workshop, the North Pole, whatever. We could use one of the floats we're already building."

Zach thought of the floats at headquarters. Holland's Christmas Lane. Evie's Toy Store's ice castle. Pipit's Candy's gingerbread house. There was also, among others, a nativity float, a winter sport float, an anime float, a nursery rhymes float, and one based on a video game.

"I guess we could try with Evie's ice castle?" Santa would probably have a hard time maneuvering from one side to the other, and the spectators wouldn't be able to see him if he was on the other side, which kind of defeated the purpose of Santa at all. "Or maybe not. Maybe I could build one?"

Holland didn't outright laugh in Zach's face, but his lips twitched before he got them under control.

Zach sighed. "Yeah, I know."

"Here." Holland pulled a piece of paper, folded in four, out of his pocket. Spreading it out onto the table, he turned the design to face Zach. "I'll fix the sleigh, load it onto a flatbed, add some snow around it, some presents, throw some three-feet tall candy canes along the perimeter, and boom. Problem solved."

"It does look pretty simple."

"Simple, but Christmassy. Pretty."

Of course. Holland would want it to reflect his skills. He wouldn't want to associate his name, his business, with something that was clearly a half-assed attempt.

"Are you sure about this, Holland? I don't want this to interfere with your Christmas Lane float."

"It won't."

Zach raised an eyebrow, disbelieving.

"It won't," Holland repeated, refolding his design and tucking it into the back pocket of his jeans. "I'm almost done building my float, so I shouldn't be too pressed for time."

"I'll agree with one condition. You let me find you some volunteers."

"Good luck with that. Everyone's already overworked this time of year."

"I'll figure it out." Zach played with the frayed edge of the binder. "Thank you. Really. I'm sorry I couldn't figure out another solution."

Holland winked at him. "Not your fault."

*A wink!* That was twice today Holland had winked at him. What did it mean? Did he do it with everyone?

He probably did it with everyone.

"You done here?" Holland stood and slipped into his coat. "Can I walk you home?"

"I live upstairs. Above the café? I moved out of my parents' at the end of the summer."

"Right. Forgot about that. Didn't like living there with just Alana for company?"

"Living together *and* working together?" Zach shook his head. "We were constantly sniping at each other, so I left rather than murder Al in her sleep."

Holland laughed and pulled a pair of leather gloves out of his coat pocket. He looked like Zach's wildest dream come true, standing there grinning, pulling on his gloves as if he had all the time in the world. He cured Zach's loneliness and Zach wanted to bask in his presence, extend their time together just a little bit.

Zach bit his lip, then blurted, "Can I walk you home instead?"

Holland's eyes crinkled when he smiled. "Thanks, but it's cold. Might as well stay here where it's warm. No sense in going out if you don't have to."

Disappointment slumped Zach's shoulders, made his body heavy. Twice he'd put himself out there today, and twice Holland hadn't taken the bait.

Guess that answered every unasked question, didn't it? Holland didn't want him.

"Right. Well…" Zach cleared the lump from his throat and forced a smile he didn't feel. "Thanks again for volunteering to make Santa's float."

"You're welcome." Holland studied him for a few seconds, eyes shrewd. He opened his mouth, then seemed to think better of whatever he was going to say before settling on, "See you around, Zach," and seeing himself out the door.

Leaving Zach all alone again.

# CHAPTER FOUR

*18 days until the parade*

TWO DAYS LATER AND HOLLAND HADN'T SEEN ZACH around parade headquarters since the damaged sleigh incident. And yet they still had fresh coffee, hot water for tea, and pastries that were brought in several times a day, even though it was only Holland and a couple other people working in the afternoon of a weekday.

"Holland?"

He felt Zach's absence acutely. Sure, they'd only worked together in this building once, but Zach had a soothing presence about him, a way of making Holland feel settled.

"Holland?"

The look that had crossed Zach's face when Holland turned down his offer to walk him home still made him wince. He'd hurt Zach's feelings. Zach might as well have offered himself on a goddamn silver platter, and what had Holland done? Rejected him.

Not once, but twice.

"Hel*looo*? Holls?"

Zach couldn't have made it clearer that he was interested in him. Holland had been so shocked when Zach had put himself out there a second time that he hadn't known quite how to respond and ended up making Zach feel like shit.

*Smooth, Holls. Real smooth.*

In his defense, he was still shocked Zach wanted someone like him at all. Clearly their age difference meant nothing to Zach, so why should it matter to Holland? Truth was, Zach was more mature than a lot of people Holland's own age.

"Yo!"

A flick on his forehead.

"Ow!" Holland jerked back and rubbed the sore spot. "The fuck?"

"I called you three times." Dev headed back to his painting project. "What do you think? Is this what you wanted?"

Holland had adapted his design for Santa's float slightly. Instead of a sleigh on snow, he'd built a raised wooden platform over the last couple of days that the sleigh would balance on, pulled by a pair of wooden reindeer he'd borrowed from his neighbor—she of the excessive Christmas decorations who always had some to spare. The platform would be painted midnight blue and dotted with stars, the sleigh made to appear like it was flying through the sky. Dev, his cousin, was one of the two volunteers Zach had recruited for him, although Holland had yet to hear from the second one, whoever it was. All Zach's text had said was Your 2nd volunteer will meet you at HQ late afternoon today. Well, it was late afternoon and no second volunteer had materialized.

"Do you think it's too dark?" Dev was saying. He picked up a piece of wood from the table and held it out to Holland. "I think I did a layer too many. Here, this is one with a layer less."

Holland inspected both pieces of wood, then handed

one back to Dev. "Yeah, the lighter one's good. Thanks."

Dev started painting the platform, side-eyeing Holland at the same time. Holland grabbed a paint bucket and took up position on the other side of the platform, opposite Dev.

"Everything okay?" Dev said. His too-long, light brown hair was held back from his face by a red bandana, and he wore an old T-shirt with holes in the armpits over baggy jeans with rips in the knees. He looked like a teenager, but he was only five years younger than Holland.

"Why wouldn't it be?" Realizing he'd forgotten a paint-brush, Holland unearthed one from his supply cabinet.

"You're distracted today."

Holland shook his head. "Just…got a lot on my mind."

"Worried about getting this done in time? Who's your other volunteer, anyway?"

"No idea. Zach said he—or she, I guess—would be here late this afternoon, so…" Holland shrugged. "Guess we'll find out soon."

"Who do you think it'll be?" Dev asked with a smirk. "I think it'll be…Curtis Crandall."

Holland stared at his cousin. "He's seven."

"So? Even seven-year-old hands are better than none. Who do you think it'll be?"

"Mrs. Shoemacker."

Dev cracked up.

"Hey, it's not out of the realm of possibility," Holland insisted. "I think she'd pitch in in a heartbeat if she knew the jam we're in."

"Maybe she does know. Didn't you say Zach had to re-port in to her today? Did he tell her? I think not, seeing as Mrs. Shoemacker—" He made a point of looking around. "—isn't here."

"Actually, I did tell her," came Zach's voice from behind

Holland. "And she has full confidence in my abilities to see the parade and fair through to completion. *With* a Santa float and sans her help."

Holland whirled.

And dropped the paintbrush on his shoe, splattering blue paint over his old runners. "Damn it."

Zach was dressed in loose jeans and black Converse. He shed his winter coat and revealed a baggy, olive green T-shirt underneath an old, unbuttoned shirt three sizes too big. If Holland googled "woodworker" he'd probably find hundreds of images of people wearing the same thing. Out of a large canvas bag, Zach removed a small toolbox, several paintbrushes, old rags, and a multi-pocket apron he slipped on over his head.

It made Holland grin.

Zach flushed.

From the other side of the warehouse, retired Mr. and Mrs. Columbus waved at Zach from where they were working on one of the town-sponsored floats and thanked him for keeping them sugared and caffeinated.

"What are you doing here?" Holland asked. "Your second volunteer couldn't make it?"

Squaring his shoulders, Zach said, "I'm your second volunteer."

Holland swallowed hard. Hanging out with Zach every day? Watching him work? Talking to him? Getting to know him beyond the surface stuff Holland already knew?

Sign him up!

Except… "Are you sure you have the time? With the café and the parade?"

"The café's the café," Zach said with a shrug. "As for the parade, Mrs. Shoemacker was right. Mr. Barry organized everything already. I just have to see things through without fucking them up." He pulled a music player out of the bag. "Should we put some Christmas music on? Get in the spirit of things?"

Holland glanced around the warehouse at the dozen or so floats and tables littered with red-and-green fabric and various decorations. "Not sure you can get more in the spirit than this place."

"Oh. Right." Zach looked up from where he was fiddling with the wireless speaker, trying to get his player to connect. "Well, we don't have to listen to Christmas music. I have other stuff."

"No, no," Holland backtracked. He hadn't meant to make Zach second-guess himself. "Christmas is fine."

"I have Top 40." Zach bit his lip and scrolled through his playlists. "Some country. Some indie stuff. Classic—I mean, uh, rock. Punk rock. Lots of it."

Dev turned a laugh into a cough.

"Have you got 'The Cowboy's Christmas Ball'?" Holland asked.

Zach's grin showed his surprise. And that adorable dimple. "Hell yeah."

Holland ignored Dev's curious gaze and watched Zach as he cued up the song, then tucked his paintbrushes into the various pockets of his apron. When he glanced up, Holland was standing there aimlessly, paintbrush in hand, smiling stupidly at Zach.

"Um." Zach ran his hands down his apron. "Is this okay?"

"Yeah. You look good. I mean, uh…" Holland coughed. "You look…ready to work."

A loud *thud* had them both turning to Dev.

"Not to interrupt whatever this is—" He waved a hand between them. "—but is anybody going to help me?" He bent and lifted a second can of paint onto the platform.

They got to work, each taking a corner of the platform. Zach hummed along to The Killers under his breath, and his butt bopped with the beat of the music. Dev caught Holland staring and raised an eyebrow. Holland paid him no mind and focused on painting.

"Holland, have you been keeping your receipts?" Zach asked a few minutes later.

"Receipts for what?"

Zach gestured at the float. "For this. Santa's float is one of the town-sponsored ones, which means the town pays for it. We were renting the one from Manchester."

"Are you still paying them even though it came broken?"

"Nope." Zach's grin was a little evil. And a lot hot. "Bob Lewis and I had a long chat about that this morning. Lighthouse Bay is being refunded, which means those funds are being redirected to you. So keep your receipts."

"I've got 'em somewhere." Holland took his wallet out of the back pocket of his jeans and pulled out the stack of receipts folded inside.

"You have them here? Hang on a sec." Zach disappeared outside, but was back less than a minute later, shivering from the cold and carrying his binder and two day planners. He held his hand out for Holland's receipts, reviewed them, then removed an expense claim form from the binder, filled it out, and had Holland sign and date it. "If I submit this tomorrow," Zach told him, "you should have a check next Friday."

"No rush," Holland said, distracted by a tab in Zach's binder with *secret* written in capital letters. "What else have you got in here?" He flipped the tab, only for Zach to slam his hand down on top of it mid-flip.

"That's not for you." Zach scowled and turned Holland

around, pushing him back to his side of the platform. "That's a secret project. My eyes only."

"Is it for the parade? The fair?"

"Maybe."

"You should tell me," Holland insisted. "Mrs. Shoemacker tasked me with helping you, remember?"

Zach scoffed. "Nice try."

"Hmm." Holland resumed painting. "I'll get it out of you. I have a thing about mysteries."

"I don't know what that means."

"I'll give you an example," Dev piped in with a grin.

"Dev." Holland put a warning in his voice.

Dev cheerily carried on. "You know those mystery packages you get at the dollar store, or, like, Hot Topic? Usually they're key chains or mini figurines? 'A mystery in every bag! Collect them all!' Well, Holland's collected them all."

Holland flicked paint off his brush in Dev's direction.

"Really?" Zach's grin was delighted. "Why? What do you do with them? Do you display them somewhere?"

"They go into a shoebox under his bed."

Holland glared at his cousin. "Seriously?"

"Why bother, then?" Zach asked.

"I just…" Holland sighed. "I don't know. It's hard to explain. It's like opening a present. The anticipation of not knowing, and then the pleasure of finding out what's inside."

"Even if whatever's inside is just going to end up hidden under the bed?"

"It's not about the item itself. It's…the discovery, I guess? I'm not explaining it well."

"Weird, right?" Dev said.

"Not really." Zach's smile for Holland was soft. "You're curious by nature."

"I guess?"

"Besides, we all have our idiosyncrasies." Zach pointed his paintbrush at Dev. "Even you."

"What? I am a perfectly balanced human being."

"You've been playing the same song on repeat while baking since you were fifteen," Holland said.

"It's a good song!"

"Aqua's 'Barbie Girl?' Really?"

"It's a classic."

Zach was laughing at them, and when Holland met his eyes, a little flutter erupted in his stomach, something he hadn't felt since his last relationship crashed and burned.

The flutter lasted until Dev said, "Did you get that job in Florida, Zach?"

Florida? Zach was looking for jobs out of state? Holland understood the need to look elsewhere. For recent graduates, competing against other recent graduates plus the rest of the workforce? The pickings were slim. You went where the jobs were.

But Florida?

There was no way Holland could do the long-distance thing again. Been there, done that, had the public social media breakup to prove it.

And hadn't Zach said, just the other day, that he wouldn't want to live in Florida?

"I didn't apply for a job in Florida," Zach said, and Holland's spirits soared. "It's in Portland."

"Oh. Jennifer Wakefield came into the bakery the other day and mentioned something about Florida."

"Alana," Zach muttered under his breath. "Never listens. No," he said, louder. "It's definitely in Portland. And I haven't heard yet, so fingers crossed."

"So you're not moving to Florida?" Holland asked,

needing confirmation. If he was going to maybe—hope-fully—start something with Zach, he needed to know he wasn't going to put his heart out there again only for it to get stomped on. Because what he felt for Zach had the potential to grow into something huge. Maybe even bigger than what he'd felt for Mika Jones, his childhood friend turned lover who'd moved to Los Angeles to pursue an acting career over five years ago. The guy Holland had intended to marry be-fore Mika cheated on him.

Holland wasn't still nursing a broken heart over it. But the effects of Mika's betrayal still lingered, and sometimes Holland thought himself too jaded for someone as young and exuberant as Zach.

"Hell no." Zach snorted. "Perpetual summer? No thanks."

"I know what you mean," Dev said. "I wouldn't want to live anywhere else. In fact, one of these days I'm going to buy the lighthouse."

"The lighthouse?" Zach looked up from his paint job. "The old, decrepit one at Harper's Point?"

"That's the one."

"You want to *live* there?" The horror in Zach's voice made Holland laugh. It was tinged slightly with relief.

"In the house next to it," Dev clarified.

Zach's mouth dropped open. "Dude, that place is haunted."

"That's what I've been telling him," Holland said.

Dev wagged his eyebrows. "That's what makes it awesome."

Hours later, Zach flopped belly-first onto the bench next to Holland's Christmas Lane float, legs sticking out the end. "Why do my shoulders hurt?"

"Because you painted four coats of cosmic navy onto the top of the platform with a paint roller?" Holland said from the food table.

"Was it four? I lost count after two. Do I smell apple cinnamon?"

Footsteps sounded as Holland approached. "You'll have to sit up if you want this."

"I don't know if I want to. This bench is surprisingly comfy."

"Of course it is. I built it."

"Really?" That got Zach moving. He sat up and inspected the bench. The seat was made of polished wood, the legs and arms curved wrought iron. The back was wooden with inlaid scrollwork made of intricately detailed iron. Zach ran his hand over the top, which rose and dipped like waves in the ocean, perfect crests swelling and gentling. "It's beautiful. Why is it in here and not in a park or overlooking the ocean?"

"It's for the park at the end of Main." Holland sat next to Zach and handed him his tea. "It's going next to the gazebo."

"Under the willow tree? I always thought a bench was needed there. It has a perfect view of the whole park." Zach clutched the paper cup in his hands, savoring the heat that seeped through. Resisting the urge to cuddle closer to Holland's warmth, he took a sip of his perfectly prepared tea and sighed deeply. He had no idea how Holland knew how he took it and didn't care. It was nice that someone paid attention.

Next to him, Holland's sigh mimicked Zach's, making

them chuckle.

"Thanks again for your help with this float," Zach said. "I don't know what I would've done without you."

"You would've figured it out." Holland stretched his arm across the back of the bench, fingers brushing the collar of Zach's shirt. Zach's heart sped up at Holland's proximity. "Tell me about this job Dev was talking about," Holland said. "The one in Portland. Not Florida, right?"

"No, not Florida." Why did Holland keep asking about that? "It's for a junior events coordination role at a hotel downtown Portland. I'd be in charge of corporate events hosted by the hotel for a hundred attendees or less. Seminars, workshops, corporate retreats, team building events, holiday parties. That kind of thing."

"And is that what you want to do?"

"Yes?"

Holland's expression was disbelieving.

"Truthfully, I think it'd be great experience." Zach shifted on the bench so he was half turned toward Holland. "But I want to plan events that mean something, you know? Recognition events or charity fundraisers or…town parades. If Mr. Barry retired tomorrow, I'd lobby for his job in a heartbeat."

"Maybe he needs an assistant."

"I'm surprised he doesn't have one, actually. It's not just the parade and Christmas fair he organizes. He does the summer farmers market, the lobster festival, the sandcastle competition, the annual Christmas tree lighting ceremony. I'm sure I'm forgetting a whole bunch. I don't know how he does it all on his own."

"I admire you for knowing what you want to do with your life," Holland said. "Not everyone's lucky enough to figure it out so early."

Zach grunted. "Most of my friends from college changed majors at least once."

"But not you."

"No, I did."

"Really?" Holland leaned back, his fingers brushing the base of Zach's neck when he moved. Zach shivered. "What'd you start out in?"

"Philosophy."

Holland squinted at him.

"I know." Zach chuckled. "Not at all me, right?"

"Why philosophy?"

"I don't know. At the time, I thought I had to study a subject that means something. Stupid, right?"

"It's not stupid to want to make a difference." Holland's voice was soft, intimate.

"Yeah, I know. It took me a while, but I finally realized there are other ways to do that."

Holland sipped his tea. "Why do you think I became a teacher? I wanted to make a difference."

Folding one leg underneath him, Zach turned fully toward Holland. "Why'd you quit? You were a good teacher."

Scoffing, Holland shook his head.

"What? You were," Zach insisted. "You knew how to make class fun. How to speak to the students without talking down to them. How to teach material so it was understandable. I always wondered why you stopped."

"It was different than I expected." Holland tapped a finger against his cup. "You expect to go into a classroom and be in charge, but the truth is you're not. The principal isn't even in charge. It's the parents who run the show. Parents and the administration. I remember sitting in a meeting and being told to limit story time because it's not valuable class time." He laughed under his breath, but it lacked amusement. "Kids deserve the magic of a story. They deserve to learn that reading can be for pleasure. But try telling the administration that. It was soul sucking. I wanted to stay for the kids, but at the end of the day…" He shrugged. "I just couldn't. I wasn't happy."

"I'm sorry." Zach squeezed Holland's forearm. "I didn't know."

Holland's lips tilted. "Not your fault."

Zach's phone vibrated in his pocket and he jolted. Removing it, he swore under his breath at the notification from the dating app he'd yet to delete—apparently it had found someone else he had an eighty-seven percent compatibility match with—and quickly swiped the alert away.

Too late. Holland had seen. His expression closed off, and he shot Zach a tight-lipped smile. "Didn't know you were into the online dating scene."

"I'm not. I mean, I was, but… I just keep forgetting to delete it." Or maybe, given that Holland didn't want him, he'd keep it and go on as many first dates as he had to until he found The One.

"Online dating not for you?"

Zach rolled his eyes. "Oh my god, let me count the ways."

"Now I need to know," Holland insisted. He nudged Zach's knee. "Come on, you can tell me on the walk home."

They bundled into their winter outerwear and found lids for their teacups before exiting the building, locking it up behind them. The stars shone, tiny points of brilliant light in a midnight-dark sky. Zach pulled his scarf over his chin and stuffed a hand in his pocket, clutching his tea close to his chest with the other.

The clock tower was lit in green and red, and every storefront was festooned with lights and decorations for the holidays. More lights were wrapped around tree trunks and lampposts. All the shops and restaurants were closed for the night, and it was just Zach and Holland heading down Main Street. It would've been romantic under different circumstances.

"Where are your gloves?" Holland asked.

"Um, in my car?"

"Speaking of your car, I heard it go put-put-putting down the street the other day." Holland paused on the sidewalk, placed his tea on a bench outside Pipit's Candy, and took off his leather gloves. "Are you sure it's safe to drive?"

Zach winced. *Putting* was certainly a good word. "I haven't had any issues recently. It's just loud lately for some reason. What are you doing?"

"You're shivering so much I'm afraid you're going to fall to pieces." Holland tugged Zach's hand out of his pocket and pulled his own glove onto it.

"What about you?" Zach's heart warmed at the gesture, but he refused to read anything into it. Holland was methodical as he transferred Zach's tea to his gloved hand and slipped the second glove on. His calluses were rough against Zach's skin, shooting tingles up Zach's arm.

"Don't worry about me," Holland said. "I tend to run warm."

That was true. Holland's hands radiated heat where they brushed against Zach's.

Done outfitting Zach, Holland picked up his tea and nudged Zach into resuming their walk. "So tell me some online dating horror stories."

"Where do I start? Oh, I know. How about with the guy who brought his chinchilla to dinner?"

"You're kidding."

"Nope. We went to a pub and got chicken wings, and

he kept pulling the bread off and putting it in his backpack. When I called him on it, he said he was feeding Libby. Then he pulls out a chinchilla, and when I started playing with it, he got mad and put it back in his bag."

Holland laughed.

"And there was another guy who showed up with laminated copies of his own poems and asked me to read and critique them."

"How were they?" Holland asked, still laughing.

"Bloodthirsty."

Holland regarded him for a second, before asking, "What it is you were hoping to find by going on these dates?"

"It's silly when I think about it, but…I guess I was looking for The One. Or at least some spark of recognition that this person *could* be The One. Isn't that how it works? You meet someone and boom! You're like 'I'm going to marry this person one day.'"

"I don't think it works that way for everybody."

"It wasn't like that for you and…uh… Crap, sorry." *Smooth, Zach.* Bring up the ex-boyfriend that broke Holland's heart.

"With me and Mika?" Holland grunted. "No, we were friends for a long time before it evolved into something more."

"I'm sorry I brought it up."

Holland bumped their shoulders. "It's fine. It was a long time ago."

Five years to be exact. Zach remembered the gossip that had swept through town at the time. Holland was generally a private person, so Zach had no idea how word of Holland and Mika's breakup had started, but he recalled hearing that Holland had seen pictures on Facebook of

Mika kissing and cuddling some other guy, only three months after Mika had moved to Los Angeles to try and make it as an actor.

To find out via social media that the person you were in love with was seeing someone else? Town gossip had spread, claiming that Holland was nursing a broken heart, and gossip hadn't linked him with anybody since. Except Clark, but it was apparently a friends-with-benefits kind of thing.

"Was it hard maintaining a long-distance relationship?" Zach asked.

"Yeah," Holland said, bluntly honest. "I understood Mika's need to try to make his dreams come true, and it sucked that he had to leave to do that, but despite that we still intended to get married someday."

Zach contemplated that for a second. "I didn't know that."

"Yeah, the long-distance thing? I don't think it's something I could do again."

Zach didn't think he'd be able to do it again either after being so horribly burned.

By silent, mutual agreement, they went passed Tiny's Panini without stopping for Zach to go home. Zach held in a secret smile. Was it possible Holland wanted to spend more time with him? As they passed Flowers by Daisy, The General Store, Rent-A-Bike, Annie's Irish Pub, Marcella's Tools & More, and entered the park, it sure seemed like it. Holland might not want Zach like Zach wanted him, but that didn't mean they couldn't be friends.

It was better than nothing.

Considering Lighthouse Bay's small size, the park was relatively large. A white gazebo strung with lights and garlands, lots of green space under a blanket of pristine snow, a paved walking/biking path, a huge playground, multiple benches. Right in the middle was a twenty-foot tall Christmas tree lit with multicolored lights and topped with a white star. They strolled through the park, arms occasionally brushing, sipping their teas. It smelled fresh and wet, and it was quiet save for the sound of ocean waves hitting the cliffs in the distance.

"When I was a kid," Holland said, breaking the peaceful silence of the night, "there was an outdoor skating rink in this park. That building over there—" He gestured at a wooden structure large enough to fit a single car into, which had fallen into disrepair. "—used to be a little warming hut with hot chocolate and snacks."

"Yeah, there are old black-and-white pictures of the old ice rink at the café on the east wall." Zach kicked at a rock. "How come they don't do it anymore?"

"One year it wasn't cold enough to sustain throughout the winter, and…" Holland shrugged. "I guess they just never bothered bringing it back after that."

"Hmm." Zach finished his tea and threw his cup away into the next trashcan they passed. "Mom and Dad used to take Al and me to an outdoor rink in Portland when we were little, but I never really liked it."

"How come?"

"I was a small kid. Didn't hit my growth spurt until I was eighteen, so I got pushed around a lot when I was younger."

"You were bullied?" Holland's voice was sharp, a whip in the night.

"No," Zach said slowly. "No, not bullied so much as… unnoticed. Since I was so small, other people didn't see me and they'd run into me, knocking me onto the ice. Eventually, I learned to skate along the perimeter, but still.

I never really enjoyed it."

"You mentioned snowboarding the other day. That's more your thing?"

Zach smiled. "I love snowboarding. You ever tried it?"

"No. I do ski, though."

"Yeah? We should go sometime," Zach said without thinking.

Holland's smile was slow to form, yet it was soft under the light of the lamp post they ambled under. "I'd like that. Maybe after Christmas, once the holiday crazy dies down and I don't have two floats to build."

Zach tensed.

"I didn't say that to make you feel bad." Holland squeezed Zach's shoulder. "Just pointing out that we're both busy. We both essentially have two jobs."

Zach: café worker and parade organizer.

Holland: town handyman and float builder.

Zach sighed. "True. I don't think I've had a day off from the café since August."

"I'm pretty sure that's illegal."

"It's my parents' café. It's not like I'm going to report my sister for overscheduling me. I'm happy to help."

"She still hasn't found anyone? I swear that *We're Hiring* sign has been in your window forever."

"I don't even think she's actively trying anymore."

"You could quit and force her hand."

Zach stopped right there on the path.

"Uh, Zach?" Holland peered at him. "I was kidding."

"Yeah." Zach huffed, breath pluming out in front of him. "It's not a bad idea, except then I'd be out of a job." No job equaled no income. His calligraphy business wasn't big enough to sustain him.

"You work for the town now, though."

"Temporarily," Zach reminded Holland. "Mr. Barry won't be gone forever."

The path took them to the other side of the park where it curved and led to a stone bridge that arched over a tiny creek that was currently frozen.

Zach hopped up to sit on the wall, the stone ice cold under his butt. "This is my favorite place in Lakeshore."

From here, he could see the entire park. Dead ahead was the town Christmas tree. On either side, Christmas Lane stretched toward the clock tower, which itself reached toward the sky in its red-and-green brilliance.

In the summer, the park was usually occupied late into the night with dog walkers, joggers, and people enjoying the summer weather. The creek could be heard bubbling gently, the trees were in full bloom and teeming with life, and the salt of the ocean could be smelled on the air.

Now, it was just him and Holland taking in the Christmas atmosphere on a cold winter night. With anybody else it could've been a date.

With Holland…

Zach wished it was a date.

It started to snow gently, fat flakes landing on their heads and shoulders. The music from John Williams's "Somewhere in My Memory" popped into his head and he scooted closer to Holland.

"I can see why you love it." Holland leaned against the wall next to him. "My favorite place was always the marina where my dad taught me to sail."

"I didn't know you sailed." Their voices were quiet in the still air, as if they didn't want to disturb the peace of the night.

"I don't. I never took to it. I didn't like being on the ocean. It's…"

"A big, scary pool of water that can eat you?"

Holland let loose a surprised burst of laughter. "Yeah. Exactly."

"So why is the marina your favorite place, then?"

"I spent a lot of time there with my dad growing up. Got lots of good memories. Come on." Holland gave Zach's arm a tug. "Let's get you home. Your nose is so red it looks like it's going to fall off."

The cold had made his nose runny and Zach sniffled. "Okay." Hopping off the wall, he tugged his scarf over his mouth and nose as they continued their walk. "How are your parents? I don't see them much."

"They don't come back often. They like living in Atlanta with my sister."

A string of lights had fallen off the bottom of the Christmas tree, lights casting eerie shadows against the snow. Zach fixed it, then stood gazing at the tree for a moment. A piece of litter had embedded itself into a branch. Zach removed it and shoved it in his pocket to throw away later.

"Christmas is my favorite time of year," he said.

"You don't say."

Something soft hit him in the back. Whirling, he gaped at a smirking Holland, then at the crumbled snowball at his feet.

"You didn't!"

Holland's smile widened. "Oh, I did. What are you gonna do about it?"

This was a new side to Holland. One Zach was totally on board with. He grinned and scooped up some snow. "It's on!" A second snowball hit him in the shoulder. He straightened, gave a war cry, and—

Where'd Holland go?

*Whack.* A snowball to the back of the head. Pieces flaked off and fell down the back of his jacket.

"Ahhhhh!" Hopping around, he tried to get it out to the chorus of Holland's laughter. "Cold, cold, cold."

Holland poked his head out from the other side of the Christmas tree. Another snowball hit Zach in the thigh.

"Oh, this is *war*, Holland!" Giving a great cry, Zach tackled Holland to the ground. Snow sprayed in an arc around them, getting everywhere. In their hair, in their boots, up pant legs, underneath jackets that got rucked up as they tumbled, exposing skin to the elements.

"Ha ha!" Zach crowed from atop Holland, where he straddled Holland's thighs, arms in the air in triumph. "I win!"

"You think so?" Holland flipped them, and all of a sudden, Zach found himself on his back, staring up at a laughing Holland.

He froze as calloused fingertips lightly brushed his cheek, sweeping away a small patch of snow. Holland's hair, mostly white with streaks of dark brown, almost sparkled in the brilliant lights of the tree. His weight pressed Zach into the snowy ground, but Zach didn't register the cold or the hard earth. Pressed together from thigh to chest, all Zach felt was Holland's hard body against his own. His heart pumped. What would he see in Holland's eyes if Zach met them? Curious and apprehensive in equal measure, Zach lifted his gaze.

Holland's eyes, the color of faded denim in the light of day, were black as the night against a backdrop of red, green, blue, and white lights that shone from the tree. Only inches away, they locked with Zach's. Zach's breath left him in a rush, fanning against Holland's face. Holland's gaze dropped to Zach's lips.

Zach quivered, waiting.

Clearing his throat, Holland stood, towering above Zach at his full six-foot-two height. He held out a hand. "Let me walk you home."

Zach slumped deeper into the snow and closed his eyes against the disappointment.

"Zach?"

Smiling gamely, Zach took Holland's hand and let Holland pull him up and walk him home.

# CHAPTER FIVE

*16 days until the parade*

Two days later, Zach sat at Mr. Barry's desk in parade headquarters early in the morning. He was alone save for a handful of retirees who'd volunteered to build the town-sponsored floats.

Without Holland to ogle as he worked, it was kind of boring. So Zach removed himself from headquarters and headed to Tiny's Panini to snag a table and get some work done.

He should've known better. Tiny's was the congregation place for early morning small-town gossip.

A chorus of "Hi, Zach" greeted him when he walked in. There was a handful of people in line at the counter where Alana and Zari served coffee, grilled breakfast sandwiches, and sold pastries.

Zach chose a table in the back corner, underneath a circular wall clock five times the size of his head, shed his winter coat, and opened Mr. Barry's binder to the *secret* tab.

And tried to ignore the conversation around him.

"I heard they drove up to Portland last week," Hank said, rapping large knuckles on the tabletop.

"They had a date." Rosie, a young single mom of two,

giggled. "Left the kids with her mom and took a mini vacation."

"Speaking of dates." Jean, one of Zach's mom's best friends, swung her chair around to face Zach with an impish smile. "How did yours go last weekend, Zach?"

Zach blinked at her. Glanced around. Every customer, except for the ones still in line, now eyed him with curiosity.

Goddamn small towns. Just because there was nothing to do didn't give everyone leave to get up in his business.

"How'd you know I went on a date?"

"Heard it from Rosie."

"And I heard it from Dev, who heard it from Jennifer."

Jennifer Wakefield, Alana's best friend, toasted him with her coffee cup. "And I heard it from Al."

Zach sighed. Stupid small towns. Jennifer was incapable of holding her tongue, and it drove Zach crazy that Alana told her everything.

"It was…fine," Zach said.

"Fine," Jean repeated. "Mm-hmm. And what was wrong with this one?"

"He referred to himself as *the Donster*."

Hank snorted. At the next table over, Charlie said, "And remind me what was wrong with the one before that? Was he the one with the unibrow?"

"No, the last one spent their entire date Instagramming their food," Michaela piped in.

"And wasn't there one who brought his sister?" Rosie said.

That had actually been a fun date. Hugh was his sister's guardian, and since he hadn't been able to find a sitter, they'd gone to an arcade in Portland. The sparks hadn't flown, but they'd had a good time.

"And there was one who didn't show up at all."

Yeah, that had been fun.

"One brought his pet, didn't he?"

Ah, Libby the chinchilla.

Seriously. He was never telling Alana anything ever again.

"He's just picky, our Zach," Jean said.

He wasn't picky. He just had trouble connecting romantically and sexually with another person. The interest was there. He *wanted* to connect, wanted to be part of a couple, a tandem, a unit. Have someone to rely on and share memories with and build a life with, but…

Maybe he was aromantic? Aromantic *and* asexual?

But that couldn't be right. He had romantic feelings for Holland. He'd had romantic feelings for a couple of people in college, but it hadn't been instant. Just like his feelings for Holland hadn't slammed into him out of nowhere. They'd blossomed over the course of the last few months, when Zach saw much more of Holland than he had since third grade, since Holland was always at the café fixing broken equipment.

Ugh. Sexuality was confusing.

"Hey, Zach," Jennifer said. "Did you get that job in Florida?"

*It's not in Florida!*

But before he could answer, Jean started talking about her brother's best friend's sister who lived in Jacksonville and did they know the Atlantic Ocean was different in Florida than in Maine?

The door opened and in walked a perfectly put-together Mrs. Shoemacker, pale gray hair coiffed to a shine, toting an extra large purse on her elbow, lips pursed in disapproval.

From the order counter, Alana stiffened and met Zach's

gaze. Zach shrugged. He had no idea. They'd decorated to the nines, so whatever Mrs. Shoemacher was displeased about must have to do with something else.

"Yoo-hoo! Alana, dear." Mrs. Shoemacker's boots click-clacked on the wooden floor. "Why isn't there any Christmas music playing, hmm?"

Or maybe not.

Alana's smile was strained. "Right. Sorry. Forgot to turn on the sound system this morning."

She did just that, and the soothing croon of Frank Sinatra's "Have Yourself a Merry Little Christmas" floated through the speakers. Zach closed his eyes and let the music wash over him, humming under his breath.

A communal groan went through the café.

"Not this one, Al," Jennifer said.

"Yeah." Jean patted Zach's arm. "We all know how weepy our Zach gets at this song."

Stupid small towns.

Holland was stepping out of Marcella's Tools & More when he heard it, the *put-put-put* of Zach's car coming down Main. Stuffing the receipt for his preordered materials into his pocket, he stepped into the middle of the street.

Zach screeched to a halt.

"What the hell, Holland?" Zach said, stepping out of the car. His eyes flashed. "I could've hit you."

Unlikely, given that he was a dozen feet away.

Holland grinned at him. "Where are you off to?"

"I'm…" Zach glanced around, and Holland easily read

the expression on his face—*are we really having a conversation in the middle of the road?*

Indeed they were. There were no other cars on the street, so who cared?

"I'm going to Portland," Zach finally said, "to pick up some materials for the town-sponsored floats."

Holland jerked his chin at Zach's car. "In that?"

Zach squinted at him. "Yes?"

"Seriously?" Could Zach not hear that rattling coming from the engine? The car, which was from the nineties, was clearly on its last legs. "Why don't I drive us instead?"

"Um…"

"I've got to pick up a few things, anyway." Lies, but Zach didn't need to know that.

"You don't think my car will make it there."

"I really don't."

"Okay. Thank you." Zach gestured at the car. "Get in. I'll drive us to your place."

Holland's house was a little two-story Craftsman bungalow at the end of a quiet, tree-lined street only a couple of minutes' drive from downtown. Skeletal branches, devoid of leaves, reached over the single lane road, meeting in the middle to create a simulated archway. This late in the morning, it was quiet, most of the residents off to work.

Zach parked in Holland's driveway, next to Holland's truck, and they exited the vehicle.

"I've got to grab a couple of things from inside," Holland said.

He led the way into the house, Zach trailing behind, head swiveling, trying to take everything in at once. Holland took his boots off, then headed into the kitchen where he grabbed bottled waters and snacks for the road—granola bars, a box of crackers, and a couple of apples. When he returned to the foyer, Zach was sitting on the floor petting Tadashi.

"I didn't know you have a cat," Zach said, grinning as Tadashi started to purr.

"He's Dev's."

"What's his name?"

"Tadashi Hamada."

Zach threw his head back and laughed. The scarf around his neck unwound, revealing the slim column of his throat. "From *Big Hero 6*?" He picked the cat up and brought him up to eye level. "You don't look much like a cartoon character, but you sure are cute."

The little black fur ball swiped a playful paw at Zach.

"Dev lives here too?" Zach asked, letting Tadashi knead at the fabric of his coat.

"Yeah." Holland grabbed a small reusable grocery bag from the closet and deposited his snacks into it. "He moved in with us when he was five, after his parents died. I was ten. When I moved out of my parents' house and bought this place, he sort of just…followed along like a lost puppy."

Dev was no longer that lost puppy, that scared, sad, broken, quiet little boy he'd been. But he still took comfort in the familiar, in family. For him, Holland, their house, and Lighthouse Bay were home.

"But he's determined to buy the lighthouse, and I think he might have enough for a down payment soon, so we'll see how long he stays. You ready to go?"

"Yeah." Zach set Tadashi down. "Bye, Tadashi. Be good." To Holland: "Got everything you need?"

Holland held up his bag. "Snacks for the road."

"Ooh, good thinking." Zach stood and brushed off the seat of his pants. "I'm starving. Breakfast was hours ago."

"Here." Holland handed him a granola bar as they headed back out into the sunlit cold.

They drove to Portland in contented silence. Zach tapped away on his phone for most of the drive, and at one point, he took Mr. Barry's enormous binder out of the backpack at his feet and started making notes in the section marked *secret* between checking his phone and updating two separate day planners.

Holland turned the radio on low, anything to distract him from the way Zach's hair fell over his forehead and how he chewed the end of his pen while muttering to himself under his breath. It proved fruitless when Zach started to hum softly, then sing along to the Christmas pop song, his voice settling into the pit of Holland's stomach like a love song.

He cleared his throat. "Where to first?"

"Huh?" Zach lifted his head and looked out the windshield. "Oh, we're here. The stores I need are downtown. Why don't you drop me off and you can come get me when you finish your errands?"

"I'm sure I'll find what I'm looking for downtown."

They stopped at a souvenir store first, where Zach bought two dozen tie-dyed T-shirts in eye-blistering colors. Then it was a boutique where they picked up what seemed like yards and yards of green and red fabric that had apparently been preordered weeks ago. After that, the Christmas store, where a college-aged part-timer took two trips with his dolly to bring out a dozen boxes. Good thing Holland's truck bed was big. How had Zach expected to fit everything into his little car?

"What are these?" Holland asked Zach as the part-timer loaded the last box into the truck.

Zach shrugged. "No idea. Something for the Drakes'

float. They're working on one of the town-sponsored ones. My notes from Mr. Barry said to pick them up today."

After the Christmas store, it was Coastal Maine Popcorn. Zach bought a bag of the chocolate bacon flavor.

"Who's that for?"

Zach's grin was full of mischief. "Me." He'd eaten most of Holland's snacks and was still hungry? "Don't worry, I'll share."

Which he did, but it turned out chocolate bacon flavored popcorn was rather odd. Holland told Zach he could keep it.

It was sometime around midafternoon, when Zach had finished his shopping, that he asked Holland for the fifth time, "Which store do you need to go to?"

And Holland deflected—again. "I'll know it when I see it."

Zach stopped on the sidewalk and sucked a piece of popcorn off his thumb, eyes narrowed on Holland. "You didn't have any errands to run, did you?"

Holland shot him a smile. "Guilty." In fact, he'd be back on Saturday to pick up materials that wouldn't arrive until then.

"Hmm." Zach started walking again, towards Holland's truck parked on the street further down, and closed his popcorn bag with a twist tie. "You were that worried my car wouldn't make it?"

"Maybe. Or maybe I just wanted to spend time with you."

Zach snorted. Tucking the popcorn bag under his arm like a football, he pulled a pair of gloves from his coat pocket and slid them on. Holland didn't fail to notice that they were *his* gloves, the ones he'd lent Zach a few days ago when they'd taken their late-night walk.

"You don't believe me?"

Zach side-eyed him. "Why would someone like you want to spend more time with someone like me?"

"I don't understand the comparison."

"You're…" Zach waved a hand at him. "And I'm…" He gestured at himself.

"You're what? A reliable, mature adult? Someone who was responsible enough a few years ago to realize that his family needed him and stayed to help instead of leaving for college like I'm sure you wanted to? Someone who jumped into Mr. Barry's role with both feet, hit the ground running, and never looked back? Someone who's kind, smart, funny, and always willing to help?"

Steps slowing, head cocked, Zach seemed to listen with every molecule in his body. "That's how you see me?"

Holland nodded. "I admire the hell out of you, Zach."

A small smile graced Zach's lips. Teeth bit into his lower lip, as though trying to contain his pleasure from seeping out into the world. "I admire the hell out of you too."

"Me?" Holland rolled his eyes at himself. "I spent most of my life trying to figure out what to do with the rest of it."

"Yeah, but you didn't quit." Zach's smile for Holland was pure admiration and something more, something deeper. Something that hit Holland in the solar plexus and caught in his throat, making it difficult to draw breath. "You kept going until you found your passion. Some people stay stuck in a job they hate their whole lives."

They reached Holland's truck. Holland opened the passenger side door for Zach, who flashed him a quick grin as he hopped inside, settling into the dark brown leather bucket seat. The popcorn bag went on the floor by his feet, next to his backpack, and he turned to put on his seat belt.

His brows went down when he noticed Holland still standing there holding the door open. "Everything okay?"

"Have dinner with me tonight."

Zach paused, seat belt strap held in one hand, and stared at Holland. He blinked once. Twice. His mouth opened, then closed again. That thing that had settled in Holland's solar plexus, hot and heavy and familiar despite not having felt it since Mika, rose up into his chest and kick-started his heart at the twin blooms of color that blushed Zach's cheeks.

"I... You mean..." Zach gulped. "Like a... Like a..."

"A date?" Holland leaned a forearm against the top of the doorframe and leaned closer, drawn in by Zach's sudden insecurity. "Yes, like a date."

Zach turned sideways in the seat, feet propped on the running board, bringing him within inches of Holland, as if he too wanted to eliminate the distance between them. "I have to work the dinner shift at the café tonight. But... tomorrow?"

"Why don't you come after your shift? I'll make us something." Tiny's Panini wasn't actually open for dinner since Lighthouse Bay had other restaurants that catered to the evening crowd. But it did offer pre-made soup and sandwiches for people looking for a last-minute solution, as long as they ordered by five and picked it up by seven. "How about...?" Holland leaned closer, biting back a grin when Zach's honey eyes flared. "Chocolate chip pancakes?"

"Breakfast for dinner?"

"Why not?" He wanted to know what Zach tasted like with lips dotted in maple syrup.

"Okay." Zach played with Holland's scarf, fingers dragging through the tassels on the end. "I'd like that."

It wasn't until Holland had mixed the dry ingredients together that he realized he was out of chocolate chips. Storing the milk back in the fridge, he left everything else sitting on the counter. Open bags of flour, sugar, and salt. The egg carton. A stick of butter. The stirring spoon poking over the edge of the mixing bowl, and various measuring cups in different sizes. Bundling into his winter outerwear, he took his truck to The General Store rather than walk to save time. Zach was due for dinner in an hour.

Of course, Lighthouse Bay being the town that it was, what should've been a ten-minute trip ended up taking more than forty-five.

First, he got stopped by Rosie, who couldn't decide what shade of nearly identical blue to paint her youngest's room in.

"What do you think, Holland? The summer ocean or the whimsical sea?"

Then Mrs. Shoemacker spotted him on her way to the cash register, basket full of vegetables. "Yoo-hoo! Holland! How's Santa's float coming along?"

And Kevin, the evening part-timer, took ten minutes to track down chocolate chips in the storage room. "I'm so sorry." Kevin puffed as he came out of the back room with a large cardboard box filled with bags of chocolate. "I didn't realize there weren't any left on the shelf."

Just as Holland was about to leave, chocolate chips paid for, feet itching to get home, the town mayor's SUV pulled to a stop on the street outside the store. He exited and waved at Holland. "I'm thinking of having a deck built onto the house this summer," he said as his large feet clomped onto the sidewalk, "but I wanted to get your opinion first. What are your thoughts on decks versus porches?"

Did no one understand that he had a date to prepare for? He'd even convinced Dev to find someplace else to spend his evening so he and Zach could have the place to themselves.

Holland spent ten minutes debating the merits of decks and porches with the mayor, slowly inching his way toward his truck at the same time, Mr. Mayor following doggedly when all Holland wanted was to get away. When the mayor switched to gazebos versus pergolas, Holland nearly lost it.

He gritted his teeth against the urge to tell the mayor to go away. Finally, while Mr. Mayor was describing his backyard in painful detail, Holland put up a hand, told the mayor he had somewhere to be, and drove away faster than you could say, "I have a date!"

Well, if there was one good thing about forty-five minutes worth of unwanted conversations, it was that it had distracted him from the nerves and self-doubt that had plagued him all afternoon.

Had he made the right decision, asking Zach on a date? The age gap between them notwithstanding, it had been so long since Holland had even considered getting involved with someone past a one-night hookup that he was left a bit shaken at the prospect of something more. Not since Mika had he felt anything past simple desire, which was all he'd ever felt upon meeting someone he was sexually attracted to in a bar in Biddeford or Portland. Not since Mika had he allowed himself to experience anything resembling actual…emotion, for lack of a better word. Oh, the desire was there; he wanted Zach. But he was also cap-tivated by Zach's internal beauty, awed by his strength and maturity, astounded by his generosity and commitment, charmed by the bouts of shyness that were so at odds with the confidence he'd found in college, enthralled by his bright eyes and sunny smile that often seemed like it was for Holland and Holland alone.

He wanted to know Zach as a *person*, not just a body to warm his bed.

And that was terrifying.

But if he looked past the nerves that made his hands sweat against the steering wheel, past the fear that kicked his gut into cramps, there was nothing but Zach, and the knowledge that if Holland let himself fall, they could have something incredibly special.

Zach called to him like nobody else ever had, not even Mika.

He pulled into his driveway with minutes to spare be-fore Zach's arrival. Grabbing the chocolate chips off the passenger seat, he climbed out of the car and bounced up the porch steps.

"Holland!"

He whirled at his name. There was Zach, bundled in a thick coat, scarf pulled over his chin, and wearing Holland's gloves. He walked up the street in the dark to-ward Holland, streetlights and Christmas decorations from neighboring houses casting him in white, red, and green, a moving holiday centerpiece. He lifted a hand in a wave; the other clutched a small bouquet of flowers to his chest, most likely purchased from Flowers by Daisy.

The sight of those flowers turned Holland's heart to mush, made little stinging hornets go crazy in his bel-ly, flying in giddy happiness at the simple pleasure of watching Zach's face light up as he trotted up Holland's driveway.

Before Holland could greet him, meet him halfway, kiss him silly...all of the above...the front door opened behind him and he suddenly found himself in a lip-lock, an eager, pushy, wet tongue down his throat, and hard, grabby hands clamped onto his butt.

# CHAPTER SIX

Z ACH GASPED. OF THEIR OWN VOLITION, HIS FEET stopped moving, and he came to a standstill three-quarters up the driveway, next to Holland's massive truck.

Some guy was kissing Holland. *His* Holland. In the glow of the house's outdoor lighting, and in the bright flare of the white fairy lights strung along the porch and supporting columns, Zach made out the side profile of a man who was about five foot ten, with a button nose, high forehead, and artfully shaggy blond hair.

Mika Jones.

But…how? Why?

Sound faded. The prickle of cold wind against his face diminished. Colors became washed out. His vision tunneled and all he saw, all he registered, was Holland kissing someone else.

What had happened in the few hours they'd been apart? Since Holland had asked him to dinner this afternoon to the present? Mika had come strolling back into Holland's life, probably all apologies and big, pleading night-dark eyes, and Holland had forgiven and forgotten? Conveniently relegating Zach back to a…a…a sidetrack?

Holland had been ready to marry Mika, so of course—
*of course*—he'd take Mika back. Had Holland been waiting for Mika to come home for the past five years? And
tonight's date was what? A way to kill time with Zach while
he waited patiently for the love of his life to return?

Zach's heart stuttered, and his shoulders sagged. His
arms hung by his sides, useless in the face of such a blow.
The flowers dangled from one hand, the perfect blooms
he'd picked just for Holland scattering to the icy ground,
falling like lost hope. Amaryllis for Holland's inner beauty.
Gardenia because its snow-white petals reminded him of
Holland's hair. Daffodils for this new beginning between
them. A bird of paradise to signify Zach's own joy. Blue iris
for hope. And a single red rose. Daisy had offered to wrap
the flowers for him, but Zach had wanted to do it himself, choosing just the right shade of blue tissue paper that
matched Holland's faded denim eyes, then tying everything
together in a delicate ribbon, white to represent the start
of something new. The bouquet was a riot of color, some
that didn't even complement each other, but Zach knew
Holland wouldn't care.

No. He wouldn't care at all.

Zach took a bracing step back. Another. Pressure built
in his chest, tightening his lungs. His eyes blurred, wet-
ness hitting his cheeks, throat burning as he swallowed
a sob. He'd spent the past couple of hours floating on an
ocean of bliss, anticipating the moment when he showed
up at Holland's doorstep for chocolate chip pancakes.
Anticipating what the evening might bring, what it might
lead to.

To have those hopes crash to the ground with a bloody
hammer left him aching. Aching and lonelier than he'd ever
been.

His breathing hitched, a choked sob breaking free as he turned and walked away from every wish he'd ever had where Holland was the star and Zach was grateful to orbit his brilliance.

There was a commotion behind him: harsh words, raised voices. Holland called Zach's name.

Zach walked faster, tears wetting his lips, and didn't look back.

Holland jerked back and wiped his mouth with the back of his hand.

"What the fuck, Mika?"

"Well, hello to you too." Mika cocked a hip, stylish oversized sweater exposing a slim shoulder, hair falling around his face in waves.

What the hell was he doing here? And more importantly…

Where was Zach?

"Zach!" Holland called to Zach's retreating back, but Zach just walked faster until he was almost running. "Zach, wait!"

Zach turned the corner…

And was gone.

"Fuck!"

"Not exactly the homecoming I was expecting."

Holland rounded on Mika. "Are you kidding me right now? What the hell are you doing here?"

"Came to visit my parents for the holidays. Thought you and I could…" Mika shrugged, sweater slipping lower. "Rekindle things temporarily?"

"Seriously? You show up after five years and expect to pick up where we left off? After you dumped me?"

Under the porch lights, Mika's eye roll was enormous. "You broke up with me."

"Yeah, after you posted pictures to Facebook of you making out with some guy. What did you expect after that?" Holland stood on the top step and peered into the distance, but Zach, unsurprisingly, didn't return.

"It wasn't serious between José and me. I told you that then. It was just a bit of…fun on the side."

"And you thought it was okay to cheat on me just because we were a few thousand miles apart?"

Mika rested soft hands on Holland's shoulders. "Baby—"

Holland shrugged out of his grip so fast he almost lost his footing on the stairs. "Don't touch me." He descended the stairs, heading for his truck.

Where would Zach go? Home, most likely. Holland could walk there in a few minutes or drive there in one. Reaching for his truck's handle, he—

"Where are you going?" Mika asked from the porch. "After that guy who was here? He your new boyfriend or something? What is he, like, twelve?"

Holland slid into the car and took a look at Mika through the windshield. Artsy, paper-thin, cowl-neck sweater not meant for Maine's winter. Shiny, black leggings. Calf-height socks. Leather slippers. He wasn't dressed for the outdoors, which meant he'd been inside for some time. Enough time to get comfortable and stake his claim.

"Fuck that."

He'd read online once that you should change your locks when your ex moved out. Nobody in Lighthouse Bay locked their doors, so Holland had never seen the need.

Now he certainly understood the appeal.

Exiting his truck, he slammed the door behind him, clomped up the porch steps, strode past an irritated Mika, and went inside. He didn't bother removing his dirty boots. Just flew up the stairs two at a time, leaving bootprints on the wood in his wake, and entered the master bedroom.

Where, sure enough, Mika had deposited his suitcase. It laid open, clothing scattered around it, some in, some out, and some organized into one of Holland's empty dresser drawers.

Mika had been busy while Holland had been gone.

Muscles bunching in anger, he dropped the package of chocolate chips he was somehow still holding onto his bed and repacked Mika's suitcase haphazardly, throwing in fancy sweaters, leggings, skinny jeans, and underwear willy-nilly. He had to displace Tadashi from a small pile of socks, but once all evidence of Mika was gone from Holland's home, he hauled the suitcase downstairs.

"What the hell, Holland?" Mika jumped out of the way as Holland dumped the suitcase onto the porch, then went back inside to the closet for Mika's coat and boots. "You can't just kick me out. This is my house too."

"Not anymore, it isn't."

"What—" Mika stumbled backward when Holland thrust his coat and boots into his arms. "Where am I supposed to go? I don't have a car."

"You got here somehow. I'm sure you can find your way…wherever. It's only a twenty-minute walk to your parents.'"

"It's cold."

"Not my problem." Holland headed to his truck once more. Turned back. Locked the front door. "I don't want you here when I get back."

"When did you get so heartless?"

Holland braced his hands against the top of the truck and hung his head between his shoulders. He sighed deeply, his breath fogging the driver's side window.

Heartless, huh? All Holland wanted was to run to Zach, to explain, to beg forgiveness, to plead for a second chance. All because Zach had somehow wound his way into Holland's heart, threaded in there like he'd left a piece of himself behind.

The wind blew, sending scattered flowers tumbling over his boots. Bending, he picked up the red rose. Across his lawn, the rest of the bouquet had been flung by the wind into every corner, finding their way under bushes or lodged against tree trunks. Holland found gardenia, bird of prey, amaryllis, blue iris, daffodils. They were a little bruised now, a little imperfect, but no less beautiful in their thoughtfulness. Each find was a stab through the chest, knotting his gut, thickening his throat with the urge to scream in frustration and regret.

Mika's slippered feet scuffed against the porch. "What are you doing?"

The paper the flowers had been wrapped in was nowhere to be seen, blown away into the darkness. Holland was grateful the flowers hadn't followed. Bundling them together, careful not to prick himself on rose thorns, he was halfway to his truck before he remembered Mika was there.

"Seriously? You're just going to leave me here?"

Swallowing hard against the urge to rail at Mika—this was all his fault!—Holland sucked in a breath and looked, really *looked*, at him.

Spotlighted under the porch light as if used to finding the best lighting to make himself stand out, Mika's usually shiny blond hair hung lank and flat. He'd always been slim, but now he was downright skinny, too skinny for his five ten height. Dark circles lined his eyes, and he held his arms crossed over his chest as if trying to hold himself together lest he fall apart. Even with the distance between them, Holland could tell that Mika's eyes, a shade of brown so dark they were almost black, were lost and alone and… frightened.

Something was wrong.

But…Zach.

Decision made, Holland leaned into his truck and placed the flowers carefully, gently, in the console between the seats, then stood behind his open door, using it as a shield. "Look, Mika… I don't know what's going on with you, but I'd like to find out. I'd like for us to be friends again. But we'll never be anything more than that."

Mika's face tightened, muscles pulling taut. He slipped his coat on. Traded his slippers for his boots, stuffing the slippers into the front pocket of his suitcase, the wheels of which bumped down the steps when he descended. He passed Holland, gaze downcast, suitcase wheeling behind him.

Holland gazed up at the stars, exhaling roughly, cursing himself to hell. "Get in."

Mika stopped at the sidewalk but didn't turn.

"Come on, get in. I'll take you to your parents." It really was too cold for such a long walk, especially when it seemed as though a strong gust might topple Mika like a broken leaf.

Mika huddled in the passenger seat, shoulders up to his ears, hands stuffed between his thighs to keep them warm, all the wind gone from his sails. Holland turned the heat on high and directed the air vents toward him.

"Thank you," Mika said, sinking deeper into the leather

seat. "And I'm sorry for showing up unannounced and scaring your…boyfriend…away."

"Zach's not my boyfriend." Holland turned what would've been a twenty-minute walk into a three-minute drive. "He's not my anything yet. But I'm trying."

"I didn't even notice he was there until after I—" Mika winced and stared out the window. "I guess I just missed you, is all."

Zach pulled into Mika's parents' driveway. "You have a funny way of showing it." Considering Holland hadn't heard from him since they broke up.

"Yeah." Mika thunked his head back against the headrest. "Can we have lunch this week, or coffee even? Maybe at Tiny's? They've always had the best espresso."

"Not Tiny's," Holland rebutted. He wasn't shoving Mika in Zach's face, not after what had happened tonight. "But yeah. Sure."

Mika's smile was thin-lipped and wan. "Thanks. And thanks for the lift." He stepped down from the truck, the wind teasing his hair. "I really am sorry I messed things up with your guy."

"I'll see you around, Mika."

Mika nodded, shut the door, and disappeared around the side of the house, dragging his suitcase behind him.

"Jesus." Holland scrubbed his hands over his face, then backed out of the driveway. It felt like forever since Zach had seen him kissing Mika, yet it had only been fifteen minutes.

Parking on the street in front of Tiny's Panini a few minutes later, behind Zach's car, he looked up at the second-floor apartment above the café. The lights were off, but that didn't mean Zach wasn't home.

Except he wasn't home. Holland knocked again. Still

no answer. It was dark in the alley, where the iron stairs leading up to Zach's apartment were located. Dark, quiet, and cold.

Damn it. He'd had his chance with Zach and had fucked it up already. Would Zach even listen to him if he tried to explain?

Zach couldn't have gone far. This was Lighthouse Bay, not New York City. Setting the flowers down next to the door, Holland cleared a spot free of snow and sat on the top stair.

And waited.

Zach drifted aimlessly through the park, feet dragging as he walked the path along the perimeter, then over the bridge at the far end, and then back toward town. Once. Twice. Three times. Four. With each loop, he sat on the stone wall of the bridge for a while, staring sightlessly at the lit Christmas tree through a haze of tears, before continuing on once his butt got cold.

He came upon the tree again on his fifth loop. The mess he and Holland made of the snow a couple of days ago, during their snowball fight, had disappeared under other people's boot prints, but Zach could nevertheless hear the echo of their laughter. He wished he could go back to that time, to when he'd thought Holland hadn't wanted him. Before Holland had asked him to dinner and Zach had thought Holland wanted him back, only to get hit with a cold dose of reality hours later.

Holland wasn't interested in Zach. At least, not like Zach was interested in him. Zach was merely a sidetrack onto something better. A distraction.

Zach sniffled and wiped his nose on the back of his glove. Holland's glove. He'd probably have to give them back now. His eyes burned.

From the cold. Not anything else.

He shoved his hands in his coat pockets. He fingered the little wrapped gift in the right one, plucking and toying and teasing it around and around. A small surprise for Holland in addition to the flowers he'd picked out. Given that Holland liked mystery things—which was a quirk Zach found endearing as hell—it had seemed like a good idea at the time. It was just a simple thing, nothing extravagant. But Holland would never get to enjoy it, and that caused a lump to form in his throat.

Stupid Mika, the Ruiner of Plans.

Although realistically, who wouldn't want Mika? Who wouldn't wait around for him for five years? From what Zach remembered of Mika from years ago, Mika was friendly and easygoing. Cheerful. Beautiful. Talented. Successful. Zach watched his television show. The man had so much charisma on TV, it was no wonder he had thousands of adoring fans. It was Zach's bad luck that Mika's charisma transferred over into real life too.

In comparison, Zach was…Zach. Event planner. Recent college graduate. Owner of a creaky car with a ducttaped bumper. Part-time café worker.

Yay.

Whatever. Just because Holland didn't want him didn't mean nobody ever would. He'd check in on his dating app when he got home and see what was up. Maybe he'd get in touch with whoever that second eighty-seven percent match was.

Oh, who was he kidding? He was never dipping his toe

into the online dating world ever again.

And speaking of home…

He left the park and headed up Christmas Lane. The stars shone, bright and beautiful, guiding him home. Now that he wasn't going around in circles in his head, he registered the cold that nipped his nose and cheeks. His toes were freezing in his boots, and he couldn't feel his chin.

How long had he been walking? He should've gone home, but the prospect of an empty apartment hadn't appealed. He could've gone to headquarters, but—

Ugh. Headquarters. He rounded Flowers by Daisy and entered the alley, the staircase leading to his second-floor apartment above Tiny's Panini only feet away. How was he supposed to face Holland ever again when he'd run away like a…like a…like something that ran away scared.

Fuck, he was too tired and cold and hurt to think of anything beyond a warm bed.

The iron steps reverberated under his feet as he climbed, and—

"Jesus!" He jerked back when he spotted the hulking shadow that stood at the top of the stairs, losing his footing and falling, foot slipping. Something twisted in his ankle and he flailed. Grabbing ahold of the railing, he held tight and stopped himself near the bottom, spread-eagled over a few steps, arm twisted up and over, anchoring him to the railing. "Ow."

"Shit!" came a voice from above.

Holland?

"Shit, are you okay?" Thundering footsteps that made the stairs vibrate echoed in Zach's sore body. "Zach?"

Cold fingers touched Zach's face. Zach batted them away and hauled himself up, tailbone protesting. "I'm fine."

"I'm so sorry." Holland helped him stand with a hand

under his elbow. "I didn't mean to scare you. I was waiting, and the light above your door went out…"

The automatic timer turned it off at ten. Seriously, what time was it?

And how long had Holland been waiting?

"Does anything hurt?"

Pretty much everything. Zach took his arm back. "I'm fine. It's fine. Everything's fine." He put weight on his twisted ankle. Thankfully it barely twinged. The rest of his body didn't hurt too badly, but he'd have bruises in certain places tomorrow.

"I'm so sorry," Holland said again. He reached, as though he wanted to sweep Zach's body to make sure he was okay, but aborted the motion. "I should've met you at the bottom when I saw you turn the corner."

"It's fine." Wow, they were a bunch of *sorry*s and *fine*s, weren't they? Zach squeezed Holland's arm. "Really, it's…" He trailed off when he registered Holland's huge, hulking body was trembling. "Are *you* okay? How long have you been sitting out in the cold?"

"The cold?" They were standing so close on the staircase that, even in the dark, Zach noticed the puzzled look cross Holland's expression before it cleared and his eyes went wide. "The cold. Yes. I'm cold."

Zach squinted, trying to see him better in the dark. He was being shifty. "Why are you being weird?"

"What? I'm not." Holland gestured upward. "Can we talk inside?"

Stiffening, Zach turned and headed up. "We don't have anything to talk about."

Holland caught Zach's wrist, bringing him to a stop. "Please." In the darkness, his voice was an unfair caress over Zach's tender heart. "Let me explain."

Sighing at his own inability to protect himself, Zach tugged free of Holland's hold and said, "Fine. Come in."

Inside the apartment, Zach left his outerwear by the door, then turned on the lamp in the sitting room and the lights in the kitchen. Closed the blinds over rectangular windows as tall as him that looked out over Christmas Lane. Fluffed a throw pillow. Got a couple of glasses from the kitchen cupboard and poured them each some water.

Anything to avoid how tiny Holland made his already tiny home feel, with Holland's tall, bulky frame essentially taking over the living room and its breathing space. How Holland made the apartment feel less…generic. Sterile. Cold. He brought life and personality to it just by standing there watching Zach with his denim blue eyes that caught the lamplight and glowed with warmth, the flowers he held providing a splash of color to an otherwise dull living space.

Wait. Those flowers…

Holland held them up. "The wrapping paper flew away, but I managed to save these. Thank you, Zach. They're…" He cleared his throat. "It means a lot to me that you brought them."

"Really?" Zach whispered, stilling when Holland entered the kitchen in easy, measured steps.

"Yeah." Holland placed the flowers in one of the water glasses, then took Zach's hands. "I'm so sorry about what happened earlier. I didn't know Mika was there. I was picking something up at the store, and when I got back… He took me by surprise." He squeezed Zach's hands. "And Mika didn't know you were there, didn't know that you and I… If he had, he never would've kissed me. He's not cruel like that."

Maybe not, but Zach couldn't get the image of them kissing out of his head. He didn't know how long he'd stood there, shocked and stung, heart clenching, before leaving, but in that time, Holland hadn't done anything to push Mika away.

He stepped back from Holland and put distance between them, striding into the minuscule living room and putting the tray table he used as a coffee table between them.

"Zach?"

Zach crossed his arms over his chest. "Thank you for explaining." It was nice of him, but nowhere in the explanation did Holland offer reassurances.

"But?" Holland came into the living room but stayed on the other side of the tray table. "What's going through that head of yours?"

"Nothing. I'm just tired. It's been a long day."

Holland cocked his head. "You don't want to come over for pancakes, then?"

"I—" Zach's arms fell to his sides. "You still want me to? But what about Mika?"

"What about him?" Even before he finished speaking, understanding lit Holland's eyes. "Zach, Mika and I aren't getting back together."

"You're not?"

"No." Now Holland smiled, slow and teasing. "You think if we were getting back together I would've left him behind to come here and wait for you in the cold for two hours?"

"I guess not, but…"

"But?"

"But it's *Mika*. You were going to *marry* him."

"Yeah," Holland said with a chuckle. "Five years ago. I promise you, I haven't been waiting around for him for five years, pining away."

Zach's heart hoped, just a little. "Okay. But what about Clark?"

Holland groaned. "Fucking small-town gossip," he muttered. "There hasn't been anything between Clark and me since our very brief stint as boyfriends in high school."

"Oh." Zach bit his lip. "But—"

"Zach." Holland moved the table out of the way and cupped Zach's face in his large, work-roughened hands. Zach whimpered at the contact, stomach fluttering with the wings of butterflies, and had the pleasure of watching Holland's eyes darken. "I promise, there's no one in my life right now."

"No one?"

"No one but you."

"Oh."

Holland didn't want Mika. He didn't want Clark. He wanted…

Him.

Holland's words were convincing enough, but paired with the flowers he'd rescued from, most likely, every corner of his front lawn?

And the fact that he'd waited *two hours* in the cold for Zach to return home? Zach moved closer, almost chest-to-chest with Holland, heart thumping madly. He grasped Holland's wrists and stared up at his gorgeous face.

"So?" Holland said, smiling. "Pancakes?"

"It's past ten."

"So?"

Zach let out a short laugh. Then, "I don't want to have sex."

And his face burned so hard it must've been the color of a fire truck.

"Oh my god." He buried his face in his hands, ignoring

Holland's laughter. "Oh my god, I can't believe I said that. I don't even know where that came from."

Holland swung an arm around his neck and brought Zach into his side. "I wasn't using pancakes as a euphemism for sex."

"I know!" Zach wailed, burying his face in Holland's shoulder. Seriously, *why had he said that*? What was wrong with him? "Why doesn't the ground open up and swallow you whole in times like these?"

Holland was still chuckling, his shoulder lifting and falling underneath Zach's head.

Zach slapped his chest. "Stop laughing. Asshole."

"I'm sorry, but…"

"But what? Ugh, never mind." Zach straightened and scrubbed his face, which no longer felt like it was on fire, but he still wanted to disappear. "Can we pretend that never happened?"

Holland pulled Zach's hands away from his face and kissed the backs of both. Zach sucked in a soft breath, then released it in a whoosh when Holland said, "No," and kissed him.

Taken by surprise, Zach mumbled something unintelligible against Holland's lips.

"No kissing either?" Holland asked. He didn't appear disappointed by it, just…curious. Cautious.

"Um…" Zach stared at him for a second. In the past, he'd liked kissing about as much as he'd liked sex, but with Holland he was willing to try. "I think kissing is okay. Maybe we can try again?"

Holland dragged a thumb over Zach's cheek, causing Zach to break out in chills, and lowered his head again.

Zach met him halfway this time, and it was…perfect. Sweet. Disney-channel worthy tame. Just lips against lips and breathing each other in.

Until Holland tilted Zach's head, slanting their mouths together, and probed at the seam of Zach's lips with his tongue.

Zach opened, a combination of excited, anxious, and curious. But, to his surprise, Holland didn't swoop in and take over. He coaxed. He teased. He seduced.

One hand settled at Zach's lower back, drawing him in, snuggling their bodies close. The other cupped Zach's neck. He was hard and firm all over and, cocooned in his embrace, Zach had never felt more cherished. And in this one simple act, where Holland held him so carefully and didn't push and pressure, Zach had never felt more desired.

They were both breathing unsteadily by the time they separated. Holland's eyes were at half-mast as he swept that damnable thumb over Zach's wet lower lip. Zach nipped it playfully, and Holland smiled at him.

"Pancakes?"

"Yeah," Zach said, leaning against Holland's body. "Pancakes."

Dev was back home by the time Holland and Zach arrived a few minutes later. He must've just gotten there, because he stood in the kitchen, eyeing the scattered debris of Holland's attempted pancake making, still in his winter jacket. Tadashi sat on his left foot.

"What happened?" he asked, raking Holland with his gaze. "Was there an emergency?"

Holland understood why he might think that. Half the

counter was covered in pancake ingredients. It looked like he'd abandoned everything and left in a hurry. Which he had.

Just not for the reason Dev thought.

"No emergency." Holland stepped further into the kitchen, Zach behind him, and placed Zach's flowers, still in their water glass, onto the kitchen table. "I had to go get chocolate chips."

"But wasn't your date, like…" Dev checked the time on the microwave. "Two hours ago? More than that."

"Yeah, we had a…hiccup of sorts."

"For two hours?"

"It's not important." Holland hip checked him out of the way.

"You're still going to make the pancakes?" Dev turned to Zach. "He's making them *now*?"

"Why not now?" Zach asked.

Dev huffed, grabbed Holland's bicep, and pulled him back. "I'll make them."

"What? Why? Shouldn't you go to bed?"

But Dev was already whipping ingredients together.

"Dev—"

"Don't argue with me. It'll take you two hours to make a dozen pancakes. It'll take me twenty minutes."

Holland sighed, acquiescing. "The chocolate chips are on my bed upstairs."

Dev grunted. He needed to be at the bakery at four tomorrow morning to start baking, and he was usually in bed by now, but if he wanted to make them pancakes, Holland was done arguing.

Because it really would take him two hours.

He turned to find Zach with his butt parked against the table. "Do you want to— Are you okay?"

Zach cocked his head. "Yeah."

"Do you need ice?"

Zach looked down to where he was rubbing the out-side of his left thigh. "No, it's okay. I didn't realize it at the time, but I think I landed on it when I fell. Doesn't hurt too much, but there'll be a bruise tomorrow."

Holland's hands started to shake again as he remembered that fall Zach had taken. Scared the shit out of him to watch Zach go down like that. He'd thought for sure Zach would go all the way down, bashing his head open on the concrete below.

Shaking his hands out, he took a breath. At least this time it was only his hands that were trembling.

"Sure you don't want an ice pack?"

"Yeah," Zach said, smiling at him. "I'm fine."

Holland jerked his head toward the back door and, over the sound of the mixer, said, "Want to see my workshop?"

Tucked in the corner of his backyard, his windowless workshop was about the size of a minivan. Only taller, about fifteen feet high, with a steeped roof. Half the space was taken over by tools and wood. That left the rest of it as his building space…which wasn't much.

Zach took one look around and announced, "You need a bigger space."

"Tell me about it." Holland turned on the space heater. "I keep meaning to knock this wall down and expand it, but I haven't had time."

But Zach was no longer listening. "Holy crap! This is what you're working on now?" He ran his hand over a waist-high, multilevel, cream and dark brown, vintage Victorian dollhouse with a lovely porch that wrapped around the side of the house, two bay windows, and delicate shutters around the glass windows. "This is beautiful."

Pride swept through Holland. Out of everything he thought he'd build for a living, he'd never once thought it'd be primarily dollhouses, and yet here he was. "Want to see the inside?"

"How?"

Holland unhooked a hidden latch and swung the front of the house open.

"Wow," Zach breathed, stretching the word out. He crouched to peer inside at the carpeted rooms on all three levels, the miniature staircases, the little kitchen at the back of the house, and the perfect little cabinets. There wasn't any furniture; that was for the lady who'd commissioned the piece to do once she received it.

Holland crouched next to Zach.

"I mean, I was never into dolls," Zach said. "But this… This is awesome." He leaned against Holland's side. "How did you get into building dollhouses, anyway?"

"A friend of my sister's in Atlanta was looking for something specific, but everything on eBay was too expensive, everything on Amazon was DIY, and ordering something custom cost too much. I offered to make her one and…it kind of flew from there. Most of my business comes from word of mouth. Moms wanting fancy dollhouses for their kids."

"Do you like it? Building dollhouses?"

"Surprisingly, I do. I like coming up with unique designs. I've never built two of the same."

"And where's this one going?" Zach said.

"To a woman in Arizona who collects Victorian dollhouses."

Zach's brow furrowed. "People collect dollhouses?"

"People collect all sorts of things."

"Mm-hmm." Zach's lips twitched. "Like you with your mystery packages."

Holland groaned. "I hate Dev."

Zach's chuckle warmed Holland's insides. "No, you don't. Actually, speaking of mystery packages…" Standing, he dug into the pocket of his skinny jeans, then thrust his hand out toward Holland. "Here."

"What is it?" Holland stood and took the gift, which was wrapped in bubbly red-and-green wrapping paper. It was small, roughly two inches by two, and weighed about as much as a couple of business cards.

"It's just…" Zach shrugged, face flushing. It wasn't quite as red as when he'd blurted out that he didn't want to have sex—when it had looked liked he'd baked under the high noon desert for twelve hours—but it was close. "I figured if you like those mystery packages, you probably also like presents, so…"

Anticipation making him grin, Holland carefully tore off the paper, pried the lid off the box, and pulled out the key chain. On the end was a small, flat, metal house with a chimney, a couple of windows, and an adorable rounded front door.

"It's not a dollhouse," Zach said. "But it still reminded me of you."

When had Zach had time to pick this up? Either way, it was perfect.

Holland reached for Zach's wrist and reeled him in, placing a kiss on his pillowy lips. "Thank you."

Zach smiled and leaned in—

"Dudes!" Dev yelled out the back door. "Pancakes are done!"

Zach leaned forward, into Holland. "Food time?"

Holland kissed him, light and easy. "Food time."

They had pancakes. Dev went to bed. Then they snuggled on the couch in comfortable silence in front of a roaring fireplace that shot sparks and made the house smell like winter.

Holland drove Zach home when Zach's eyelids began to droop. Parked on the street in front of Tiny's Panini, they kissed lazily under a streetlight decorated with a wire star shot through with tiny white lights. Zach pulled back and smiled at Holland, honey eyes darkened to brown. When Holland asked what he was smiling about, Zach said he was happy.

And as Holland watched Zach climb the stairs to the apartment to make sure he got in okay, he realized that with Zach's simple words—"I'm happy"—Zach had handed him a precious and terrifying gift.

# CHAPTER SEVEN

*15 days until the parade*

MIDMORNING THE NEXT DAY, HOLLAND STRODE INTO Dev's Bakery thinking the morning rush would be over by now, but he found Dev's two weekday morning part-timers, Rosie and Jean, assisting a long line of customers. Holland waved at them as he strode past the twelve-foot counter, half the gleaming display cases showcasing a dozen different kinds of bread, the other half pastries and baked goods. Iron shelves built into the wall behind the counter held yet more varieties of bread. On either side of the shelves, chalkboards in wooden frames listed prices and daily specials.

A red garland hung the length of the counter, and atop each display case sat a small snowman family made of felt. Christmas music played, a jaunty pop tune Holland didn't recognize.

At the back of the bakery, past the counter, Holland went through the door into the kitchen where he found Dev piping red icing onto a series of chocolate mini cupcakes. A red bandana tied his hair back, and he wore a white apron over washed out jeans and a T-shirt. Dev's baking song, Aqua's "Barbie Girl," played softly through

Dev's portable speakers.

"Hey." There were two counters dominating the middle of the kitchen, twelve feet by twelve feet each. Holland hopped onto the clean one.

Dev grunted at him.

Holland drummed his heels against the counter and waited Dev out, the *thump, thump, thump* of his feet against the metal cabinets echoing throughout the room in tune to Barbie Girl singing about life in plastic being fantastic. Bored, he took his phone out and reread this morning's text message from Zach. Hi :)

Grinning, he texted Zach back. Hi! Sleep well?

"If you don't stop that, I'm never making you pancakes again," Dev growled.

Holland stilled his feet as Zach's reply came through. No. Couldn't sleep.

Holland: Are you sore? I knew I should've given you an ice pack yesterday.

Zach: Huh? Oh, haha. No I'm fine. Just . . . there's this guy. And he's sort of got me tied in knots. Made it hard to fall asleep. [blushing emoji]

Holland: A guy, huh? Is he an old white-haired guy who makes toys for a living?

Zach: No. He's an ALMOST white-haired guy who crafts beautiful, unique dollhouses and who stepped in to help with Santa's float last minute...and who makes my heart beat too fast.

Holland grinned at his phone.

"You're gonna make me barf with all that lovesick sighing you're doing over there."

"You know," Holland said, "for a baker, you lack a single romantic bone in your body."

"I don't know what one has to do with the other."

"Aren't bakers supposed to be romantic?"

The look Dev shot him was incredulousness mixed with confusion.

"No?" Holland scratched his jaw. "That's a stereotype?"

"I don't think that's an anything," Dev said, attention back on his cupcakes. "I think you just made that up."

Dev had piped white icing around the perimeter of the cupcake tops while Holland wasn't paying attention and was now putting the finishing touches on the tips of the red icing he'd piped into a lopsided cone: a dollop of white icing. Santa's hat.

"Those are cute."

Dev groaned. "Everybody wants Christmas themed pastries as soon as December hits."

"Can I help?"

"What's the rule in my kitchen?" Dev asked without pausing.

Holland rolled his eyes. "Don't touch anything. Yeah, yeah."

He went back to texting Zach while Dev finished his cupcakes, and sent him a series of heart-eyes emojis.

What he really wanted was to ask about the no-sex thing, but that wasn't a conversation they should have via text message. *I don't want to have sex* could mean anything from *I'm asexual* to *I'm waiting until marriage* to *I want to wait until we know each other better.*

Or none of the above.

Because it could also mean something worse, something that had caused trauma to the point where Zach simply *couldn't* have sex.

God, please don't let it be that. Just the thought of Zach going through some kind of sexual abuse made bile clog Holland's throat.

Dev muttered something indecipherable, then, louder, "There. Done." He picked up the tray of cupcakes and headed out front. Holland followed.

The customers were all gone, and Rosie and Jean were removing empty trays from the display cases and moving food around to make it look fuller. When they spotted Dev, they cleared a spot for the mini Santa hat cupcakes, and Dev slid his tray into the display case.

"Why don't you guys take a break?" Dev suggested. "I'll watch the front."

"Don't mind if we do," Rosie said. "We're going next door to order lunch in advance. Want anything?"

"No thanks. But can you bring Alana a bag of ciabatta buns? They're almost out."

The women packed a clear plastic bag full of buns, grabbed their winter gear from the back, and headed out.

"So?" Dev pulled a hardcover notebook from the shelf underneath the cash register and made a note inside. "What brings you by?"

"Hmm?" Distracted by the sample plate next to the cash register, Holland lifted the domed lid, snagged a cube of bread, and popped it in his mouth. "Holy shit! This is the sourest sourdough bread I've ever had."

Dev arched an eyebrow. "It's Zach's favorite."

"I'll take two."

Minutes later, round loaves of bread paid for against Dev's protests and securely tucked into paper bags, Dev said, "Seriously, what's up? Thought you were over at the McPhees today, fixing their sink."

"I was there earlier. Didn't take long. Just wanted to come by on my way into headquarters and say thanks for the pancakes last night."

"You know how I feel about people baking around me."

Holland knew Dev was a control freak who hated when people didn't follow recipe instructions. Holland followed them. It just took him a while to get to the end product.

"What was your hiccup last night, anyway?"

"Ah. That." Holland leaned a hip against the counter. "Don't worry about it. That's a story for another time."

"But—"

The door opened behind Holland, cutting Dev off and letting in the cold. By the scowl Dev shot over Holland's shoulder, Holland had a pretty good guess who'd just entered.

"Hey, small fries!"

Clark.

Dev shot him the finger. "Hey, Sasquatch."

Clark threw his head back and laughed, dark hair flowing over his shoulders. "Sasquatch. Good one. I like it, smalls."

Hands on his hips, Dev glowered at Clark from behind the cash register. "What do you want?"

"Why, my biweekly loaf of fruitcake, of course."

"Of course," Dev parroted. "I don't know how you can eat so much fruitcake. Nobody likes it *that* much."

In fact, Clark, Holland knew, despised fruitcake. Dev knew it too. If only he'd realize it and put two and two together.

Holland leaned against one of the glass displays and watched his best friend watch his cousin slice and package a loaf of cake. Whereas Clark's smile had been teasing when he'd walked in the door, it was melancholy and soft while Dev wasn't looking, his eyes pulling down, as though he was looking at something he knew he'd never have.

Realizing Holland was staring at him, Clark blinked once and said, "What?"

He was surrounded by idiots. "Why are you dressed for the North Pole?"

"Tourists from Toronto want a personalized walking tour."

"Of Lighthouse Bay? It's literally this street."

Clark shrugged. "That's what I said."

"Here's your biweekly dose of dried fruit buried in flour and butter." Dev held out a hand. "Four ninety-nine."

Clark handed him a bill with a mock bow. "Here's ten. You may keep the change."

"You're so generous," Dev said, voice bland. "Almost as generous as that time you left me exactly a tiny corner of the fresh brownies."

"You're still not over that? Not my fault Holland ate it all."

"What? Lies." Holland straightened. "Don't pretend you're some kind of angel."

"Evil angel, more like," Dev muttered.

Clark leaned over the counter, closer to Dev. "You're going to have to be nicer to me when we get married."

Dev closed the distance between them, bringing them inches apart, mutiny on his face. "I'll marry you when a hippo drives a motorcycle out of my sphincter."

Holland swallowed a laugh. One day, Dev would give in to Clark. Holland just hoped he was around to witness it.

The door opened again, and if Dev's scowl for Clark had been ferocious, the one he leveled on the newcomer was downright murderous. "Did you forget something when you moved away five years ago? Your heart, maybe?"

Stopping in the doorway, Mika looked momentarily flummoxed at finding both Dev and Clark glowering at him as though he'd just shit in their shoes, but then he squared his shoulders, face settling into determined lines, and stepped the rest of the way inside.

Mika might as well have stepped off the cover of a magazine. Dark jeans, a granite-colored, knit button-up sweater open at the throat, revealing the black turtleneck underneath. Completing his outfit was a navy peacoat with deep pockets and loafers in a dark chestnut. His face wasn't as shadowed today and his hair was stylishly coiffed.

The door closed behind him, shutting out the cold and the voices of passing pedestrians. "At least I had the guts to leave and make something of myself."

"Guys," Holland warned.

Clark straightened from his lazy perch against the counter. "Oh, hell no. Nobody gets to insult short stack but me."

"Nobody gets to insult me at all." Dev crossed his arms over his chest. "Especially in my own bakery. Everybody out."

"What'd I do?" Holland asked.

"You can stay."

Mika huffed. "Look, I only came to—"

"You heard mini mouse." Clark turned Mika around by the shoulders and directed him toward the door while Dev actually growled at the nickname. "Out you go."

"You too," Dev informed him, pointing at the door.

Clark turned wounded eyes on Dev. "What'd I do?"

"You know what."

"Guys," Holland tried again.

"If I could just—"

"Why *are* you here?" Clark interrupted Mika to ask him. "Come to rub your success in our faces?"

"What? No—"

"Come to win Holland back?" Dev guessed. "I can tell you right now—it won't happen."

"Guys."

Mika was starting to get more and more agitated, fidgety. Feet shuffling. Hands clenching. Breaths coming quicker. Holland recognized the signs. Mika had something to say but didn't know how to say it.

Dev snapped his fingers. "Or maybe you came to break Holland's heart again."

"Why don't you just go back to Tinseltown and pretend you never heard of Lighthouse Bay," Clark suggested. "You've been doing that so well, so far."

"For once, Clark and I agree on something," Dev said.

And Mika finally exploded. "I have cancer!" Hunching in on himself, he mumbled, "And I just…wanted to come home."

Fear, unlike anything Holland had ever experienced before, took root in his blood and spread outward, infecting everything until he thought he'd vomit. That dreaded C-word of terror. Stomach curdling, he took two steps closer to Mika but, not knowing what to do—hell, what to say—he stood there useless while the silence turned deafening.

"Mika, I—" Throat closing, he swallowed hard. It might have been five years since they'd spoken, but they'd meant everything to each other once, and Holland didn't want Mika to die. Holland liked to think that he'd been more than a distraction on Mika's way to something bigger and better, and he was pretty sure he was right. Mika couldn't have faked his way through their friendship and eventual relationship for that long. He was a good actor, but Holland knew him well enough to know when he was putting on a show.

He wasn't putting one on now.

Mika avoided eye contact, eyes bouncing from the line of stools tucked under a high table across from the counter, to the store windows, to the floor, to his own hands. His breathing came too fast, and his face had turned a blotchy red.

"Doesn't give you the right to be a jerk," Dev said, breaking the uncomfortable silence.

Holland whipped his head around and stared at is cousin in surprise and horror. "Dev!"

"What? Just because he's dying, it doesn't give him a free pass."

Mika's breathing hitched.

Rosie and Jean chose that moment to return from their break, walking into a situation so tense Holland was surprised they hadn't felt it from the other side of the door. They glanced at each other, at them—doing a double take when they spotted Mika—then back at each other.

"Who died?" Rosie asked.

And Mika started to cry.

In a quiet corner of Tiny's Panini, Holland and Mika sat at a small round table cradling hot mugs of tea. Dev's expression had gone from hard to contrite when Holland had shuffled a softly crying Mika out of his bakery twenty minutes ago, taking him next door. Sure, Holland hadn't wanted to bring Mika here, not when Zach was working, but it was close, warm, and served good food, which Mika looked like he needed.

Zach's eyes had widened when he saw Mika, but anxiety quickly turned to concern when he spotted Mika's red eyes and the tear tracks on his face. He'd brought over two mugs of tea, an egg salad sandwich cut into squares, a small bowl of pasta salad, and a plate of Christmas sugar cookies. Holland squeezed his hand in thanks and winked at him. Zach's smile was wan as he left them alone, but it was something. No doubt he was wondering what was going on.

Frankly, Mika was a bit pathetic sitting across from Holland with hunched shoulders, eyes on his mug, and the occasional sniffle. He looked better than he had yesterday—less limp and fragile—but still pale and still too skinny. His back faced the room, keeping his expression hidden from the few customers enjoying a late morning coffee.

Holland reached across the table and took Mika's hand, warming the cold fingers in his own. "I'm sorry." He'd known, hadn't he? Last night. Just looking at Mika, he'd known something was wrong. And he'd almost let Mika walk home by himself in the cold?

*Smooth, Holland. Way to be a friend to someone who so obviously needs one.*

"I'm sure it's not your fault Dev turned into an asshole."

Holland choked on a laugh. "That's not what I meant."

Mika sighed, long and slow. "Yeah, I know."

"How long have you known?"

"A couple of weeks. I haven't slept much." He picked at one of the sandwich squares.

Holland swallowed hard, then asked the question he didn't want an answer to. "How bad is it?"

Lips pressing together in a thin line, Mika took in a deep breath through his nose and straightened from his half slump over his mug. "The doctors said they caught it early. They don't think it's spread, but they won't know until they do the biopsy after the holidays."

"Why wait so long?"

"Apparently that's early, considering the backlog in hospitals these days."

"What's the treatment look like?" Holland asked. Giving Mika's hand one last squeeze, he let go and snagged a sandwich square. "Chemo?"

Mika shrugged. "Won't know until after the biopsy. They need to know how bad it is first."

"I'm glad you came home for this."

"Yeah." Mika's laugh was grating in its self-deprecation. "That was a surprisingly easy decision. Most of my friends in LA distanced themselves from me as soon as I told them, as if cancer's contagious or something." He rolled his eyes. "Whatever. You and Clark have always been my best friends anyway. At least you were, once. Oh, and Dev."

*Oh, and Dev.* Poor Dev. Always an afterthought, at least when it came to their little group. Growing up, it'd been Holland, Clark, and Mika—the queer kids against the rest of the world. Dev, five years younger, had chased after them relentlessly, wanting to be included. But when they were younger, a five-year age difference had seemed enormous. What sixteen-year-old wanted their eleven-year-old cousin tagging along?

But it'd been Clark that Dev had been enamored with. Clark he'd wanted to play with, go to the playground with, who he baked cakes and pastries for. Yet Clark hadn't given him the time of day, always more interested in his girlfriend or boyfriend du jour.

Until recently. In the past year or two, Clark had *noticed* Dev in a way he never had before. It was so obvious to Holland that Clark's constant teasing was his version of flirting with Dev. However Dev—too used to Clark's rebuffs—couldn't see it.

When he finally figured it out, it was going to be awesome.

"I meant what I said yesterday," Mika said. "I really did

miss you. I guess I hoped you missed me too."

"I did," Holland admitted, and Mika's eyes lit. Then Holland said, "At first," and Mika dropped his gaze. "The way we left things, Mika…"

"It sucked." Mika leaned his forearms on the table and sat forward, a wry smile on his lips. "You never asked why I cheated on you."

Holland tilted his head, considering. "No, I guess not. At the time I was too hurt to care." Time and distance had turned hurt into regret, and curiosity outweighed everything. "Why did you?"

Mika stuck a finger into the sandwich plate and sucked the crumbs off. Holland pushed the plate closer, hoping Mika would eat actual food and not just the debris.

"I was lost when I got to LA," Mika said, voice soft. "Alone, confused, tired. And every time we spoke, it felt like I was a chore to you."

"What?"

"It was while you were managing that bar in Biddeford, hating every second of it. When we spoke, you were always grumpy and short with me, and… I'm not explaining this well."

"I made you feel like you didn't matter," Holland said, belly cramping into knots. "Fuck. Mika, I'm so sorry." He'd never meant to hurt the person who'd meant the most to him. Mika had left right around the time Holland's work at the bar had been starting to drag him down into misery, and for a time, he'd taken it out on everyone. He hadn't realized he'd pushed Mika away in the process.

Shrugging, Mika played with the handle of his mug. "I didn't sleep with someone else to hurt you, Holland." His dark eyes met Holland's. "I honestly thought you were done with me. It wasn't until after you broke up with me that I realized I'd been wrong."

"Shit." Holland scrubbed his face hard, his beard scratching against his palms. "We both fucked this up, didn't we?"

Mika's answering smile was rueful. "I thought we could pick up where we left off before I left, but…" He glanced over at the order counter where Zach was making something at the fancy coffee maker for the only customer in line.

Holland smiled. "Yeah. But."

Eyes dark in an otherwise pale face, Mika scrutinized Holland. "You happy?"

Holland couldn't help but track Zach as he passed the coffee to his customer in a takeout cup, then wiped coffee grounds off the counter. His dark blond hair was mostly tamed today, and around his waist, he wore a forest green apron with the café's logo on the front, with a pair of black skinny jeans, a pale blue long-sleeved T-shirt, and bright blue Converse. With no other customers needing immediate attention, Zach pulled Mr. Barry's binder from underneath the counter, opened it up, and started jotting down notes.

"Yeah. I'm happy."

"Good. You deserve to be."

"So do you." Holland pushed the plate of cookies closer to Mika. If he wasn't into the sandwiches, something sweet might tempt him. "You'll get past this, Mika. I know it."

Gulping hard, Mika sent him a game smile. "I'm glad I decided to come home, but I'm not sure what I'll do while I'm here."

"Don't you have, I don't know…scripts to read or something? A show to rehearse for?"

Mika shook his head. "I took a leave of absence from the show until I know more about what I'm facing, so I'm basically aimless. Know anyone who's hiring?"

"Actually…" Holland looked at Zach again. "Yes."

There was nothing subtle about the way Zach kept looking over at Holland chatting with Mika. And Holland didn't even notice, which meant…

He was done with Zach already?

He was getting back together with Mika?

None of the above and he was simply catching up with an old friend? Boyfriend. Whatever.

And what was wrong with Mika that he'd come in here in tears? Was he sad because Holland wouldn't get back together with him?

It was petty, but just the thought bolstered Zach. Clearly he was a terrible person.

"What are you looking at?"

"Gah!" Startled from his thoughts, Zach jumped and scowled at Alana. "Don't sneak up on me like that."

Alana followed Zach's line of sight. "You're not still crushing on Mr. Stone, are you?"

"You make it sound so dirty when you call him *Mr. Stone* like that." Zach closed his binder and put it on a shelf underneath the counter.

"It *is* dirty." Alana placed a tray of pre-made sandwiches in the display case and adjusted the case's temperature.

"Why?"

"For starters, he was your teacher."

"So?"

Zach barely remembered third grade. What adult did? He remembered bits and pieces—the grasshopper on his leg on the first day of school. The class project where they'd all raised their own caterpillars. His caterpillar dying before it morphed into a butterfly. How devastated he'd been that he'd killed something so vulnerable. Learning the multiplication tables up to the number nine, because Holland had a trick for each one. The quilt they'd sewed as a class as a donation to the sick kids wing of the hospital. Spending recess alone on the swings in the school playground because the other kids in his class didn't want to play with him.

And he remembered Holland being larger than life and seeming so much older and more mature than Zach's nine-year-old self. But Holland would've been the same age as Zach was now when he taught back then.

Weird.

"So?" Alana scoffed. "And secondly, he's fifteen years older than you."

"Why does that bother you so much?"

"Why *doesn't* it bother you?"

Because the age gap was inconsequential. Holland didn't *feel* older. He treated Zach like a peer, an equal, not as a younger, less experienced child or as a stupid kid with a crush. And, coincidentally, they were at similar points in their lives, both starting new careers and trying to make a life for themselves.

Holland had the house and savings from years of professional experience under his belt, while Zach lived above his family's café with scarcely a cent to his name and had college debt up to his eyeballs… But what did that matter when you connected so viscerally with someone? What did it matter when Holland made him feel accepted for the first time in his life? Accepted and, more importantly, understood. What did it matter when Holland made his heart pound, his palms sweat, and his stomach bounce in joy? When Holland made him feel so wonderfully *alive*, like he belonged.

Zach only hoped he made Holland feel the same way.

But explaining all of that to Alana would be like holding a conversation with someone whose only language was Greek.

So he responded with, "Why should it?"

"I…" Alana paused at that, appearing truly stumped. "I don't know, I guess…" She tucked a flyaway length of hair into her ponytail. "It's a lot of years."

"Again… So? There's, like, twenty-six years between Harrison Ford and Calista Flockhart."

Alana waved a hand. "Celebrities aren't real people."

"Really? Because there's one sitting right over there."

But Alana was already walking away, done with the conversation. "Oh, Mom called," she said over her shoulder. "They're not coming for Christmas."

"What?" Zach hustled to follow her through the swinging door and into the kitchen where Zari, one of Al's part-timers who was a college student in Portland, was making this evening's preordered dinner sandwiches. "What do you mean they're not coming? Why?" It was Christmas— how could his parents not come home?

Alana headed to her workstation and started cleaning up, putting away the rest of the vegetables, storing the bread in airtight containers. "They decided to spend it with their friends in Florida. They'll come visit in the new year."

"But—"

"Here." She handed him a wet cloth. "Make yourself useful."

Zach stared at her balefully, then over at Zari, who shrugged and went back to work. "I—"

"And since Mom and Dad won't be here," Alana went on from inside the walk-in fridge, "I'm going to head to

Sugarloaf with some friends for a few days."

His sister was ditching him for Christmas to go *skiing*? "What about the café?"

"You'll be here, won't you?"

Now, wait just a second!

"You and Zari," Alana said.

Zari blinked up from her sandwiches. "Wait, what?"

"You guys can hold down the fort." Alana came out of the fridge rubbing the cold from her arms, kicking the door closed behind her.

"Um, you already approved my time off for the holidays," Zari said.

Alana snapped her fingers. "Right. You and Marcus and Jodine, then," she said to Zach, naming her other two part-timers.

Zach threw the cloth onto the table with enough force to send Alana's detritus scattering in every direction, falling onto the floor and onto Zach's Converse shoes. "Did it ever occur to you to ask?"

"Ask who? You? Why? I already know you'll be here."

It was like being kids again, when Alana expected him to do her science homework because a) he was good at it even though she was a year ahead of him in school, and b) since he didn't have any friends, he had nothing better to do. Never mind that he'd never actually *liked* science. Enjoying something and being good at it were two very separate things.

He crossed his arms over his chest. "What if *I* have plans to go skiing with friends over Christmas?"

"Do you?" Alana cocked her head as though she'd never considered that he might have a social life.

Which he didn't. But that wasn't the point.

Before he could answer, the little bell they kept on the

counter rang, summoning them to the front.

Holland and Mika stood there, and just the sight of Holland had Zach calming. He even managed a smile, although it wasn't huge. It must not have been very successful because Holland nevertheless looked at him funny.

"You okay?" he asked.

Zach smiled for real then. "I'm fine."

"Is everything okay?" Alana asked.

"Yeah." Holland tore his eyes away from Zach with what seemed like real effort. "Alana, are you still looking for a part-timer?"

Alana perked up. "Yes! Got someone in mind?"

Holland gestured at Mika.

"Are you moving back to town?" Alana asked.

"For the foreseeable future," Mika said.

"What about your TV show?"

"I've taken a leave of absence." He shrugged when Alana raised an eyebrow. "Personal reasons. If it helps, I worked here throughout high school and college."

Zach stiffened as Alana seemed to seriously consider it. He was supposed to work with Holland's ex? Why would Holland even suggest that?

*Please say no, please say no, please say no.*

On the other hand, it meant fewer shifts for him. He'd have to stick around until Al found a second person; if he left now, it'd be Mika who was run off his feet. But it was a step in the right direction, though why a TV star would want to work in a small-town café was beyond him. Maybe he was researching for a part?

*Please say yes, please say yes, please say yes.*

"Do you have a few minutes to chat?" Alana asked, and she and Mika disappeared into the kitchen where there was a tiny office tucked into a corner.

It was quiet in the café that time of day, after breakfast but before lunch, when it was empty. Zach rested his forearms on the counter next to the register and leaned forward. On the other side of the counter, Holland mimicked him, bringing their faces close.

"Hi," Zach said.

"Hi." Holland rubbed a thumb between Zach's eyebrows. "What's wrong?"

"Nothing. Just Al and I arguing over who's going to run the place over Christmas."

"Have you considered closing for a few days?"

"I guess we could, but the few days before and after Christmas are a huge profit maker for us. Lots of tourists; lots of visiting families. I don't do the books, so I don't know how much of a loss we'd take if we closed, but I don't think Al would go for it, anyway. Which leaves me running the place."

Holland rested a hand on Zach's arm and swiped his thumb back and forth. Even through the material of his shirt, Zach felt that touch to his bones.

"Alana won't help?" Holland asked.

"She's going skiing with friends."

Holland frowned. "Over Christmas?"

"Yup. Anyway." Zach nodded in the direction of the kitchen. "Everything okay with Mika?"

"No," Holland said on a sigh. "He got some bad news recently."

Even knowing it was none of his business, Zach wanted to ask, but he didn't. Besides, from the way Holland's mouth opened, closed, opened, closed again, it was clear he was debating how much he should divulge.

"It's fine." Zach squeezed his hand. "You don't have to tell me. Just… Is he okay?"

"Hopefully he will be."

The words struck a chord, making Zach think of his mom, of those first few days after she was diagnosed with cancer right around his high school graduation. Of how he'd let "Hopefully she'll be okay" slip out of his mouth, and his dad had scolded him and told him there was no *hopefully* about it—she *would* be okay.

"Is he sick?" he asked Holland.

Holland let out a deep breath and leaned that extra inch forward, resting their brows together. "Yeah. He said they caught it early, though."

"That's good. That's really good. My mom's was caught early too, and she's fine now. Cancer-free." She'd gone through a biopsy, surgery, radiation, and chemo, and was now on a list of meds as long as Santa's naughty or nice list, but she'd beat it.

"Can I tell Mika that?" Holland asked. "Might make him feel better, because right now…he's not doing so well."

"Of course."

"Thank you." Holland pulled back, took a quick glance around the empty café, then placed a quick, chaste kiss on Zach's lips. Zach's heart jumped from that brief contact alone. "I've got to head out. See you at headquarters later?"

"Sure."

Holland winked at him before heading to the door. When he reached it, he called back, "Don't let Alana run you ragged."

Zach chuckled humorlessly. "I'll try."

Then Holland was gone.

A few hours later, Zach stood at the snack table in parade headquarters and made a couple of teas. Activity was high in the building with many of the volunteers working on their floats. With the parade only fifteen days away, it was all hands on deck. Somewhere behind him, a loud *clank* sounded as someone dropped what sounded like steel against the concrete floor. Conversations among volunteers, instructions called over shoulders, and good-natured ribbing could be heard over the Christmas music coming through the speakers on Zach's desk.

On his way back to his desk, he stopped by The General Store's float, which was the same every year—a huge mechanical hammer hammering a nail. Frank Wilson, the owner of The General Store, was giving it a fresh coat of paint.

"Hey, Frank."

"Zach," Frank said from on top of his float. "Got any more of those cinnamon scones?"

"Dev brought in some fresh ones not long ago. They're on the snack table."

Frank rubbed his hands together.

"I've got you down as a volunteer to help set up the fair on the evening before the parade," Zach said. "I just wanted to confirm that you'll be there."

"Will there be cinnamon scones?"

Next was a stop at Evie's Toy Store's ice castle—an ice castle made of wood, but nobody cared—where Evie's husband, Tom, was taking a break. He sat on a chair, feet propped on the float's platform, and munched on a sandwich.

"Hey, Tom. Do you and Evie still plan to host a booth at the Christmas fair?"

Tom eyed him, chewing slowly, and said, "Will there be sandwiches?"

The winter sports float was next, where one of the part-timers from the sporting goods store off Main Street was burning the store's logo onto a large sheet of wood with a wood-burning tool.

"Maven, are you guys all set with the Lighthouse Bay-branded knit hats to hand out at the parade?"

"Sure," Maven said, never looking up from her work. "But only if Dev's handing out cake pops again like last year."

And finally, the nativity float.

"Hi, Mrs. Doohip."

Mrs. Doohip, a music teacher at the elementary school, beamed down at him from her perch near the top of a ladder. "Zachary! I've been meaning to come by your desk to chat. My students are looking forward to singing at the fair in a couple of weeks. I'm so glad you suggested it."

"They agreed to do it?"

"Of course!" She peered at him through her glasses. "There'll be candy canes and apple cider for the kids, won't there?"

So the way to secure his volunteers' cooperation was through food. Good to know for next year.

Except—as much as he wanted to—he wouldn't be doing this next year. This job wasn't his. He was a temporary replacement. Next year he'd be planning corporate holiday parties for the Gold Stone hotel chain in Portland.

Hopefully.

If he got the job.

Which might be his after tomorrow's second interview with the director of events, the human resources director, and the corporate events manager. Apparently, he'd made a short list of three candidates they couldn't decide between. He couldn't imagine what else they needed to know after last week's hour-long interview, but if they wanted to see him *five* more times before making a decision, he was on board. Whatever it took to get him out of the café.

When he got back to his corner of the building, he found Holland on a step stool painting Flowers by Daisy's shutters purple.

"I just realized the stores are facing the wrong way," Zach said, coming to a stop next to Holland.

Distracted, Holland hummed a question under his breath.

"The stores," Zach explained. "They're not facing the street."

"Huh?" Blinking, Holland pulled back and rubbed a hand over his jaw, leaving a speck of purple behind. "Oh yeah. I wanted the spectators to be able to see the shops. There's nothing interesting about the backs of them, so I turned them around."

"How come you didn't build a giant dollhouse for your float?"

"Two reasons." Holland descended from the stool and dropped his paintbrush onto the overturned lid of the paint bucket. "First, we've already got an ice castle and a ginger-bread house."

"True." Zach handed him one of the teas in his hand. "Here."

Holland smiled his thanks and brought the mug up to his nose, inhaling deeply. "Second, a dollhouse implies dolls, and life-sized dolls are scary as fuck."

A surprised laugh escaped Zach. "You could've used kids from town. I'm sure there are a whole bunch who would've loved to dress up as a doll and be in a Christmas parade."

"Thought about that, but I couldn't work out a design in my head that left room on the float for people to stand on. Why?" A teasing smile played over Holland's lips. "You don't like my float?"

"Please," Zach scoffed. "It's the best one here."

"You might be biased."

"No. I thought that before we, uh…" Glancing around, confirming no one was close enough to hear, he whispered, "…started dating."

Holland winked at him. "I still think you're biased." He took a small sip of tea, then turned for the bench against the wall. "Sit with me for a bit? I need a break."

"You okay?"

Holland grunted, slouching onto the bench. "My back hurts from bending over and painting shutters all afternoon. God. I must sound so old saying that."

"Not really." Zach sat next to him. "I've been working so much, I don't remember what it's like for my feet not to hurt."

"You working tomorrow?"

"Yeah, in the afternoon. After my interview."

"Interview for what?"

Zach gave him the details, blushing when Holland smiled wide with delight. "That's great, Zach."

"Yeah."

"You're not excited?"

Zach shifted on the bench. "I am, but… I don't know who the other candidates are, so I don't know how to make myself stand out above them."

"I don't think you have anything to worry about," Holland said, voice soft. Intimate. "You've always stood out above everybody else."

Overcome with emotion, Zach bit his lip to hide a grin as his belly leaped with butterflies. He wanted to lean over and kiss Holland, right on the jaw above that spot of purple paint, but they hadn't discussed whether or not they'd keep their new relationship a secret for now, so he stayed in his corner of the bench. "That's the nicest thing anyone's ever said to me."

Holland held his gaze and there was something in it that made Zach's heart feel light, that made him want to crawl over to Holland and snuggle against that hard chest, tuck his head underneath that strong chin, and just…be. With the way Holland was looking at him, he'd totally let him…if not for the two dozen other people in the room.

Clearing his throat, Holland sipped his tea, then said, "How are you getting to Portland tomorrow?"

"My car?"

Holland groaned. "Take my truck."

"Are you sure? But what about you?"

"I'm fixing the Seagulls' bathroom fan tomorrow, then talking to the mayor about a pergola, and then I'll be here for the rest of the day. I can walk everywhere."

"If you're sure…"

Holland discreetly squeezed Zach's thigh. "I'm sure. Don't take that death trap car of yours as far as Portland."

Zach snorted. "Okay. Thank you."

"I'm just looking out for you," Holland told him before his expression went positively stricken—denim blue eyes huge, he straightened from his slouch and waved a hand around like he could erase his last sentence from existence. "But not in, like, a dad kind of way."

"Ugh." Zach made a face. "Why would you say that to me? What's wrong with you?" He stood and went over to his desk, sitting in his chair and fighting off a shudder. "Ew."

"I guess you don't have a daddy kink?"

"Just stop talking."

Holland laughed.

# CHAPTER EIGHT

*14 days until the parade*

THE NEXT DAY, ZACH DROVE AWAY FROM HIS SECOND interview with the Gold Stone hotel chain with an assignment—to plan a fundraising event for a hundred people. He got to select the cause and location, but next Saturday he had to present a cost-benefit analysis as well as his strategy behind his choices of venue, food, invitation list, entertainment, and party favors or door prizes.

Next Saturday. A week from now. He had to plan a complete fundraiser—research locations and costs and best practices—while working on the Christmas parade, the Christmas fair, fulfilling orders from his Etsy store, and putting in shifts at the café.

When would he have time to breathe? Or see Holland?

He parked Holland's truck on the street outside of the Lighthouse Bay Town Hall. An older home a few minutes from Main Street, it also housed the town's visitor center. Inside, a teenager was manning the customer service counter while a couple of tourists browsed through the display of brochures.

"Hey." Zach nodded at the teen. "Is Mrs. Shoemacker

in today?"

"Yoo-hoo! Johnathan!"

The teenager—Johnathan, presumably—huffed.

"I'll just follow the sound of her voice," Zach said, doing just that. He followed a hallway to its end where a door on the right with a placard that read *Lighthouse Bay Business Improvement Association* led into what had probably been this house's dining room at one point. Against one wall was a fireplace. Opposite it was a small table with one of those fancy coffee makers that brewed by the cup. There were six desks in the long space, all of them unoccupied.

All but one.

Mrs. Shoemacker sat behind a sturdy wooden desk, purple cat eyeglasses perched on her nose, and her gray hair pulled into some sort of twisty thing at the back of her head.

Zach knocked on the doorframe.

"Zach." She adjusted her glasses. "Is everything all right with the parade?"

"Oh yeah, everything's fine." He took the chair in front of her desk. "Do you have a few minutes? I wanted to ask you about something."

"Sure."

He told her about his assignment for his job interview, then finished with, "I was wondering if there are any fund-raising events the BIA is planning that I could base my presentation on?"

"Well, there will be a couple next year. As I'm sure you know, proceeds raised from the lobster festival are directed to families who have lost loved ones at sea. And—"

"The lobster festival," Zach interrupted. "Can I use that?"

Mrs. Shoemacker hemmed and hawed. "I don't know,

Zach. You know Mr. Barry's the one who organizes it."

"No, I know. And I don't want to step on any toes. I just figured that if I was going to put together a plan for a fundraiser, it might as well be based on something real. I can even pass my business plan on to you once I'm done to share with Mr. Barry. I'm sure he's got it covered, but he might find something useful in there."

She chuckled. "Okay, Zach. Why not? Let's see what you come up with. Here." Rising from her chair, she crossed to a desk with a small name card that had Mr. Barry's name on it, opened a drawer, and pulled out a binder that, while not as thick as the Christmas parade/fair one, was still quite hefty. "Why don't you take this?" Mrs. Shoemacker handed it over. "It's Mr. Barry's notes from the last two festivals. It'll give you a starting point."

Zach beamed at her. "This is great! Thank you. Hey, is the mayor in by any chance?"

The mayor wasn't in, not on a Saturday, but Zach coincidentally bumped into him on the street on the way back to Holland's truck. He had a box from Dev's Bakery tucked under one arm and a leash in the other.

Zach crouched to greet the hyperactive little Chihuahua that tried to climb his leg. "Hey, Scout." The dog rested his front paws on Zach's knees. "Mr. Mayor."

"Good to see you, Zach. Is Holland with you?"

The dog whined when Zach stood abruptly. Had the mayor somehow figured out Zach and Holland were dating? How had they given themselves away? "What, uh… What do you mean?"

The mayor gestured at Holland's truck. "Isn't this his? I thought he and I were meeting at my house."

"Oh!" Oh wow. Zach hadn't realized that the prospect of the whole town knowing about them would freak him out so much. Not that he was embarrassed to be with Holland. In fact, he wanted to advertise it from the rooftops that Holland had finally *seen* him…but maybe not just yet. "No, I borrowed his truck to go to Portland."

"Ah. Your car still giving you trouble?"

Scout whined at Zach's feet, so Zach bent to scratch his head. "You know about that?"

The mayor laughed. "We've all heard your car putting around town."

Zach sighed. One of these days he'd get it looked at. After the holidays maybe, when he wasn't as busy.

"Did you find what you were looking for inside?" Mr. Mayor eyed Zach's binder. "I see you've got one of Mr. Barry's binders."

"Yeah." Zach straightened. "It's for a project I'm working on. Actually, I was looking for you as well. You're still going to play Santa at the parade and the fair?"

"Of course!" The mayor's white beard twitched when he smiled. "I'm looking forward to it. My grandkids are coming, you know."

"And you'll still be one of our judges for the float competition?"

"Oh yes, I wouldn't miss that. Remind me when that is again."

"Two o'clock on the day of the parade. That gives the judges an hour to survey the floats and fill in the score sheets before the parade starts. The winner will be announced at the fair."

"Perfect." The mayor whistled for Scout, who'd wandered as far as his leash would allow to sniff at a snowbank dotted with yellow. "I've got to head off to my meeting with Holland. Good luck with whatever's in that binder, Zach."

He left, and Zach had a minute of indecision over what

to do with Holland's truck. Keep it for the rest of the day and drop it back off at Holland's after his shift at the café? Or drive it over to the mayor's, who lived down the street, since Holland would be there soon anyway?

He kept it. He liked having a tangible connection to Holland, something to tie them together. Plus, the truck smelled like Holland, and being surrounded by his scent was comforting. He also liked that Holland had added the small house key chain onto his key ring.

The café was already packed for the typical busy lunch hour when Zach walked in a few minutes later, after a quick stop upstairs to change out of his suit and into jeans and a T-shirt and his mint green Converse. The line up had mostly been dealt with by the time he arrived, so Alana sent him to the back to fill panini and soup orders.

Which was where Mika was also working. He had a series of buns spread out in front of him, as well as lettuce, five different deli meats, tomatoes, pickles, apples, and assorted condiments, and was working based off an order sheet, making tonight's preordered sandwiches.

"Uh, hi?" Zach said.

Mika smiled wanly. "Hey."

Let the awkward silence commence. Except Mika didn't let it get that far. "Alana said you could train me on the cash register later today."

"She what?" An order came through on the menu screen that was hooked onto the corner of Zach's workstation. He slipped on a pair of clear plastic gloves and got to work making a turkey, avocado, and pesto panini with a side of raw veggies. It kept him from acknowledging how annoyed it made him that Alana always *assumed* instead of *asking*. Almost annoyed enough to ignore how gross and slimy the avocado felt, even through the gloves.

"Is that okay?" Mika asked. "It's just that the register is different than the one your parents had when I worked here, and even if it was the same, it's been, like, seventeen years or something since I worked here—"

"It's fine," Zach said, interrupting Mika's ramble. "After the lunch rush but before the preorder pick ups?"

Mika's smile was more genuine this time. "That'd be great. Thanks."

Sure. Because it wouldn't be weird at all working with Holland's ex.

"Listen." Mika snapped off his own gloves, then walked over to Zach, wiping his palms on his apron. "I wanted to apologize for the other night. I didn't see you standing there when I kissed Holland."

Zach stiffened.

"Honestly, I didn't even know he was seeing anyone new," Mika continued. "I promise I'm not here to cause trouble between you. Holland mentioned that he told you what's going on with me?"

Holland and Mika had been *talking*? Beyond yesterday's quiet chat before Mika had asked for a job? Jealousy roared, a big, ugly freight train that made his shoulders lock and his teeth clench. It was stupid—Holland had told him that he was over Mika. But that was before Mika had popped back into his life unexpectedly. Had his reappearance unburied the feelings he used to have for Mika?

No. Zach had to believe they hadn't. Had to get over his insecurity and believe Holland was telling him the truth when he said he was over Mika.

Zach put the sandwich in the panini press and set the timer. "Not the details," he told Mika. "Just that you're sick."

"I got diagnosed with cancer a couple of weeks ago." Mika swallowed roughly, throat clicking audibly. "I came home because I don't want to go through it alone."

Alone. Was Mika alone out there in LA? It seemed impossible. Mika had always been charming and vivacious, and he had a fan following that could rival Jensen Ackles's. But fans didn't equal friends. And if there was one thing Zach knew, it was what it was like to be friendless. To feel alone in a sea of people, wishing you belonged. To want closeness so desperately that you searched for it everywhere.

Sympathy overshadowed jealousy, and he placed a hand on Mika's where it rested on the table. "You won't." The timer on the panini press beeped, and he lifted the lid and carefully slid the sandwich onto a plate. "You know, when my mom was diagnosed, and even when she was going through treatment, she kept busy. Kept working as much as she could, and even got involved in volunteering a couple of times a month. She said staying active kept her mind off what she was going through." He brought the plate out front, and when he came back into the kitchen, Mika was standing where Zach had left him, contemplating his hands.

"No offense or anything, Zach," Mika said. "But I don't think working here is what's going to keep my mind off things. I mean, it's fine for now, but for the long term, I think I'll need something a bit more challenging."

Zach snorted a laugh. "I'm not offended, are you kidding? I can't wait to quit this place." Two orders came through in quick succession, and he got to prepping new sandwiches.

"So, why don't you?" Mika asked, heading back to his own workstation.

"Can't afford to."

"Yeah, I remember what that was like after college, with debt coming out of my ass."

Zach spread cranberry mayo over a couple of slices of bread and eyed Mika, who probably made more for filming two episodes of his TV show than Zach would ever see in a year. "It must be nice not to have to worry about money."

"Yeah," Mika acknowledged. "But—and this is going to sound totally cliché—money doesn't buy happiness. Sometimes it doesn't even buy contentment."

"You don't like being an actor?"

"I like being an actor. I don't like all of the backstabbing and politics that is Hollywood."

"What's next for you, then?"

Mika's lips tilted in a wry smile. "Wait for test results that'll tell me whether or not I'm dying?"

As a joke, it was a bit morbid for Zach's tastes, but if Mika needed humor to help him get through a life-changing diagnosis, who was he to judge?

"Sounds depressing," Zach said, trying to match Mika's affected levity. "And boring. How do you feel about building parade floats?"

"Are you sure about this?"

Holland peered past Zach to contemplate Mika. Zach and Mika had arrived at headquarters—together, of all things—after their shifts at the café, smelling of coffee and deli meats, and carrying trays of sandwiches and cookies for the volunteers.

"I'm sure." Zach fell onto the bench next to Holland's Christmas Lane float, groaned in what sounded like relief, then fell sideways, resting his head on his arm.

Tucked into a corner and out of anyone's direct line

of sight, Holland gave in to temptation and ran his hand through Zach's hair. The strands were soft against his fingers, silky and smooth, but wet in a few places. It must've been snowing outside.

"Are you okay?"

Zach grunted.

"Tired?"

Zach grunted again.

"Have you had dinner?"

"No." Zach moaned. "But if I eat another sandwich, I'm going to hurl."

"I'm just finishing up here," Holland said. "I was going to make fettuccini Alfredo for dinner for Dev and me. Want to join us?"

Zach visibly drooled. "I smell," he said, apropos of nothing.

"Yup."

"Gotta go home and shower first."

"Shower at my place," Holland offered. He hated Zach's apartment. It was small and cold and impersonal. There was nothing of Zach's personality anywhere. Just generic furniture and decorations. The only nod to Zach was the string of Christmas lights strung around the window and a shelf holding baskets filled with pens, ink cartridges, and more paper than Holland had ever seen in one place. Otherwise, the apartment was as sterile as a model home. For someone who loved Christmas, Holland was surprised Zach didn't have a Christmas tree. "I'll even provide you with an ice-cold beer before you get in."

"Twist my arm."

Laughing, Holland nudged him up. "Come on, let's get out of here."

On the way out, they stopped by the snack table.

Holland waited for Mika to finish his conversation with Mrs. Columbus before grabbing his attention. He looked better today, calmer, if tired from a full day at Tiny's Panini.

"Good thing I never saw these floats in their half-built stages when I was a kid," Mika said, eyes bouncing from float to float to float. "It would've ruined the magic of Christmas."

"Zach says you're going to help me with Santa's float," Holland said.

"Yeah?" Mika glanced from Holland to Zach and back. "If that's okay? He said you needed the help, and…" He leaned sideways to look past Holland at the Santa float that was only a third complete. "Looks like he's right."

"I'm always right," Zach mumbled.

Holland swallowed a laugh, and Mika chuckled out-right, his smile for Zach warm.

"Are you sure about this?" Holland asked. "Shouldn't you be resting or something?"

Mika crossed his arms. "I'm sure. Frankly, I could use the distraction."

"Okay then. Want to meet me here about eight tomor-row morning?"

Mika's nose scrunched. "Eight? On a Sunday? Sunday's the day of rest."

"Not during Lighthouse Bay parade season, it isn't."

"Fair enough. Sure, I'll see you then." He turned to leave, but Zach reached out and snagged the sleeve of his jacket.

"Do you want to join us for dinner?"

Surprised, Holland turned to look at him, eyebrows raised. Even Mika gaped at him.

Zach back-pedaled and addressed Holland. "I mean, if you have enough food." He winced. "Sorry, I should've asked first."

"There'll be more than enough," Holland said. To Mika: "Join us."

"Are you sure?" Mika looked like he wanted to accept, but also like he wanted to run away. "I don't want to interrupt date night." He whispered the last two words while glancing furtively around.

"You're not," Zach said. "Dev'll be there too. Come on." Turning, he headed for the door and tossed Holland his truck keys over his shoulder.

"Guess I'm having dinner with you guys," Mika mumbled.

Holland barely heard him, too busy staring after Zach. Who knew such a take-charge attitude would turn him on?

Mika knocked into him on his way past, following Zach. "Wipe that smitten grin off your face if you're trying to keep your relationship a secret."

Holland tried, but it was hard.

Outside, Mika got stopped by someone else who wanted to say hello and welcome him back to town. Holland caught up to Zach in the parking lot. "Thank you," he said, giving Zach's hand a discreet squeeze as they walked toward Holland's truck. "For inviting Mika. I know it must be weird for you."

"It is," Zach admitted, his smile rueful. "But he seems like he could really use a friend right now."

Holland sighed at the thought of what Mika was going through. What he'd *yet* to go through. The unanswered questions must've been driving him crazy.

They jumped into the truck and, a few seconds later, Mika joined them, hopping into the back. A few minutes after that, Holland was pulling into his driveway just as Clark was coming down the sidewalk.

CHRISTMAS JANE | 133

"Yo!" he called when he was close enough.

"Hey," Holland called back, slamming the truck door behind him. "What are you doing here?"

"I was too lazy to cook. Thought we could order a pizza or something."

"It's not pizza, but I'm making fettuccine Alfredo."

"Sweet! Even better. Mika!" Clark slung an arm around Mika's shoulders and planted a kiss on his temple. "Sorry Dev was a jerk yesterday."

It was as close to an apology that Mika was going to get from Clark. Mika knew it too. He pushed Clark away with a laugh. "Get off me, asshole."

Dev had filled a large pot with water for the pasta, but that was it. He hadn't even turned on the burner. As he constantly said, "I'm a baker, not a cook." So getting him to fill a pot was an accomplishment in itself.

Holland grabbed a beer from the fridge, let Mika and Clark make themselves at home, and led Zach upstairs to his bedroom.

Zach's head was on a swivel, taking in everything from the framed pictures on the dresser, the round clock with the Eiffel Tower motif on the wall, the blue-and-white striped bedspread. The bedroom wasn't all that interesting—blue walls, a dresser in mahogany wood, a king-sized bed topped with half a dozen fluffy pillows—but it had more personality than Zach's entire apartment. Holland's college degree hung on the wall next to the window. A TV dominated the wall space across from the bed. A wood shelf above the bed showcased some of his favorite novels. And on a corner of the dresser sat a handful of key chains, his favorites from those mystery packages he was always picking up that Dev constantly teased him about.

He pulled a pair of boxers, sweatpants, and a T-shirt

from his dresser and left them on the bed for Zach. Then, because he felt like it, he pulled Zach to him and held him close, slipping his hands under Zach's T-shirt to caress the warm skin of his waist. He still smelled like coffee, but also like something uniquely Zach and a hint of soap. He was sinewy and perfect against Holland, and Holland held him tighter.

Zach mumbled something Holland didn't catch and snuggled into Holland, giving Holland his weight, and burying his face in Holland's neck. He sighed deeply and all of the tension in his body left with it, leaving him a limp noodle in Holland's arms.

"How was your day?" Holland asked into Zach's hair, because this was the first minute they'd had alone since Zach came by to pick up the truck this morning. "Did you get the job?"

Zach groaned. "No. I got an assignment. I have to plan a fundraiser for a hundred people and present it to them next week."

"Can I help?"

"I don't know yet. I haven't had a chance to start working on it. But I'll let you know." Zach pulled back, his honey eyes warm when they met Holland's. He placed a tiny kiss on Holland's lips. "Thank you."

Holland stared at him for a few moments, his heart in his throat as he got lost in Zach's eyes. "I…"

"What?" Zach kissed him, high up on his cheekbone, a sweet, barely there brush of lips that made Holland's breath stutter in its simplicity.

He shook his head, the words he wanted to say lost somewhere between his heart and his mouth. He swiped Zach's lips with his thumb, then followed that up with a kiss, tilting Zach's head to get a better angle. Zach opened

CHRISTMAS JANE | 135

for him, fingers digging into Holland's hair. Holland kept the kiss slow, savoring Zach's soft moans. Zach ran a hand over Holland's jaw and down his neck as if craving the feel of Holland's skin and Holland pressed into him, seeking more contact.

This was so…right. Odd also, given that Mika was right downstairs. To have his ex here, reminding him of exactly what he didn't want—someone with a constant foot out the door as he sought something *more*. More than Lighthouse Bay. More than Holland. And to have Zach right in front of him, embodying everything he did want. Companionship. Acceptance. Understanding. Friendship.

Love.

He'd loved Mika once. But, over time, it had faded, become something that made him hurt, made him itch, especially with the way things had ended between them. And yet, clearing the air between them meant he could look back on that time of his life with fondness and remember the good times rather than the bad.

But Zach… Zach was *here* and he was *real* and he wasn't going anywhere. He had a way of brightening up Holland's day with his quiet strength and tired smiles. Being in his presence was like getting a jolt of adrenaline—it got Holland's blood moving, made him want to sit and shout that Zach's smiles were forever going to be for *him*, and nobody else.

What he felt for Zach wasn't explosive. It wasn't what Dev and Clark would have one day if they ever got their heads out of their asses. It was quieter. Gentle. A leaf blowing in the wind. A gently burbling creek. A quietly burning flame.

It was like they were building a bridge from two different sides. A bridge that was beautiful and intricate but had a solid foundation of core steel where it met in the middle.

Holland nipped Zach's lip, making Zach laugh.

"Gah!" Out in the hallway, Dev had come out of the bathroom and was backing away from Holland's open door with a hand over his eyes. "Can't you close the door? I don't want to see my cousin making out with some guy."

"Zach's not *some guy*," Holland grumbled after him.

"You know what I mean. Door! Closed!" Dev disappeared down the stairs.

Zach kissed Holland's cheek and grabbed the clothes off the bed and the beer off the dresser. "I'm going to shower. Get rid of the coffee smell." He headed for the en suite bathroom. "Give me five minutes."

"Take your time," Holland said, waiting until the shower started before going back downstairs.

Clark was nursing a beer in the kitchen while Dev and Mika were having a quiet conversation in the living room. Holland nodded in their direction. "Everything okay there?"

"Yup," Clark said. "Dev's apologizing for being the biggest bag of dicks there ever was."

Holland grunted and hip checked Clark out of the way so he could get to the pans.

"Where's your boy?"

"He's not a *boy*," Holland retorted, bending to remove a pan from the cupboard.

Clark waved his hand. "You know what I meant. Where'd he go?"

"Shower. He smells like coffee. If you're going to stand around, can you make yourself useful and get the cheese and cream out of the fridge?"

Holland got to work, and between the two of them, they had the sauce thickening in the pan and the water boiling for the pasta within a few minutes. Zach's footsteps sounded on the stairs, and Holland found himself grinning like an idiot before the man himself even walked into the room.

"You got it bad," Clark muttered.

"Fuck off," Holland said good-naturedly.

"Your shower's amazing!" Zach bounced into the kitchen, wearing a pair of beat-up leather slippers he'd unearthed from…somewhere. Under Holland's bed, maybe. He was only a few inches shorter than Holland, yet the sweatpants and T-shirt hung off his slimmer frame. His smile turned soft when he spotted his flowers still sitting in their water glass on the table. They were a little wilted, but no less beautiful. "How do I get that kind of water pressure?"

"Holland can probably fix that for you," Dev said, coming into the kitchen, Mika not far behind him. They were both grinning, so things must've gone well.

"Or you can just shower here," Holland suggested.

Zach grinned at him and hopped onto the counter. "Got anything to munch on?"

Holland pointed at the bread box. "There's some sourdough in there."

"Dev's?"

"Of course."

Tadashi made an appearance, padding into the kitchen to wind around their ankles and then settle at Dev's feet.

"Why are you all standing around? Here." Holland passed the cheese grater to Clark. "Grate some extra cheese and put it on the table. You two—" He pointed at Mika and Dev. "—set the table."

"What about me?" Zach asked.

"You can be my cheerleader."

"Holland, Holland, he's our man. He makes dinner

better than anyone can."

They all cracked up, making Zach grin at them as if they'd given him a prize. Holland kissed him quickly because he could before going back to stirring the sauce.

"Anyone have any objections to shrimp in their pasta?"

He got enthusiastic approval.

"Dev, can you get the shrimp from the freezer in the basement?"

"On it." Dev disappeared downstairs.

"Oh, and bring a package of fettuccini," Holland called while turning the temperature down on the boiling water. Taking a look at his hungry customers, he amended, "Make that two."

"And can you bring up my snowboard?" Clark said from the top of the stairs. "I think I left it here last time we went. Should be in the back next to Holland's skis."

"And while you're down there," Zach said. "A money tree."

They laughed again, and Zach bit his lip to hide a pleased grin.

"You're all a fucking riot!" came Dev's voice from downstairs, sending them all off again.

"Have you ever contemplated your own mortality?" Holland stood at the window in his living room and waved at Clark and Mika as they got into Holland's truck. Clark would drop Mika off, then bring the truck back before making the short five-minute walk to his own house. Dev had already gone up to bed, claiming a headache.

"Can't say that I have." Zach nursed an apple cinnamon

tea and admired the ornaments on Holland's Christmas tree.

"Me neither," Holland said as the truck backed out of the driveway. "At least not until recently." Until Mika had come home with cancer.

Zach wrapped his arms around him from behind and hooked his chin over Holland's shoulder. "Are you okay?"

Was he? After dinner, he'd pulled Mika aside while Zach cleared the table and Dev and Clark washed the dishes.

"I wanted to apologize," Holland had said. "For the way I treated you back then. You didn't deserve the brunt of my anger just because work was shitty."

"I…" Mika blinked at him. "Thank you."

"And the truth is," Holland continued, finally owning up to five-year-old feelings, "I was so pissed that you left."

"You… What?" Mika crossed his arms and sat on the arm of the couch. "But you *encouraged* me to go, to follow my dreams."

"Because I *did* want you to go. I wanted you to find whatever it was you needed. To be happy. To start your career. But that doesn't mean that I wasn't pissed that you couldn't do that here. I know it makes no sense, okay?"

Mika waited a beat, eyes on the floor. "You never said anything."

"I know. I was afraid of telling you how I really felt. Afraid that, if I asked you to stay, you'd say no."

Mika shook his head. In the kitchen, Dev, Clark, and Zach were chatting about something that made Zach laugh, and the sound reached into Holland's chest and settled there like an old friend.

"Don't make the same mistake with Zach that you made with me," Mika had said, nodding toward the kitchen. "Talk to him. Tell him what's in here." He poked Holland on the left side of his chest. "Otherwise you might push him away by mistake like you did me."

Holland shook off the memory. "I'm scared for him." He answered Zach's question—*Are you okay?*—and threaded his fingers with Zach's.

"I know how that feels."

Shaking off his mood, Holland turned in Zach's arms and cupped his face. "How are *you*? You look tired. Long day?"

"Yeah." Zach fell into Holland, resting his head on Holland's shoulder. "I should've gone with Clark so he could drop me off too instead of making you go out later."

Holland ran his fingers through Zach's soft hair. "Or you could stay the night."

Zach pulled back, chewing on his lip, eyes wary.

"Just to sleep," Holland clarified. "Since you already told me you don't want to have sex."

Groaning, Zach slumped onto Holland's chest. "Can we forget that ever happened?"

Holland chuckled. "No. In fact, I'd really love an explanation."

Zach mumbled something against Holland's T-shirt.

Running a hand up and down Zach's back, Holland leaned closer. "I didn't catch that."

Straightening, Zach squared his shoulders. The color in his face could rival that of an overripe tomato as he said, "I don't like sex."

"Oh." Holland processed that for a second. He'd known there was something more to Zach's blurted *I don't want to have sex* from the other day. But "I don't like sex" wasn't a scenario that had crossed his mind. "Okay. Like, all sex? Or just penetrative sex? What about blow jobs?"

If anything, Zach went redder. "Um, I've never had

one. A blow job, I mean. But I didn't like penetrative sex. Ugh." He pulled the neck of his T-shirt up, covering his face. "Why can't lightning strike me down right now?"

"Don't say that." Holland squeezed his arms. "It's okay."

Zach peeked up at him, the T-shirt sliding back down to rest wrinkled against his body. "Is it? But you like sex, don't you?"

"Yes. Very much so. But that doesn't mean we can't figure this out." How they'd figure it out was unclear as of yet. Holland didn't need to jump right into sex at the start of a new relationship, but for him, sex was an important part of a trusting, stable relationship. It established a level of intimacy reserved only for someone equally as committed to him as he was to them. Maybe he and Zach weren't there yet, but the possibility was. "If you don't mind me asking… Why don't you like it?"

Zach's shoulders jerked in a shrug that broadcasted how uncomfortable he was. "It hurts."

"It *hurt*?" Oh, Zach. Holland brought his hands up and kissed the knuckles. "I'm sorry your partners didn't take care of you." More words almost tripped off the edge of his tongue. About how some selfish assholes shouldn't be allowed to engage in sexual activities, and how Holland was older and more experienced and knew how to make it good.

But that wasn't what Zach wanted to hear right now. Not during this particular conversation, and not at this early stage of their relationship.

Zach averted his eyes. "It was college."

"That's not an excuse for ignorance. Thank you for telling me." He wrapped Zach in his arms, fitting Zach against him. Zach snuggled deeper, nosing into Holland's neck. "You never answered my question, though. Stay the night?"

"I'd like that."

"Come on." He kissed Zach's temple. "Let's head up."

They shut off the lights downstairs, leaving the Christmas tree lights for last. When Holland straightened from unplugging the cord behind the tree, he spotted a slim, flat package wrapped in dancing penguins wearing Santa hats sitting underneath the tree. "What's this?" There was a sticker with his name on it but nothing else.

Zach started up the stairs and threw a teasing smile over his shoulder. "I don't know. What it is?"

"Is it from you? How'd you get it here? When? Do I have to wait until Christmas to open it?"

Zach's laugh trailed down the stairs. "You can open it now."

Grinning, Holland took the package with him upstairs. It was only about an inch thick, but it was tall and wide and surprisingly heavy. A book of some kind if he had to guess.

Zach was sitting on the bed in Holland's boxers when Holland entered the bedroom. Leaning back against the headboard, long legs stretched out in front of him, he was a sight Holland wanted to see lying right there, on Holland's side of the bed, again and again and again.

Maybe forever? Was it too soon to think of forever? Probably.

He pressed a kiss to Zach's lips before sitting next to him and carefully peeling back the festive wrapping paper. "You sure I shouldn't wait until Christmas?"

"I'm sure." Zach leaned their shoulders together.

The paper came away, falling to the bed between them, revealing a hardcover sketchpad. Bemused yet touched, Holland opened it up to the first page. "I use these to sketch the dollhouses before I build them. How'd you know?"

"There's one in your workshop," Zach said. "I noticed

it when we were in there the other day. All the pages are almost filled."

"Yeah, I've been meaning to pick up another one but keep forgetting. This is perfect." Holland kissed Zach's temple. "Thank you."

"You're welcome."

# CHAPTER NINE

*12 days until the parade*

BY THE TIME ALANA UNLOCKED THE DOOR TO THE café at seven on Monday morning, Zach was putting the finishing touches on the Christmas tree he'd set up in a corner next to the window. One more blown glass ornament just so, a white dove over here, an adjustment to the string of pearls. He plugged in the lights and voilà! It was officially Christmas at Tiny's Panini.

Alana stopped next to him and grinned wide. "This is beautiful, Zach. I love the blue and silver color scheme."

Blue and silver... Like Holland's eyes and hair.

Wow. He was utterly pathetic.

"Thanks for doing this," Alana said on her way to the order counter. "Mrs. Shoemacker has been bugging me about it all week. Oh, hey! You might get your wish soon and be free of this place. I got a whole bunch of new applications this weekend for some reason. Some of them look promising. I've already got a handful of interviews lined up for this week."

"Oh, really?" Thank God. Those job ads he'd sent to every college within a fifty-mile radius had panned out.

The front door opened, letting Rosie and Jennifer into

the restaurant. They pushed a couple of tables together, then hung coats and scarves over the back of an empty chair.

"Morning, Zach," Rosie said. "Hear anything about the job in Florida yet?"

Before he could tell her that the job wasn't in Florida, the door opened again. Charlie and Hank walked in, then Jean behind them, completing the Tiny's Panini morning quintet. More often than not, others joined them, but it was always the five of them at the core, even on days Jean and Rosie worked at Dev's Bakery next door.

Zach retreated to the kitchen to get away from the crowd and spent three hours fulfilling breakfast orders that came in one after the other, almost faster than he could keep up. It was mind-numbing work. Slice open a bun. Slap on lettuce, tomato, and an egg. Bacon, occasionally. Toast in the panini press. Add some hash browns. Walk to the front.

Repeat ad nauseam.

He wouldn't smell like coffee at the end of his shift today. Instead, he'd smell like fried potatoes. He wasn't sure which was worse.

Zari had come in before things got too crazy and was currently tidying up her station where she'd been frying up eggs. Marcus was working the dishwasher.

His phone rang in his pocket after the breakfast rush, when he was cleaning up and putting things to rights. *Mom* the screen read.

"Hey, Mom." He turned the volume down on his portable speakers and sat in the chair in the minuscule office space, leaving the door open in case any orders came through.

"Hi, sweetie. How are you? How'd your interview go on Saturday?" Her voice was warm and bubbly, and a pang hit

Zach in the heart. It had been four months since he'd seen his parents and yet it felt like much longer.

"It went really well," he said. "But I have a third one this weekend. Hopefully I'll know after that."

"A *third* interview? Well, they're certainly thorough. I hope they're not just stringing you along."

"Yeah, that makes two of us. How's Florida?"

They chatted for a few minutes about mundane things, and when his mom asked what was new in his life…

"I'm seeing someone," he blurted without thinking.

His mom gasped. "You are?" Her pleasure and surprise were clear through the phone, her voice going up to a squeak. "Oh, I'm so happy! Dwayne!" Zach pulled the phone away from his ear as she called for his dad. "Dwayne, Zach has a boyfriend!"

"He's not my—"

"Oh, I'm so *happy*," she repeated. "Dwayne!"

"I heard you the first time," came his dad's deep, grumbly voice. They must've been sharing the phone now. "Anybody we know, Zach?"

"Uh…"

"Tell us about him," his mom demanded. "What's he like? What does he do? Where'd you meet? This is so exciting!"

His dad said, "It is pretty momentous."

They'd reacted the same way when he'd gotten into college.

"Did you meet online? Isn't that how all the kids are meeting these days?"

Zach snorted a laugh and made a mental note to finally delete the dating app off his phone. "No, Dad. We, uh, we've known each other for a while."

"So it is someone we know. Is it that weird kid who eats

his boogers?"

"The one who works at the sporting goods store?" his mom piped in.

"That weird kid only ate his boogers in kindergarten," Zach said. Poor Nick would never live it down.

His dad grunted. "Is it that boy you had a crush on in first grade?"

"What boy did I have a crush on?"

"The one with the floppy hair."

"That literally could've been anybody in my class in first grade."

"I don't remember his name."

"Oh, stop it," his mom said. "Let Zach tell us himself."

"But I like this game," his dad muttered.

"So? Who is it, Zach?"

"It's, uh, Holland."

Silence.

He could only imagine them on the other end of the line, standing on a sunny porch in perfect-weather Florida, sharing bewildered glances over the phone.

It was his mother who broke the silence, voice tentative as she said, "We only know one Holland."

Zach rubbed his forehead. "Yup." Maybe this had been a bad idea. Should he have waited to tell them in person? On the other hand, at least this way he didn't have to see the looks on their faces, whatever they might be. He was leaning towards concern and/or disapproval.

"Holland…Stone?" His dad's tone was so confused it was almost funny.

"Holland Stone," Zach confirmed.

Silence.

Why, no, this wasn't awkward at all.

The silence went on for so long that Zach said, "Are you

guys still there?"

"Yes," his mom said slowly. "Yes, we're here. Just…"

"Holland Stone?" his dad said again. "He's my age."

"He's fifteen years younger than you, Dad."

"Which makes him fifteen years older than you."

"I don't understand." His mom's voice was so small it made Zach hunch into himself.

"We just…" Zach shrugged, at a loss for words. He'd known they wouldn't understand. He should've kept their relationship to himself for a while longer instead of having it tainted by his parents' disapproval. "We click."

"You click…" Her voice trailed off. "Do you think…?" She paused and started again. "You don't think you might be happier with someone your own age?"

"I've never really connected with people my own age, Mom." Zach picked at his jeans. "You know that. I mean, have you ever known me to even have a best friend?"

"No. We always thought that was strange, your dad and me. How you didn't have more friends."

His dad grunted.

"Holland and me…" Zach floundered, lost. "We just… we get each other. We fit. Other than you guys, he's the first person to truly understand and accept me as I am."

"Alana accepts you," his dad argued.

"Accepts me, yes. Just like I accept her. But we've never understood each other." He loved his sister to bits, but he'd never understood how she couldn't see clearly outside of herself and her circle.

"Okay, well…" His mother paused for a second. "As long as you're happy?"

"I'm happy, Mom." For the first time in his life, he felt like he actually belonged somewhere. "I'm happy."

"Good." His dad's voice was gruff. "If you're happy,

Zach, then we're happy for you."

"You are?"

"As long as he's treating you right, we don't have anything to worry about."

"He's great, Dad. You'll see next time you're here." Was it bad juju to plan ahead like that? To assume that they'd still be together whenever his parents visited next?

"Speaking of the next time we'll visit…" His mom cleared her throat. "I don't know if Alana told you, but we won't be coming home for Christmas this year."

Zach slumped in his chair, shoulders sinking. "Oh." He'd hoped Alana'd been kidding or had heard them wrong.

"We're so sorry, sweetie. Turns out we waited too long to book our flight and now the prices are ridiculous. We'll come visit the second week of January and celebrate the holidays then. How does that sound?"

Zach forced a smile. They couldn't see it, but maybe they'd hear it in his voice. Maybe it'd hide the fact that he wanted to cry with disappointment. "Sure! Sounds great."

They said their goodbyes shortly after.

He stared at the phone in his hand. So. That could've gone worse. They hadn't outright told him he was making a mistake with Holland. They were happy he was happy. And it sounded like they meant it.

*Please let them mean it.* He'd spent the past twenty-four years of his life trying to fit in. To find that place where he belonged. Outside of his parents, Holland was the first person to truly accept him as he was. Even Holland's friends had adopted him into their circle. They joked with him. They included him in conversations. They asked his opinion. And, yesterday, they'd dragged him away from where he'd been working on his secret project at Mr. Barry's desk in headquarters, shoved a paintbrush in his hand, and ordered him to help with Santa's float.

Not because they needed the help. They'd had everything under control.

But because they wanted to hang out with him.

It was… He didn't know what it was. Surreal. Exciting. Fun. Unexpected.

Terrifying. Because it could all get taken away if they decided he wasn't worth it. He tried not to think about that.

Was it weird that he got along better with people older than him? Clearly he'd been born in the wrong decade.

Michael Bublé's "Have Yourself A Merry Little Christmas" came on the radio. Zach rested his head back against the chair and closed his eyes, letting the lyrics of his favorite song weave life into him.

Holland walked into Tiny's Panini via the back door, toolbox in hand, shaking snow off his hair and shoulders. According to his weather app, there was a storm aimed directly at coastal Maine that would hit later this week, dumping a massive amount of snow in a short period of time. But in the meantime, fat flakes fell lazily from the sky, coating everything in a sheet of snow and turning the town postcard-perfect.

"Hey, Holland," Zari called. She was helping Marcus load the industrial-sized dishwasher on the far side of the kitchen. "Alana's in front. Said something about the sink acting up again?"

"Thanks." But frankly, he wanted to see Zach first.

Yet Zach was nowhere in sight, which meant he was probably out front. Holland made his way through the kitchen to the door that led into the café, but stopped when he heard a sniffle from the direction of the minuscule room Alana used as an office.

Zach sat in the office chair, eyes closed, cell phone in hand, tears making tracks down his face. Dropping the toolbox with a loud clatter, Holland rushed to him and sank to his knees at Zach's feet.

"Zach? What's wrong? What happened?"

Zach blinked his eyes open slowly, as though Holland had interrupted him mid-nap. "Huh?"

"Are you okay? Are you hurt?" Frantic, Holland ran his hands over Zach's arms, his shoulders, into his hair, feeling for bumps or bruises or scrapes. Anything that would cause Zach pain.

"He's fine," Alana said from behind him.

Holland turned to stare at her. Zach was obviously *not* fine! "What?"

Alana opened a cupboard underneath one of the long counters and pulled out a bag of paper coffee cups. "He's fine. It's just the song."

"I don't understand."

Zach sniffled.

"The song," she repeated. "It makes him cry."

"What song?" But he heard it then, coming from a small portable speaker on the desk—"Have Yourself A Merry Little Christmas" sung with a smooth, velvety voice. He whipped his attention back to Zach. "You're crying because of a *song*?" Jesus. Relief swept through him, making him dizzy with it.

Alana scoffed. "Ridiculous right?"

Holland stiffened, but before he could come to Zach's defense, Zach said, "It just makes me ache." He swiped his hand under his nose.

"For what?" Holland asked, running his hands up and down Zach's thighs.

"A merry little Christmas?" Alana said sarcastically.

"No." Zach wiped his eyes on his shirtsleeve. "Someone to spend my Christmases with."

His eyes were still swimming, and he looked equal parts embarrassed and mournful. Holland melted, heart thumping in tune to Zach's sniffles. Cupping Zach's face, he kissed him softly. Gently. Trying to get across without words what Zach meant to him.

Pulling back, he said, "Don't ever change."

Zach stared at him, smile sweet. "'Kay." His eyes were shiny and warm and everything he felt was right there on his face for Holland to see. Holland could get lost in those eyes, in how they lit up just for him.

"Eep!"

Jolting at the sound, Holland stood and caught Alana watching them with big eyes from the office doorway.

"You kissed my brother!"

"Yes?" Shit. Had Zach not told her yet?

She leaned sideways to peer around him at Zach.

Zach smiled feebly and waved.

"Okay, whatever." Alana shrugged, but she was still frowning. To Holland: "You'll still fix my sink, right?"

Well. That could've gone worse.

"Sorry," Holland said when she went back into the restaurant with her cups. "I didn't mean to out our relationship to your sister. I wasn't aware she didn't know." They hadn't discussed keeping their relationship a secret, and Holland had thought they were in that "our relationship is so new, so let's keep it to ourselves for now" stage. But although they were keeping things need-to-know, Holland's closest friends knew. Was Zach...embarrassed to be with an old guy?

"It's okay." Zach stood and walked into his arms, resting his head on Holland's shoulder. "I just wanted to keep it to ourselves for a while. As soon as Alana knows, Jennifer knows, and then the whole town."

"I didn't think of that."

"I told my parents on the phone earlier," Zach announced.

Holland pulled back from Zach to find his eyes. "You did?" Not embarrassed to be with an old guy, then?

"Uh-huh. They were a little concerned at first because of the age difference. But I think I talked them around."

"Good. I don't want your parents to hate me for corrupting their son."

Zach rolled his eyes. "Please. I'm incorruptible."

Laughing, Holland retraced his steps and picked up the toolbox he'd dropped. "Want to help me fix the sink?"

"No. But I'll watch you fix the sink."

"That can't be much fun for you."

Zach grinned and led the way through the kitchen door. "Oh, you don't even know."

# CHAPTER TEN

*10 days until the parade*

STARING AT HOLLAND'S BUTT WAS TRULY A PLEASURE. Zach followed Holland up the stairs of his front porch and itched to reach out and squeeze that butt. But he didn't.

Because he was a chicken.

And because he didn't want to seem like a tease. He'd already told Holland he didn't want to have sex.

Except, with Holland, he kind of did.

What did that even mean?

Turned out, it was a good thing he was a chickenshit— inside Holland's house, Dev and Clark were having an argument in the living room.

"I'm not gonna screw it up," Clark was saying.

"Do you even know how to bake?" That was Dev, but he sounded off. Like his nose was stuffed full of wool.

Zach raised an eyebrow at Holland in inquiry as he hung his coat in the closet. Holland merely shrugged.

They headed toward the raised voices. In the living room, Dev sat on the couch in sweatpants and a hoodie. He was half-wrapped in a thick throw, and a box of tissues sat next to him with used ones bunched into balls on the floor. His nose was red, his eyes were bloodshot, and he was shivering.

"You look worse than you did this morning," Holland said.

"He won't let me help." Clark crossed his arms and scowled at Dev.

"Help with what?" Holland called over his shoulder as he went into the kitchen.

"The bakery. He can't open it tomorrow like this. He almost fell flat on his face twice in the half hour I've been here. But he won't let me help."

"Do you even know what flour is?" Dev demanded.

Clark growled.

"I can help," Zach volunteered.

Holland returned with a plastic bag and handed it to Dev, who stooped stiffly to pick his tissues up off the floor, dumping them in the bag.

"Thanks, Zach," Dev said. Except with his cold, it sounded like *Tanks, Dak.* "But I know you've got enough on your plate already."

True, but… "Who else can open up the bakery for you? Rosie or Jean?"

Dev sighed. "No, they can't start until eight, and neither can my other part-timers. Nobody's able to start at 4:00 a.m. to get the baking going." He rested his head back against the couch. "Except me."

"I can." Zach sat on the arm of the love seat.

Dev contemplated him for a second. Then sneezed. "You know how to bake?"

"Sure. Just follow the recipe, taste test, and if it's not right, add more flavor."

Dev's eyes went huge.

"I'm kidding," Zach said, laughing. "Of course, I can

bake." As if he'd ever improvise.

"Okay. Thanks, Za—" Dev broke off to hack up a lung.

"Seriously?" Clark glowered first at Zach, then Dev. "How come you're letting him help but not me?"

Dev rolled his eyes. "Zach's been working in his family's café since he could walk. He knows what he's doing."

"You sure about this?" Holland asked Zach. "You've been up so late the past few nights working on your presentation. Plus with the parade and the fair... And won't Alana need you at the café at some point too?"

"I've got the afternoon shift tomorrow," Zach said. "So I can spend the morning baking at Dev's. Although..." He addressed Dev. "I won't be able to bake as fast as you, so I'll need some help."

Slumping against the couch, Dev closed his eyes and waved in Clark's general direction. "There. You got your wish. You can help Zach tomorrow." A pause, then: "Don't fuck it up."

Clark huffed. "You're going to have to be nicer to me when we get married, half pint."

"I'll marry you when Mrs. Shoemacker stops starting every conversation with *yoo-hoo*." Shifting to the other end of the couch, Dev lay down with his back to them and tucked himself under the throw. "Go away now. I need a nap. Zach, we'll talk later about what to bake first, and where everything is, and whatever else you need to know."

Considering it was after seven p.m. already, Zach wasn't sure what Dev meant by *later*. Either way, Zach pulled his little pocket day planner out of his back pocket, removed the mini pen from its little slot, and jotted down tomorrow's shift at the bakery. Not that he needed the reminder, but he liked to keep a record of things.

Tadashi padded into the room, hopped onto the couch

and over Dev's legs, and settled into the empty space between Dev's body and the couch.

Holland jerked his head in the direction of the kitchen, and Zach and Clark followed him out of the room, turning the living room light off on their way out.

"Is there something else wrong with Dev?" Zach asked quietly. "He seems unusually cranky lately."

"It's the holidays," Holland said, pulling three beers out of the fridge. "His parents died just before Christmas when he was five, when they were coming back from an event in Portland."

Right. That was before Zach was born, so he didn't know much about it. But he could empathize. His own parents were spending Christmas in another state and he was upset about it. It'd suck a lot more if they were dead and they never got another Christmas together ever again.

Wow. Way to put things in perspective. Time to get over it. He wasn't the center of their universe anymore. And that was…okay. In fact, it was good. Good for them, living their own lives away from the business that had run it for over forty years. Zach had been living his own life too for the past four years while he was away at college, coming home only for the odd weekend and on holidays. And Portland wasn't as far as Florida. He could've come back anytime. Hell, he could've stayed home and commuted, but…he'd wanted to be on his own for the first time in his life, to discover who he was. To become independent. To grow.

He pulled out his phone while Holland and Clark chatted around him and sent a group text to his parents. *I miss you guys, but I hope you're having a good time in Florida. Looking forward to seeing you in January :)*

# CHAPTER ELEVEN

*9 days until the parade*

"WHAT THE HELL IS THIS?" CLARK HELD A RECIPE for red velvet cupcakes up to his face.

It was five thirty the next morning and Zach had been at Dev's Bakery for an hour and a half already, baking everything from breads to scones to pastries to sweets. It was nice. Soothing. An empty restaurant with only himself for company. Christmas music playing softly from his cell phone. Detailed recipes to follow. An organized kitchen with labeled cabinets and drawers, making everything easy to find.

He liked baking at Dev's way better than making sandwiches next door. Baking was exact. A science. It was just as messy as cooking—flour had a tendency to get everywhere, and he didn't like getting egg whites on his hands—but it was easier to clean. By contrast, little bits of lettuce tended to stick to everything—including his hands, ew—and chopped vegetables got juice everywhere. And cauliflower... Don't even get him started on cauliflower.

Baking allowed him to think as he worked. Whereas cooking just made him twitch and make faces whenever something icky landed on his hand.

It had been a peaceful morning until Clark had shown up a few minutes ago, bringing his outdoor voice and penchant for commenting on everything.

"What's two hundred and twenty grams of flour?" Clark waved the recipe at Zach. "Why isn't this written in American?"

Zach pointed at the industrial fridge. "There's a conversion chart taped to the front there."

"A conversion chart." Clark headed over to it. "I bet you Dev doesn't even need this. Probably had them all memorized by the time he was ten."

"He was baking even then?"

"Oh yeah. From scratch too. I don't think I've ever seen him use box stuff."

"What's the story between you two, anyway?" Zach asked, sifting flour into a giant metal bowl.

Clark pursed his lips. "I could ask you the same thing about Holland."

Zach chuckled. "Fair enough. I guess I'm just…trying not to get my hopes up. With Mika back and all."

It was stupid to still be insecure about Mika's return, especially when Holland had assured him that he didn't have any lingering romantic feelings for him. But every time Zach saw Holland and Mika together, it was a reminder that Zach wasn't…well, Mika. Charming. Friendly. Talented. Full of life despite the crap he was going through.

And Zach was…quiet. Kind of a loner. Enjoyed being by himself. Liked things precise and orderly. So desperate for affection that he'd slept his way through college and mistaken sex for love.

Ugh. He hated that about himself. Although *slept his way through college* might be a bit of an overstatement. He hadn't been quite that bad, but when there were multiple guys who'd slept with him only to dismiss him without so much as a "See you later" the next morning, it did things to one's self-esteem.

That was his own fault, though, for sleeping with people he didn't have feelings for. Not even sexual attraction. Just…*want*. He'd *wanted* companionship. He'd *wanted* someone to call his own.

He'd *wanted* to be wanted back.

Seriously. He was pathetic. It was a good thing Holland couldn't see all the self-doubt rolling around in his head.

And if Holland did leave him for Mika, Zach had no one but himself to blame. Who kept throwing Holland and Mika together? Oh yeah, that was him. Inviting Mika to dinner and suggesting he help Holland with the Santa float. It was just that Holland had told him how he, Clark, and Dev had reacted to Mika's sudden reappearance, and Zach *got it*. He got how devastated Mika must've been to come home with the threat of cancer hanging over his head, hoping for support from his friends, only to find them less than enthused over his return. Zach had spent most of his life without friends. Mika didn't need to go through that too, not on top of everything else.

It was Zach's own damn fault that he had an excess of the nice gene.

"Mika?" Clark cracked two eggs, one after the other, into a bowl. "What about him?"

"Well, he's back, and he and Holland were together for a few years, and—"

"You don't need to worry about Mika," Clark interrupted. "Trust me, Holland's not going there again."

"How do you know? Holland said he wanted to marry him."

"Yeah." Clark scoffed. "Five years ago. But five years

is a long time to get over someone. He hasn't been sitting around pining for Mika that whole time."

Yeah, Holland had said something similar, hadn't he?

"They're working their way to being friends again," Clark went on, "but that's all it'll ever be."

"How can you be sure?"

For possibly the first time in Zach's recollection, Clark's eyes went serious as he looked at Zach from across the counter. "Because I've seen the way he looks at you. You make him glow." He raised his hands at Zach's incredulous eyebrow raise. "I know it sounds cheesy, but it's true. Pay attention next time you see him."

Zach poured the wet ingredients into the dry ones and used a large wooden spoon to mix everything together until it was *just blended—do not over blend*. "I will. And way to deflect from the topic of you and Dev, by the way."

Clark's grin was sly. "I thought so."

They worked in silence for a few minutes, or as silent as it could get with Clark muttering recipe directions to himself over the music from Zach's phone. After a while, Zach got so used to it that he tuned it out, to the point where he startled when Clark whooped.

"I did it!"

Jerked out of his own head, Zach paused in filling the muffin tins. "Huh?"

Clark held his baking tray out to him. "Check it out."

He'd shaped his croissants into penises.

"Dev's going to kill you," Zach predicted.

"He'll never know." Clark slid the tray into the oven.

"In this town? Everyone knows everything about everybody."

"True. How's the prep for your presentation going?"

Zach dropped his spoon, stomach sinking. "Tell me

not everybody knows about that."

"Don't think so. Holland mentioned it last night. What's it for?"

"A job interview. I need to plan a fundraiser for a hundred people. I'm almost done." He'd been working on it off and on since receiving the assignment. Turned out to be surprisingly easy too. Basing it off an actual town event had been a brilliant idea, if he did say so himself. Not only did he have Mr. Barry's notes from the last two years to go on, but he knew everyone in town, so he knew exactly who to talk to about donating both food and time. "Actually…" He played with the edge of a recipe card and regarded Clark.

"What?"

He told Clark about the lobster fest, then said, "I thought I'd add a silent auction element to the festival to raise more funds. Almost every shop on and off Main has donated something, plus we've got a free week of classes at the yoga studio and a bunch of other experiences. Is there anything you'd be able to donate?"

Clark was an outdoorsy guy. He ran walking tours around town for the tourists for fun and worked as a biologist at the wildlife refuge south of town.

"How about a pair of passes to the refuge?" he said, peering at a set of teaspoons as if they held the answers to the universe. "I'd have to talk to administration about it before committing, but if they agree, the winners would get free parking plus access to all of the activities for the season."

"That'd be great, Clark. Thanks." With everything the town was donating instead of being paid for, like they were last year—seriously, what was Mr. Barry thinking paying everyone when they were happy to donate their time and products to a good cause?—he'd be saving the town heaps of money.

The Gold Stone hotel chain would have no choice but to hire him now.

Hours later, after leaving the bakery midafternoon in Rosie and Jean's capable hands, working a shift at Tiny's Panini, and then finalizing some details for the Christmas fair, Zach sat on the bench next to Holland's float in parade headquarters—which he'd started to think of as *their* bench since they spent so many evenings chatting on it lately. Sipping an apple cinnamon tea, he let himself sink into the bench and relax for the first time all day.

His shift at Tiny's had been a short one, so for once he didn't smell like coffee. He thought he might smell like yeast or sugar, but Holland had assured him that all he smelled was Zach, whatever that meant.

Speaking of Holland, the man himself was on the other side of his float, tinkering with something that was making him curse. Whatever he was doing was probably unnecessary anyway. To Zach, the float looked as ready as it could be.

"What are you going to do with this float once the parade's over?" Zach asked.

"I don't know," came Holland's voice from the other side. "Seems a shame to destroy it. I mean, it's huge. Maybe I'll see if the elementary school wants it. It's big enough for the preschoolers and kindergarteners to run around in. They might like it for playtime."

"I think they'd love it. They'll need to find room for it, though." Zach got up to make a tea for Holland and was bringing it over to him when Holland emerged from the far side of the float, hammer in hand.

"Thanks." Holland winked at him before taking a sip.

They were still keeping their relationship on the down low in front of everyone outside of Alana and Holland's friends, so Zach didn't reach out and take Holland's hand like he wanted to. Instead, he resumed his slouch on the bench, patting the empty spot next to him.

Holland dropped the hammer into his toolbox, then sat, exhaling a breath as he did so. "It's done."

"No shit?"

"No shit."

"Just the Santa float left to finish."

Holland stretched an arm over his head, revealing a stretch of abdomen when his T-shirt rode up. "Yup. They're getting rid of this bench soon, by the way."

"Huh?" Zach tore his gaze away from Holland's skin. "What? Who's doing what?"

"This bench," Holland said, looking at him with a question on his face. "They're finally moving it to the park tomorrow."

"Who's they?"

"No idea. Probably someone from parks and rec. Mrs. Shoemacker came by earlier to tell me."

"Why tomorrow?" Zach asked. "Will they even be able to install it? Isn't the ground too frozen?"

Holland shrugged. "Beats me. I was just commissioned to build the thing. Hey, what's this?" Setting his tea on the ground next to the bench, he stood and grabbed a small wrapped package that sat on his float, propped against the flower store. He waved it in Zach's direction. "Where'd this come from?"

Zach sipped his tea. "I dunno."

The lines around Holland's eyes were more pronounced when he squinted. "You don't know, huh?"

Shaking his head, Zach hid a smile behind his mug.

"Hmm." Holland brought it up to his ear and shook the package gently. "Then I guess whoever left it won't mind if I open it."

"I'm sure they won't."

Grinning, Holland tore into the snowman wrapping paper. He kept sneaking peeks at Zach, smile on his face, eyes full of life and laughter. With the color in his cheeks and the way he barely paused for breath before lifting the lid on the box and pulling out the small tube nestled inside, he looked like the grown-up version of a three-year-old on Christmas morning.

"Wood glue?" Holland said, holding up the tube.

"Maybe someone thought it might come in handy. Since you build dollhouses and all."

Holland hummed. "Thoughtful, yet functional." He sat next to Zach again and squeezed Zach's thigh. "Thank you. You don't have to keep buying me gifts."

"I know." Zach threaded their fingers together. "But I like the look on your face when you unwrap them."

Holland kissed the back of Zach's hand and Zach's heart jumped. "Ready to head out?"

Zach was putting on his scarf when he spotted it, a flat, slim package, roughly three inches by six, wrapped in paper with tiny snowflakes on it, sitting on his desk. "What's this?"

Holland grinned at him as he shrugged into his coat. "I dunno."

"Really? You don't know?" Zach slipped a nail underneath the tape. "Think whoever left it will mind if I open it?"

"I think they'd want you to."

Zach snorted a laugh and opened his gift, revealing a pocket day planner for next year. "A calendar?"

Standing on the other side of Zach's desk, Holland bent over to get a better look at it, forehead furrowed. Yeah, he wasn't fooling anyone with that innocently confused expression. "Someone must know you pretty well."

"What makes you say that?"

Holland turned his head toward the wall, where Zach had three different calendars pinned. Then he rearranged a couple of items on Zach's desk, uncovering two separate day planners. "And I bet you have a pocket-sized one in your pocket," he said.

Busted.

"You're cute." Holland leaned across the desk and brushed Zach's lips with a kiss in full view of the other volunteers. And Zach couldn't bring himself to care. "You know, most people use their phone calendars these days."

Zach finished pulling on his coat and tucked his new planner in its inner pocket. "Yeah, I know." He came around the desk and headed out with Holland, getting a wink of approval from Mrs. Columbus. He smiled shyly and stepped outside into the frigid night air. "But I like paper ones. I feel like I can see the bigger picture that way." Lifting Holland's arm, he settled it around his own shoulders and snuggled into Holland's body.

"Sleeping over tonight?" Holland kissed his temple.

"Yeah. But only because I like your shower."

Holland laughed.

# CHAPTER TWELVE

*7 days until the parade*

THE CAR SPUTTERED.

"No." Zach started it again with the same result. "No, no, no, no, no."

This was what he got for spending last night in his own crappy apartment, rehearsing to the walls his presentation for the Gold Stone hotel chain, instead of at Holland's where it was cozy and warm, and there was food other than sandwiches, and a cat to play with. Although, realistically, it was probably the fact that he hadn't used his own car in over a week, and it had sat unused for so long that it had finally died on him.

Outside the car, thick flakes of snow fell steadily from the sky, so dense Zach could barely see three feet ahead. The storm they'd been predicting since earlier this week had finally landed overnight. There was already over ten inches of snow on the ground, with another foot and a half to two feet expected.

But job interviews waited for no man, and snow or no snow, he needed to get there.

Resting his forehead against the steering wheel, he stroked the dashboard. "I just need you to make it to

Portland. Okay? That's it. You don't even have to make it back. Someone can come get me, or I can get a hotel room. I just need you to make it there. Okay? What do you say?"

The car said no. Typical.

He called Holland again, and again it went straight to voicemail. The one time he needed Holland's truck rather desperately and Holland's phone was either off or dead. He didn't have time to walk over to Holland's, so it was either get his car to start or…cancel the interview.

Yeah, no.

Why hadn't he asked Holland last night when Holland had sent an encouraging Knock 'em dead text? To be honest, he was surprised Holland hadn't mentioned it himself given how much he hated when Zach used his own car. But, to be fair, Holland had gotten a commission yesterday morning for a Victorian dollhouse that needed to be ready for Christmas and he was a bit stressed by the whole development, especially since he hadn't quite finished Santa's float yet.

Straightening, Zach took a deep breath in through his nose, released it through his mouth, turned the key, and—

"Yes! Thank you, thank you, thank you."

Shit, it was slippery. Okay, it was fine. He had snow tires, he'd planned ahead and given himself extra time to get there, and there was no one on the road because everyone was smarter than him and hibernating indoors, which meant he didn't have to worry about traffic.

He double-checked his pocket before he got too far out of town, making sure his thumb drive with his presentation was in it. His laptop was on the passenger seat, just in case they didn't have one ready at the interview. Zach had laughed his ass off yesterday when Holland had asked him if his presentation was laid out on a poster board or if it was all in his head.

"The USB stick is where it's at nowadays," Zach had said, patting Holland on the chest.

He mentally went over his presentation as he drove, speaking certain parts aloud to ensure the right emphasis on certain words.

"And not only did I save the town money by asking vendors to donate products and time for the event itself as well as the silent auction, but also by getting the Lighthouse Bay Post, as well as newspapers from the surrounding areas, to agree to a non-profit rate for the daily advertisements that run prior to the event."

He flexed his hands on the steering wheel.

"I totally got this."

The interviewers won't know what hit them.

Goodbye, Tiny's Panini. Hello, real job.

Hitting the breaks gently, he slowed as the snow thickened, swirling around the car like angry bees. His anxiety kicked up a notch. Shit, he never should've gone out in this. Why hadn't the interviewers rescheduled for another day? He'd waited all morning for that phone call, but it hadn't come. Hence his dangerous trek into Portland, which went against what every radio station had said this morning.

"It's extremely slippery, visibility is at a record low, and we still have more of this to get through before the storm heads north," the weather lady had said. "Police are advising residents to stay indoors and cancel all nonessential travel."

Whether his interview was nonessential or not was debatable.

The car coughed.

"Oh, shit."

He was barely out of town, hadn't even reached the

highway yet, when his car died. Just turned off. While he was driving.

That was a thing?

"Fuck my life."

No wonder Holland hadn't wanted him driving it.

What the hell was he supposed to do now?

He so totally didn't have this.

He managed to pull over onto the side of the road before the car came to a complete stop. Groaning, he pressed his fingers into his eyelids, cursing his stupidity, the weather, the Gold Stone hotel chain, and anything else he could think of.

And, of course, his cell phone had no signal. Either the weather was playing havoc with it, or he was in that stupid dead zone between Lighthouse Bay and Portland where there wasn't any service. Probably the latter, because that was just his luck.

With nothing but fields interspersed with the occasional tree on either side of the two-lane road, his options were to bunk down in his car until someone found his cold, dead body—probably tomorrow because he hadn't passed a single person since he'd left home—or get out and walk back to town.

Except he wasn't dressed for the outdoors. He was dressed for an interview. Shiny, black loafers. Navy suit. Pale green shirt paired with a forest green tie. And a knee-length peacoat that wouldn't protect against the elements.

His parents had given him an emergency kit for his car last Christmas. He was pretty sure it was in his closet at his parents' house.

Goodbye, real job. Hello, Tiny's Panini. For the rest of his life apparently.

Pulling a scarf and Holland's gloves from the outside

pocket of his laptop bag, he gathered his bag, exited the car, and started walking.

Holland was sawing wood in his workshop when his phone finished installing its software update. Fucking finally. Two hours was a record. Usually it only took a few minutes.

He was hunting down the measuring tape when his phone booted up and buzzed.

Buzzed again.

And again.

And a fourth time.

A fifth.

Then two pings.

"The hell?"

He really wasn't that popular.

Five missed calls, a text, and an alert from his weather app. As if he needed an alert to tell him how bad the weather currently was.

Four of the missed calls were from Zach, one from Marcella's Tools & More, and the text was from Dev. Why is Zach driving that piece of shit car of his out of town?

Zach was *what* now?

Dev had to be wrong. Zach wouldn't go out, not in this, and certainly not in that piece-of-crap car of his.

But to get to his interview?

Shit.

Abandoning his project, Holland ran out of his workshop and across the lawn, ignoring the cold and the snow but unable to ignore the hard knot of worry in his gut. He was already dialing Dev's phone number as he came through the back door of the house.

"Hey."

"What do you mean Zach drove out of town in his car?" Giving his boots a quick wipe on the rug in front of the door, Holland strode through the house, snagged his winter jacket, and left via the front door.

"Just what I said," Dev said, all traces of his cold gone from his voice, although the cough lingered.

"When was this?"

"Forty-five minutes ago? An hour? Marcella saw him too. Tried calling you, but she said it went straight to voice-mail. Where's he going in this weather?"

"His job interview." Holland hopped into his truck and slammed the door closed. "Shit! I wanted him to take my truck, but I forgot to mention it… Goddamn it." He'd been so distracted with his new commission yesterday that it had slipped his mind. And poor Zach had called four times this morning, no doubt for this exact reason, while Holland's stupid phone had been updating. "I gotta go, Dev."

"What are you gonna do?"

"Follow his trail. Make sure he got there okay."

"Why? If he was in trouble, wouldn't he call?"

"I just…" He put the phone on speaker and searched his pockets for his keys. "I have a bad feeling." A bad feeling that sat like lead on his skin, making him feel heavy. Weighted.

He hung up with Dev and called Zach, but the call wouldn't connect. No straight to voicemail, no *This number is not in service*. Not even a ring. The sense of doom doubled.

Best-case scenario? He'd get to Portland, park, and sit in the hotel lobby, where Zach would find him on his way out after his interview. They'd laugh at Holland's overprotectiveness, Holland would be all embarrassed yet relieved, Zach would kiss him sweetly, and they'd stop for tea at a cozy coffee shop before heading home.

Worst-case scenario… His stomach took a dive.

He couldn't go there.

Shit, where the fuck were his keys? Not in his jeans pockets, not in his jacket. He threw the jacket into the back and checked the center console, underneath his seat, above the visor, in the cup holder.

"Are you fucking kidding me?"

Back inside the house, they weren't on the hall table or on the key rack that hung on the wall next to the door. Not in his bedroom.

He ran a hand through his hair. Yanked hard. Growled into the still air.

"Okay, okay."

Scrubbing his hands over his face, he focused on regulating his heart rate. Okay. Retrace his steps.

He'd dropped Zach off at his apartment last night after they'd worked in headquarters for most of the afternoon. Driven home. Unpacked the truck bed and brought the materials for his new dollhouse commission into his workshop out back. He hadn't gone inside, not yet, choosing instead to bring his materials around the side of the house to the back.

Now, he tracked snow through the house as he followed, in reverse, the path he'd taken only a few minutes ago while on the phone with Dev.

But the keys weren't in his workshop either.

"What the hell?"

Why did the world insist on being an asshole right this second? Zach could be hurt, and Holland was trapped in his own house.

Okay. Breathe. He'd dropped off materials, then gone inside, leaving his boots by the back door, and gone into the fridge for a beer.

And of course. There were his keys. Sitting innocuously on the top shelf of the fridge.

"I hate you so much right now."

Whether he was talking to himself or to his keys or the weather remained to be seen.

If anything happened to Zach while his stupid keys had been dicking around with him, Holland was going to commit murder.

The snow had thickened while he'd been inside, reducing visibility to near whiteout conditions.

"Shit."

His hands clenched around his keys as he made his way back to his truck. Fear and anxiety paced a cold, sharp path from his stomach to his heart.

Navigating deserted streets wasn't as easy as it sounded when those streets were thick with snow and slippery to boot. His truck could handle it, but he was extra careful in case he missed Zach stranded on the side of the road. Not to mention, he didn't want to get into an accident, further delaying him from finding Zach.

Zach was fine. Probably. He'd left before the worst of the storm had started, so chances were he'd made it at least halfway to Portland by now.

Zach was not fine. His car had broken down and he was stranded on the side of the road with no heat, no cell signal, and no rescue.

Holland's ping-ponging thoughts couldn't settle. Zach was fine. Zach wasn't fine. The two scenarios churned in his head until his hands shook on the steering wheel.

The world went into slow motion. In his hyperaware

state, everything became crystal clear. The uniqueness of every snowflake that fell on his windshield. The *phew-phew, phew-phew* of his windshield wipers. The heat from the air vents brushing along his bare hands. The ache in his hands as they clutched the wheel. His choppy breathing.

The further out of town he went with no trace of Zach, the bigger the stab of worry knotted his throat.

Zach's toes were numb. His nose. His fingers. His lips. His ears.

The storm worsened as he walked back to town, his bag slung over his shoulder and bumping into the backs of his knees. Visibility became almost nonexistent. Snow melted down the back of his neck. His feet were soaked. He shivered so hard that it was difficult to put one foot in front of the other.

Snow pelted his face, scraping his cheeks raw. He wanted to check his phone to see if he'd made it back into an area with a signal, but he couldn't uncurl them from their cramped position where they were tucked under his armpits. The strap of his bag fell to his elbow. Zach didn't stop to rearrange it. If he slowed, he'd never start up again.

Maybe he was being a bit melodramatic, but the further he went, the colder it got. The windier.

It was like looking down a long tunnel, with the tunnel getting longer and longer, even though he was walking toward the other end.

That was what this felt like. Like despite walking toward Lighthouse Bay, the town felt further and further with each step. Not a single car had passed him since he'd

176 | AMY AISLIN

started his walk.

He should've stayed in the car. Someone would've found him, eventually. He briefly considered turning back, but at this point, he didn't know if he was closer to his car or to town.

Why hadn't he gone by Holland's this morning and asked to borrow his truck face-to-face?

He had no excuse except that he hadn't wanted to be late for his interview. Well, now he wouldn't make it, and whose fault was that?

A fantastic job opportunity ripped away, and all because he hadn't wanted to waste the few minutes it'd take to detour to Holland's.

He'd gambled timeliness against safety and lost.

His feet were wet and heavy, and it was getting harder and harder to put one foot in front of the other. He didn't dare speed up, not in his useless dress shoes that didn't have any grip. Just kept a steady pace.

Zach kept his gaze dead ahead. Right foot. Left foot. Right. Left. Right. Left. Ignore the stinging pain that shot from his toes to his calves. Ignore his leaking nose. His frigid ears and fingers.

Holland was going to kill him for taking his car out, especially in this weather. That was, if said weather didn't kill him first.

Because hypothermia was a real threat.

The closer Holland got to Portland, the easier it was to convince himself that Zach had made it in one piece.

It was safer to keep thinking that rather than let his

thoughts lead him down the worst-case scenario path. Because his thoughts weren't discriminatory.

Zach was hurt.

Zach's car had stalled.

Zach was stuck in a ditch and couldn't get the car doors open.

Zach had crashed, hit his head, and passed out.

Zach had crashed, hit his head and, in his concussion-induced state, was now wandering aimlessly in the cold.

Zach was dead.

Zach had gotten car-jacked.

Each scenario was more unlikely than the last, but that didn't stop his panicked thoughts from spiraling out of control.

His shoulders ached from holding himself stiffly as he drove, but he couldn't relax. Not until he found Zach. He was still hoping for his best-case scenario: finding Zach at the hotel in Portland, safe and sound and with a new job in his pocket.

Except he spotted a figure walking on the side of the road less than ten minutes later. For a second, he thought he imagined it, the whiteout making it difficult to see past the end of his truck. But no. There, hunched against the cold, shoulders up to his ears, arms wrapped around himself, hands tucked into armpits, was Zach. The collar of his peacoat was popped, but it was no match against the wind and snow. His eyes were on the ground as he walked, slowly, mechanically, like it took inhuman strength to put one foot in front of the other.

Jesus, he wasn't even wearing boots. Had he planned on walking the entire way back to town? The drive was seven or eight minutes on a good day, but the walk? In this weather?

Holland didn't bother pulling over. Just stopped the truck in the middle of the street and scrambled out, leaving the engine running. "Zach!"

The wind swept his voice away, but Zach must've heard him anyway because he stilled, cocking his head.

"Zach! Jesus." Sweeping Zach into his arms, Holland shielded as much of Zach's body from the wind as he could.

Zach held himself stiffly, rigid as a two-by-four, but he nuzzled his face into Holland's neck, seeking Holland's warmth.

"You're okay." Heart pounding, Holland rubbed his hands over Zach's arms and back, trying to warm him, to get his circulation going.

Zach slumped into Holland and moaned.

"Okay. You're okay. Come on." He led Zach to his truck, keeping him secured under his arm and using his bigger body to block the worst of the wind.

Zach could barely lift his foot onto the running board, and when he did, it slipped. Holland nearly had to shove him inside, but once he did, he ran around the front to the driver's side, jumped in, and pointed every vent in Zach's direction. Zach sat folded over, eyes scrunched closed, shivering uncontrollably. The paleness of his face was concerning, as were the dry red patches on his cheeks. It looked like someone had taken a sander to his skin.

Holland turned the heat on full blast. Reaching into the back, he grabbed the coat he'd flung back there after getting into his truck earlier and draped it over Zach. Then he rubbed Zach's thighs. Took off Zach's gloves, uncurled his fists, and rubbed his hands. Blew on them.

Zach whimpered and leaned closer.

"Are you okay?"

The strange sound Zach made sounded painful.

"M-m-m-my toes."

Shit, his feet must be freezing. And soaked. Holland redirected the air so that the heat came from the bottom vents. Then he gave in to the need and pulled Zach into his arms, hugging him over the center console.

"Jesus, you scared me." His heart was still thundering, *boom, boom, boom* against his ribs, making it hard to breathe.

"S-s-sorry."

"No, I'm sorry." He rubbed Zach's back hard, hoping the friction helped. "Let's get you home."

The drive home was slow going. He was eager to get Zach in front of a roaring fireplace, but he didn't want to skid off the road on the way. Zach shoved his messenger bag aside and bent to slip his shoes off. It took him three tries with hands that shook, but soon he was out of shoes and socks and sitting cross-legged in his seat, toes tucked under his thighs, and hands wrapped around his feet. Holland itched to reach out and ruffle Zach's hair, shaking it free of snow, but he kept both hands on the wheel, aware that any distractions might cause an accident.

Zach's shivering hadn't abated completely by the time Holland pulled into his driveway, and he was hit with the occasional shudder that made the entire car shake. He picked up a wet sock, wincing when it dripped water onto the floorboards. The lost expression on his face when he looked at Holland gripped Holland's heart in a vice and didn't let go.

"Wait here." Holland left the car running so Zach wouldn't be without heat, went into the house, and returned a minute later with a thick pair of wool socks and a pair of his old boots. Crouched on the passenger side, he helped Zach get them on, picked up his bag, and ferried Zach indoors, where he stripped Zach out of clothing that was wet—which was everything except socks, boxer briefs, and his shirt and tie. Holland wasn't so freaked that he couldn't appreciate the sight of Zach in nothing but underwear and a shirt, but the way Zach trembled had Holland leading him into the living room, sitting him on the couch, and burying him under a pile of blankets. He got a fire started, cursing himself six ways to Sunday as he worked. How could he have forgotten that Zach's interview was today and he'd need Holland's truck to get there? He'd known Zach's car was one good pothole away from death.

He turned to apologize again, but instead of blame, all he saw in Zach's gaze was a plea. A plea that snagged Holland, hooked its claws deep, and had him taking a lurching step forward. Another. And another. Zach watched him the entire time, gaze never leaving him, and he was in Holland's lap before Holland had even fully situated himself on the couch.

With Zach safe in his arms, Holland let himself breathe for what felt like the first time since his conversation with Dev. He kissed Zach's temple.

Zach shifted, moving aside some of the blankets, and resettled against Holland's chest without the blankets between them.

Holland rubbed Zach's arms through his shirt. "You okay?"

"Mm-hmm." Zach nodded against Holland's throat. "How did you know?" His whisper was rough, hoarse. Like he'd lost his voice to the storm.

"Dev said he saw you head out of town."

"But how did you *know*?"

Holland didn't have to ask what Zach meant. "I don't know. I just did. I knew something was wrong."

"Thank you," Zach said and kissed the hollow of Holland's throat.

Holland swallowed roughly and tightened his embrace. "I'm so sorry, Zach. My phone was updating when you called this morning. That's why I missed your calls."

Zach patted his chest. "It's okay."

"I'm just glad I found you."

When Zach straightened, there was a teasing glint in his honey eyes and the dimple in his left cheek made an appearance. "Would you have kept going all the way to Portland if I hadn't broken down?"

"Yes. I wanted to make sure you were okay." Holland let his head fall back against the couch. "And yes, I realize how overprotective and vaguely stalkerish that sounds."

Zach chuckled. "Hey, do you know where my bag went? I need to call and explain why I didn't show up for my interview."

"Should be on the floor there."

Holland held on to Zach as he reached for his bag, dragging it closer by the strap then digging through it until he found his phone.

"They left me a voicemail," Zach said, thumbing the screen. "Probably to tell me I'm a huge disappointment and they never want to see my face again."

God, Holland hoped that wasn't true.

And he was proven right as Zach listened to the message, his eyes widening, getting bigger and bigger the longer the message went on. Then he grinned fiercely and squeezed Holland's shoulder before hanging up. "They rescheduled the interview for Tuesday because of the storm." He scowled then. "Why couldn't they have called before I left home? Ugh."

"Maybe the storm hadn't hit Portland as bad yet."

"Maybe. Look at this." Zach held his screen out to Holland but turned it back around before Holland could read the text. "Alana says I don't have to come in later because it's not busy. She's going to close the café early. Wow. Miracles do happen."

Holland choked on a laugh.

Zach grinned back at him. Until a shiver overtook him.

"Why don't you take a hot shower?" Holland suggested. "Get warmed up."

"That sounds heavenly," Zach said, but he made no move to get up. Instead, he snuggled back into Holland. "In a minute."

"Yeah." Holland inhaled his scent and finally let go of the tension in his shoulders. "In a minute."

A minute turned into fifteen as they sat quietly on the couch, not really talking. Just enjoying being together in the quiet as the storm raged outside and the fire burned inside, filling the house with the lovely scent of burning wood.

Zach snuggled further into Holland. It was pure dumb luck that Holland had found him. Thank God Dev had seen him on his way out of town. Never mind that—thank God Dev had told Holland about it. And while he was thanking God—and whoever else was listening—if there would ever be a better time for Holland to listen to his instincts, Zach couldn't think what it could be.

He would've made it to town. Eventually. He wouldn't have given up. But he probably would've had frostbite in a few places. As it was, he'd already been unable to feel his fingers and toes when Holland found him.

He hadn't seen Holland pull up. Hadn't heard him stop the truck. And at first, he'd thought his name on the wind had been a hallucination brought on by extreme cold, if that was even a thing. But then Holland had materialized out of nowhere, wrapping Zach up in his heat, whisking him away, keeping him safe. He'd clearly been terrified. Zach had no idea what kind of nightmare scenarios Holland had created in his head, but they must've been pretty bad. Holland probably hadn't realized it, but he'd been shaking just as much as Zach. Just for different reasons.

That Holland cared that much about him made his palms sweat. He was most of the way in love with Holland already, and he thought Holland might feel the same way too.

Eventually Zach found himself upstairs in Holland's bedroom. Ignoring the drawer that held a few of his own clothes, he went for Holland's and got a pair of sweatpants, an old T-shirt, and a hoodie. He wanted to be surrounded by Holland. Mired in his scent. He'd burrow into Holland's skin if he could and stay there forever, where Holland would have to keep him. Always.

He wanted…Holland.

That was it. Holland. Everything else was just gravy.

Abandoning the clothes to the bed, he descended the stairs, socked feet silent on the wood, nerves drumming a tempo in his belly. In the kitchen, Holland leaned against the counter, ankles crossed, eyes on the electric teakettle. The little light was on, Zach noticed. Holland must've been waiting for it to boil. On the counter, next to the kettle, was a box of apple cinnamon tea, a carton of milk, and a small bag of sugar.

Holland was making him his favorite tea. Heart

melting, Zach couldn't stop the sappy grin if he tried.

He must've made a sound, because Holland looked his way, straightening from his slouch against the counter. "Hey. Everything okay?" His denim eyes raked Zach up and down, taking in that Zach was still dressed, and he frowned. "What's wrong?"

Zach gulped. Squared his shoulders. Ignored the dancing butterflies and eventually found his voice. "I want you to shower with me."

As a euphemism for *sex*, s*hower* wasn't so bad.

Okay, it was awful, but nevertheless, it took Holland no time at all to figure it out.

His eyes darkened, swirling with a mixture of uncertainty and desire. Zach understood the uncertainty—he had blurted out, rather forcefully, that he didn't want to have sex. Except that he did. But only with Holland. The sexual attraction had blossomed slowly the more time they spent together. And although Zach was nervous—hell, now he shook for an entirely different reason—he knew Holland wasn't like those other guys, the ones from college who'd barely spared him a thought, even while they were having sex. Holland would take care of him. Be gentle with him. And he wouldn't toss Zach away the next morning like a used condom.

"Zach, I…" He looked so lost, standing there in his kitchen, arms hanging limp.

Zach played with one of the buttons on his shirt and dropped his gaze to the floor. "It's okay if you don't want to."

"No." Holland's laugh was confused rather than humorous as he rubbed his hands over his face. "I definitely want to. But I thought you *didn't* want to."

"Turns out that I do want to. With you." Zach shrugged when Holland stared at him. "I don't understand it either."

Holland strode to where Zach stood in the doorway, shifting from foot to foot, and cupped Zach's face in his calloused hands. "Are you sure?"

"I'm sure." Zach held onto Holland's wrists, brushing his thumbs against the inside. Holland's eyes darkened, burning with need and want. Zach's knees threatened to buckle.

Silently, Holland led him upstairs. While Holland gathered something out of his night table, Zach went into the bathroom and started the shower, then undressed. He was standing there in nothing but skin when Holland walked in. Holland didn't hesitate. He strode toward Zach, steps purposeful. Grabbing the back of his T-shirt, he pulled it over his head, revealing a glorious chest lightly coated in a mix of white and dark brown hairs. Zach swallowed hard. He'd stayed over enough that they'd seen each other naked before.

But never for this express purpose.

Zach wanted Holland's skin all over his.

He got his wish a minute later. Ensconced in the shower, hot water raining down on them, steam swirling and fogging up the glass shower walls, the mirror, the window, Zach had never felt as safe, as protected, as cherished as he did with Holland's strong body against his, Holland's arms cradling him close. To date, Holland's kisses had been sweet. Nice. Sometimes sensuous. But this… This was an inferno, a bomb going off. Zach moaned into Holland's mouth and gave as much as he took.

Hands skimmed along wet skin. Mouths sucked water off shoulders and chests, laving a path up throats. Fingers teased. Gasps and sighs. Breathless moans. Eyes meeting, an exchange without words.

Done with their shower, they stepped out and dried off.

In the bedroom, Holland had placed lube and a condom on the nightstand. Their presence only made Zach more desperate for Holland.

The bed was fluffy and cool against Zach's back, a contrast to the fire and desire blazing a path through his veins. He was electrified, coming undone. And when Holland entered him at last, and his legs were wrapped around Holland's hips, their eyes locked, the feeling of belonging that hit him was so strong he squeezed his eyes closed and hoped Holland didn't notice his tears.

It turned out that when sex was done right, it only hurt for a little bit before it got good.

Really, *really* good.

Zach floated on a cloud of bliss as he helped Holland make lunch, sneaking peeks at his man in between chopping carrots to go with the egg salad sandwiches Holland was building. Holland caught him looking and winked. Zach blushed as if they hadn't just spent a naked hour doing fun things to each other.

In the short amount of time they'd been seeing each other, Holland must've figured out how Zach felt about wet things sticking to his hands, because he went ahead and peeled the carrots before asking Zach to chop them. That way he wouldn't get nasty carrot shreds on him.

How was it possible to want to melt into a puddle of goo and kiss someone senseless, all at the same time?

He placed a dozen carrot sticks on each of the two plates Holland had set out, then hopped up to sit on the counter. His backside twinged a little, but it was a nice ache.

A little reminder of Holland and the way he'd treated Zach with respect, with gentleness, running his hands reverently over Zach as if unable to believe that Zach was in his life.

"What's that smile for?" Holland asked.

Zach swung his legs. "I'm happy."

Holland's answering grin lit Zach up inside.

# CHAPTER THIRTEEN

*6 days until the parade*

WHEN ZACH AWOKE THE NEXT MORNING, HE KNEW without checking a clock that he was late for his shift at Tiny's Panini.

He grumbled into his pillow, forcing his eyes open. He'd set his alarm on his phone last night. Why hadn't it gone off?

Next to him, Holland rolled over and plastered himself against Zach's back. "Good morning," he rumbled in Zach's ear.

"Not good," Zach whined. Despite knowing he had to get up—damn, he probably didn't have time for a shower—he snuggled deeper into Holland.

"Not good?" Holland kissed Zach's shoulder and fitted his legs into the back of Zach's. "I think it's good. Great, even. Every morning is great when I wake up next to you."

"Awww." Zach turned over and nuzzled into Holland's throat. "I like waking up next to you too. Did you know you only snore when you're on your left side?"

Holland grunted. "Did you know you get a little furrow right here"—he ran a thumb between Zach's eyebrows—"when you sleep?"

"I do?"

"Uh-huh. Like you can't turn your brain off, even in sleep."

That sounded about right.

Zach took another minute to bask in the heat emanating from Holland's body. Seriously, the guy was a living, walking furnace. It was why Zach had snuggled up to him with no blankets between them yesterday on the couch after Holland had rescued him. Holland did a better job of warming him than any blanket ever could.

Zach sighed deeply.

Holland squirmed. "That tickled."

Chuckling, Zach flopped onto his back and stared at the ceiling. "I gotta go to work." Frankly, he was surprised Alana hadn't blown up his phone, demanding where he was.

"No, you don't." Holland propped his head on his hand to peer down at him.

"I do," Zach said, miserable. Please let him blow the interviewers away on Tuesday. More than wanted, he *needed* that job. He was sick and tired of being a slave to the café. He wanted his evenings and weekends back. Hell, his mornings too, where he and Holland could laze around in bed with nowhere to go.

"No, you don't," Holland repeated. He nodded at something on the night table next to Zach's side of the bed. Yeah, he had a side of the bed! "Check your phone."

Zach reached for it. Squinting at the bright screen, he read the text from Alana that had come in two hours earlier. Mrs. Shoemacker activated the BIA phone tree. Businesses on Main are to remain closed for the day on account of the weather.

"On account of the weather?" Getting out of bed, he

went over to the window, pulled the curtain aside, and—
"Holy crap!" The world had gone white. Everywhere. Snow
clung to rooftops, awnings, tree branches, lampposts, electrical boxes. It was piled two-, maybe three-feet thick on
the sidewalk and road. And it was still falling. Fast too. Foot
and paw prints marred the perfection of the sidewalk, but
other than that, it was pristine.

He fell back into bed. "Wow. So that means…"

"It means…" Holland rolled on top of him. "The café's
closed."

"Closed?" Zach spread his legs and Holland sunk deeper into him, their morning wood bumping. Heat crept up
Zach's spine. "But Al never closes it."

Holland dipped his head and nipped Zach's collarbone.
"By order of Mrs. Shoemacker."

"You mean—" Zach shivered as Holland ran his hand
up Zach's calf, his thigh, to dig fingers into his butt. "I don't
have anywhere to be today?"

"Nowhere but here."

Carding his fingers through Holland's hair, Zach
brought his head up. "Awesome," he said before their lips
met.

Sitting around doing nothing all day was great in theory,
and Holland was sure it worked for some people.

People who didn't have other commitments.

The storm was still raging outside and showed no signs
of slowing. His weather app said it was supposed to peter off
this evening, but for now, the wind blew, snow fell, and he
wasn't looking forward to the eventual driveway shoveling.

After spending the morning fooling around in bed, he and Zach had watched a movie with Dev, the three of them sprawled on the couch with chips and tea. Coffee for Dev. Because he was weird.

Then Zach had pulled his pocket day planner out of his peacoat and started typing on his phone, bemoaning the fact that he'd left Mr. Barry's binder in the back seat of his car. Which was still stuck on the side of the road west of town. They'd have to get it at some point, but for now, Zach didn't seem too worried about it.

The space heater was on in Holland's small workshop, making the air stuffy and close, but it was better than the alternative: working in the cold. Zach had wanted to keep him company, so he'd set himself up in a corner, out of Holland's way, on a small table Holland often used for sketching.

"I'm surprised you're okay working in here," Holland said, marking measurements on a square piece of wood with a pencil. "What with the dust and all."

"Dust is fine." Zach muttered it absently, too involved in his work to even glance up. "Comes off easy."

Holland was pretty sure he was getting better at anticipating the kinds of messes that made Zach twitch. Dry stuff—dirt, dust, crumbs, flour, sugar—was fine. Even a messy room didn't bother him much. Piles of books, dirty clothes, dusty dressers, full garbage cans, loose change—all easy to clean.

But the wet stuff—or, rather, stuff that clung? Nope. Lettuce bits, condiments, sticky granola bars, wet grass, mud, wet hair. Even flour that stuck to wet hands. And cauliflower. *Especially* cauliflower.

Zach had very particular thoughts about cauliflower.

And god forbid the food on his plate touch other food.

Once, Holland had seen him toss away a perfectly good red grape because it was a darker color than the rest of the batch.

Frankly, Holland was a little surprised Zach didn't have a problem with Tadashi's cat hair.

And then there were the intangible messes—missing a deadline, an unread email, keeping the lights on when leaving a room, arriving late, an unfinished task. All unacceptable.

His quirks were rather adorable.

It wasn't OCD… At least, it didn't appear that way, not to Holland. It was more a desire for organization, and an offshoot of that was remaining clean.

But it begged the question—what was he doing with Holland, who was essentially a huge mess? At least, he had been. Flitting from job to job to job until he found something he could make a living at. Zach hadn't done that. Would never do that. Chances were he'd researched and dissected and created endless lists before deciding on event planning when philosophy hadn't worked out. Which was a very clever career choice for two reasons: first, it would never go out of style. People would be planning parties until the end of time. And second, it allowed Zach to color between the lines. To use spreadsheets to his heart's content. To have napkins that matched the tablecloths that matched the theme.

Whereas Holland often overbooked himself, was awful at keeping track of his earnings and expenses, and thought coloring between the lines was boring as hell. He'd tried that when he'd worked as a teacher, but the administration's rules had sucked the life out of his soul. He'd tried it while managing a bar, but he disliked dealing with suppliers who didn't keep their word. And then while doing the books for

Bud, from whom he'd learned the art of woodworking.

It was ironic that he could do the finances for someone else but couldn't keep track of his own.

Holland watched Zach from the other side of the workshop while Zach was oblivious. Now that he knew what it was like to truly *be* with Zach, he wanted more of it. More making love, sure. But also more touching, more kissing, more snuggling on the couch. He almost went over to Zach's corner to nuzzle his neck, to tease him into giggles and, maybe, a make-out session. But Zach wouldn't thank him for interrupting. And that was okay. It forced Holland to concentrate on his own work. He also had a looming deadline. Also for someone he hadn't been able to say no to—a reference from his sister.

But Zach's lip biting as he worked distracted him. That red lip caught in Zach's teeth made Holland's mouth water. He wanted to nibble on that lip, then suck it into his mouth to soothe. Yet the way Zach concentrated so fiercely on his work said "I'm busy. Come back later." So Holland stayed on his side of the workshop.

The way Zach held his fancy pen was odd. It rested lightly in the space between his thumb and index finger, and with his index finger only slightly bent, the pen was supported by his thumb and middle finger. He barely moved his fingers, instead shifting his entire arm as he wrote. He tended to slouch over his project, but then he'd catch himself and straighten up again.

His art—and calligraphy *was* art—was simple, yet beautiful. Clean lines, teasing flourishes. It was incredibly precise. Holland could understand why Zach would be attracted to it.

"Shouldn't you be working?" Zach asked without looking up.

Okay. Maybe not so oblivious.

"When did you start doing calligraphy?"

"In high school." Zach finished one greeting card—*Thank you* written in lovely, flowing letters—and started on another. "High school was…not the greatest."

Holland's heart froze. "Oh?"

"It was elementary school all over again. Just with more people."

Lighthouse Bay had its own elementary school, but the high school was in the neighboring town and served half the county.

*Elementary school all over again.* For the three years Holland had taught at Zach's school, Zach had been the lonely kid who hung out on the swings in the playground at recess because no one wanted to include him in their games. He was the one who spent rained out recesses quietly drawing at his desk, reading, or helping the teacher with some task. He was picked last in gym class, ignored during class presentations. And nobody ever had any snacks to trade with him.

It had never made any sense. Zach was smart. Kind. Eager to help. Quieter than the other kids in his class, though, and much more serious, which perhaps explained why he had trouble making friends. He wasn't seen as fun.

And if high school had been much of the same, had he been the kid sitting alone in a huge cafeteria at lunch? The one no one wanted to partner with for group projects? The one who was never invited to parties?

No wonder he'd picked up a hobby that kept him busy. And shrewdly, he'd chosen one that earned him some money on the side. He'd told Holland earlier that he'd had to close his Etsy shop temporarily since he'd taken over for Mr. Barry, and his only outstanding order was a set of thank you cards for Mrs. Shoemacker.

"I should've said no when she asked," Zach had grumbled. "But have you ever tried saying no to Mrs. Shoemacker?"

"High school wasn't…friendly?" Holland asked him now.

"Not that it wasn't friendly. It just wasn't genuine. Drama for the sake of drama. Gossip. Cliques. Backstabbing. I knew even then that the friends I made were for high school only, and I'd never see them again after graduation. I mean, it's a small town, so I see some of them around sometimes. But I'd never call them to hang out."

"Hmm."

Zach must've been born in the wrong generation. It was the only explanation Holland could think of. Because he knew from Dev, Clark, and Mika that they liked Zach, not just for Holland, but as his own individual person.

"Where did you learn?" Holland asked. "Calligraphy, I mean."

"Books. YouTube videos." Zach was so bent over, his nose was practically touching the paper.

"You're slouching again."

Zach grunted and straightened, throwing Holland a quick smile. "Thanks."

"So you're self-taught, then?"

"Uh-huh."

"Me too. Well, sort of," Holland amended.

That caught Zach's attention. "Yeah?"

"I learned the basics of working with wood from someone I used to work for," Holland explained. "But I taught myself to build dollhouses."

"Do you think you'll get this one done in time?"

Holland blew out a breath and sat on the stool behind

him. "I think so. It's for a friend of my sister's who lives in Portland, so I don't have to worry about shipping it. And she's not looking for anything fancy. Doesn't even want me to paint it."

"Why not?"

"Her seven-year-old daughter is into art. Nancy wants to…well, basically give her daughter a blank canvas in the form of a dollhouse for her to personalize however she wants."

"Cool. How's Santa's float coming? I keep meaning to ask."

"It's done. Well, all of the individual pieces are done. Mika, Dev, and I just need to assemble it onto the platform. We'll do that tomorrow."

"And what about your Christmas Lane float?"

"That one *is* done." And it was amazing, if he did say so himself. He had a real chance of winning the float competition.

"Yeah, you said that a few days ago, but you keep tinkering with it."

Holland's chuckle was self-deprecating. "Yeah. I just want it to be perfect." It was like his sister, a freelance editor, had once said while working with a particularly nitpicky author—eventually you have to stop editing and accept that the book is as perfect as you can make it. The same idea applied to his float. Eventually, he'd have to stop tinkering and proclaim it as perfect as could be.

He stood and stretched his back. "Wanna get out of here?"

The expression on Zach's face was so incredulous it made Holland laugh. "And go where?"

"Come with me and I'll show you."

Zach's lips pinched, and he glanced down at his

unfinished project.

Holland grabbed his tape measure, pencil, and handsaw. "Why don't you finish that and then we'll go?"

"Okay."

They worked in silence for the better part of an hour, each of them busy with their own tasks. Yet Holland never forgot that Zach was there, just a few feet away. Despite how quiet he was, even when switching the cartridge in his pen, Holland was aware of his presence like he was aware of his own name. It was nice to have company while he worked. It was like being at headquarters, him working on his floats while Zach sat at Mr. Barry's desk doing… whatever he was doing. Something secret he wouldn't tell Holland about.

What did he have to do to get Zach to stay with him forever?

"I'm done," Zach eventually said. Setting down his pen, he raised his arms over his head and stretched. "Where are we going?"

Ten minutes later, the incredulousness was back on his face, making Holland grin at him as he handed Zach his gloves. Holland's gloves, actually. The ones he'd loaned Zach a couple of weeks ago. That Zach was still wearing them caused all sorts of funny feelings in his chest.

"Are you serious?" Zach had a few items of clothing in Holland's bedroom, yet he wore a pair of Holland's sweatpants, a hoodie, Dev's winter boots, and one of Holland's spare winter coats.

"Yup." Holland grabbed his own gloves, then opened the front door. "After you."

Zach slipped past him, heading outside. Holland closed the door behind himself and turned to find Zach smiling up at the sky, snowflakes falling onto his face, his shoulders, his hair. When he stuck his tongue out to catch the snowflakes, Holland's stomach flipped, then settled.

Perfect. Zach was utterly perfect.

"You were right," Zach said. "Getting some fresh air was a good idea. Even if it is damn cold."

Holland couldn't help himself. He strode toward Zach, cupped his face, and kissed him like he'd wanted to back in the workshop an hour ago.

Breaking the kiss, he said, "Let's build snowmen."

"Um." Zach's breathing was unsteady. "Okay?"

They built seven. A mom and dad, three kids, a baby, and a dog that looked more like a pig than any house pet Holland had ever seen.

Zach fell over laughing.

"What?" Holland kicked snow at him. "You're not allowed to make fun of my puppy. You gave your snowman nipples."

That just sent Zach off into more peels of laughter.

Holland tackled him and they went tumbling on the front lawn, almost killing their snowbaby, and getting snow everywhere. They came to a stop next to one of the snowkids. From his position on top of Zach, Holland took in Zach's flushed face, the tumble of hair peppered with snowflakes. His eyes shone with light and laugher, glowing bright and merry under the overcast sky.

Placing a hand on either side of Zach's head, Holland leaned closer to him. "What's that smile for?"

God, that smile was everything. And when it revealed the dimple in Zach's left cheek, it made Holland crazy.

Zach ran a thumb over Holland's cheek. "I'm happy."

Holland's heart turned over, stomach spasming as the words sank into his veins. He never got tired of hearing them, of the joy that spread through him when Zach looked at him like he was special and wanted. He was always, *always* conscious of the fact that by giving Holland his happiness, Zach was offering him a precious gift that was in equal parts terrifying.

Because Holland was terrified of fucking it up.

# CHAPTER FOURTEEN

*5 days until the parade*

MONDAY MORNING EVENTUALLY CAME, AND WITH IT, the end of the snowstorm. But a cold front moved in, the frigid air nearly stealing Holland's breath the second he stepped outside.

After quite literally digging his truck out of the driveway, he and Zach drove to headquarters to get started on their day. In the passenger seat next to him, Zach called the owner of the town's garage and asked him to pick up his car.

They were the first to arrive at headquarters. Everyone else was probably still trying to get out of their driveways, but Holland had gotten up before the sun, first working on his dollhouse commission, then making breakfast for Zach—which they enjoyed in bed, thank you very much—before they showered and headed out.

Zach shivered as he entered the building. "God, it's freezing in here. And where's that draft coming from?" He turned on the space heaters interspersed throughout, took his gloves off, and held his hands out to the warm air. "I miss summer already."

Holland unwrapped his scarf from around his neck and headed for his float in the back. "I thought you liked winter. For snowboarding."

"Yeah." Zach trailed behind him. "I like the snow. I don't like this freeze-your-balls-off temperature."

It got colder the further back they walked, and a gust of wind smacked Holland in the face with its strength. "The draft's coming from back— Holy shit!"

Zach plowed into him when he stopped abruptly. "Oof. Sorry. What…?" He strode forward, mouth hanging open, eyes huge. "Oh my god. Oh my god. Holland." The horrified expression on his face sunk into Holland, sunk his stomach to his feet. Sunk his future into oblivion.

It was confirmation that yes, it really was as bad as it seemed.

Sometime during the snowstorm, a small section of the warehouse's roof had caved in. Shouldn't have been a big deal, and any other time of year it wouldn't be. But now? Today? With Holland's Christmas Lane float right there?

"Oh god, Holland." Zach hooked his hands under the edge of Christmas Lane's platform and pulled. The float didn't budge. Squeezing his eyes shut, grunting with the effort, Zach pulled and pulled, neck straining. But he was no match against an eighteen-foot platform topped with pounds and pounds of wood.

"Zach, stop." Holland wrapped his arms around Zach's waist and steered him away. "You'll hurt yourself."

"But we need to get it out of the way."

There was no point. The damage had been done. The right end of Holland's float, the last few feet that featured the stores on the corner of Main and Holly, plus the park, were ruined. Gravel, wood, metal, piping—all of it had fallen onto that end of the float, crushing buildings, tearing holes through fabric awnings, flattening the gazebo, shattering the glass windows he'd ordered custom made. Not to mention the pile of snow that had soaked into the wood and into the artificial grass of the park. The miniature pine tree he'd gotten from Flowers by Daisy that was the centerpiece of the park had survived, although it was tumbled onto its side. Some of the lightbulbs on the multicolored fairy lights had splintered, but those could be replaced. And much easier than the rest of it.

He blew out a breath. "Shit."

"Your beautiful float." Zach was almost in tears, trembling with repressed fury and sadness.

"It's okay."

"No, it's not!" Zach stiffened and pulled away. "The back third is ruined, and the parade's only five days away. There's no way you can fix this, finish Santa's float, and complete your dollhouse commission in time."

"Don't worry." Holland rubbed Zach's shoulders. "I'm sure I can figure it out. Mika, Dev, and Clark will help. You'll still have a perfect parade."

The scowl on Zach's face was spectacular. "That's not what I'm worried about, you ass!" It was growled through clenched teeth. "I want you to win the damn float competition."

Oh. *Oh.* Wow. Holland was an idiot. Here he'd thought Zach was upset about messing up the parade, when really he was worried about Holland.

Holland's shoulders loosened and he offered a conciliatory smile. There'd been a time not so long ago when he would've panicked at the sight of his half-wrecked float. He *needed* to win the competition. But did he? If he took a step back and looked at himself, his business, his finances… Sure, he wanted to be a bigger name, but he didn't need it. The commissions he was already getting, after less than two years in business, were keeping him afloat. And sometimes he was overbooked.

So yeah. Winning the competition would be nice. But it wasn't necessary. If he were honest, the competition had taken a back seat ever since Zach had stepped into his life.

Because no competition was more important than his relationships. Not just with Zach. But with Dev and Clark. And Mika too. If there was one thing Zach had taught him over the past couple of weeks with his obsession with calendars, adorable eccentricities, dimpled smile, eagerness to help, and dedication to everything he set his mind to, it was that Holland wasn't as broken as he'd thought, as he'd considered himself for the past five years. Since the debacle with Mika.

And sometime in the past couple of weeks, winning had become unimportant in the face of spending time with Zach.

Before he could say any of that to Zach, Zach marched past him to the front door of the warehouse. "I can fix this."

"Zach—"

"I'll be right back."

"Where are you going?"

"To round up the troops!"

"What troops?" Holland muttered as the door closed behind Zach.

Who returned a moment later, sheepish smile on his face. "I need your truck keys."

Twenty minutes later, a couple of guys arrived to patch up the roof.

Half an hour after that, Mika walked in with a bounce in his step. "Zach's out there doing damage control. It's friggin' awesome!"

An hour after *that*, they'd removed the roof debris from his float, piling it out of the way for removal, broken down the remaining bits of the crushed buildings, and were soaking up the melted snow from the artificial grass with towels when Zach came in…

Trailed by half the town.

"What the…?"

There was Clark—who was supposed to be at work—in the lead. Dev was right next to him. Who was running the bakery, then? Behind them were Hank, Rosie, Jean, and Charlie—the morning crew from Tiny's Panini. Only Michaela was missing, but since she was a judge for the competition, she wasn't allowed inside headquarters until the day of.

And then there were about a dozen other people, mostly volunteers who'd already completed their own floats. Some of them carried huge thermoses of coffee and, presumably, hot water that they set up on the snack table.

And Zach, with trays of breakfast sandwiches from the café.

Holland raised an eyebrow at Mika.

Mika grinned back. "Damage control."

Everyone was chatting and laughing, and as they surrounded Holland's float, the conversation continued without pause, switching from whatever topic they'd been discussing to brainstorming ideas on how to fix it.

Holland stood stupefied as Zach divided the team and assigned them a float, half on Santa's, half on Christmas Lane. Then he pointed at Holland and said, "What do you need us to do?"

But Holland couldn't speak. Couldn't think. All he could do was stare at Zach in amazement while his heart grew two sizes, then fell right at Zach's feet. This was the guy—the charming, spectacular, utterly *perfect* guy—who would own Holland's heart forever.

A quizzical expression crossed Zach's features, and he looked behind him, as though wondering who the hell Holland was staring at with the lovesick grin on his face.

As if Holland would ever look at anyone else.

"Do you think he's all right?" someone behind him whispered as the silence dragged on.

"I think he's got a certain man on the brain," someone else said.

Clark grunted. "Isn't it always about a man?"

"No," Dev muttered a touch sharply. "For you, maybe. But not for Holland."

With his lip caught between his teeth, Zach paced up to him. "Is everything okay? Did I mess up? I was just trying to help."

Holland cupped his face, hauled him forward, and kissed him in full view of everyone, ignoring the catcalls and one shout of "Get a room!"

"You're perfect."

"Um." Zach blinked, pink dotting his cheeks. "Later we'll talk about your skewed definition of *perfect*, but for now, maybe tell us what to do?"

Holland kissed him once more—just because he could, and because Zach hadn't seemed to mind Holland kissing him in front of everyone—then addressed the volunteers who'd shown up last minute to help him.

God, he loved this town.

What felt like a zillion hours later, Zach locked up Tiny's Panini and dragged his feet toward the alley and the staircase up to his apartment. He had two missed calls from

Holland and a text that said Call me when you finish work. Zach called, but it went straight to voicemail.

His afternoon shift at the café had been predictably boring, but he was still invigorated from this morning, so he continued straight instead of going home, heading for the park.

The first thing he'd done this morning after leaving headquarters was call a couple of guys to fix the roof. He couldn't believe it had collapsed, of all things. God. Then he'd called Mika and told him to get himself to headquarters pronto and help Holland fix his damaged float. Then he'd gone to every store down Christmas Lane, rounding up anyone who'd be willing to help. And the look on Holland's face when he'd arrived back at headquarters had been priceless. An unexpected kick to the nuts would've surprised him less.

Honestly, he couldn't believe Holland hadn't been more upset by the damage to his float. Zach was plenty heartbroken for the both of them, it seemed. Maybe he'd freaked Holland out by going into fix-it mode, and that was why he'd appeared so surprised.

Zach hunched his shoulders against the cold and kept walking, the air refreshing after being cooped up indoors most of the day. It was just as cold as it'd been this morning, but with the Christmas decorations in every store and the stars shining overhead, it felt magical.

Laughter and raised voices echoed out of Annie's Irish Pub. Zach paused on the sidewalk, hands stuffed in his pockets. He couldn't see much through the stained glass windows, just enough to make out a large crowd inside.

Every part of his being wanted to walk in there. To be included. To feel like part of a crowd. Monday night was trivia night at Annie's. He knew everybody in town. He

CHRISTMAS JANE | 207

could walk in there right now, choose any table to sit at, and be welcome.

But still. Something held him back. Some deep-rooted fear that he'd be rejected for daring to intrude. That he'd be laughed at for even trying to make friends.

In elementary school, a group of kids had begrudgingly included him in a game they called Fun Ball, which essentially included throwing a tennis ball at a wall and then… something. He'd never found out. Because when he'd tried asking for the rules of the game, he'd been ignored. Like he hadn't spoken at all, yet he knew everyone had heard him.

He'd felt invisible.

Had spent his entire elementary school career feeling invisible.

High school hadn't been quite as bad, but he hadn't enjoyed it either. He hadn't felt invisible so much as…not good enough. When the people he'd called friends laughed at him for using a fork and knife to eat pizza, it splintered something inside him that had already been fragile.

And college. College hadn't been awful. In fact, he'd liked it. He'd found a crowd of people who were his type, but more than that, who were nonjudgmental and accepting. Not including the guys he'd had one-night stands with, of course. That was entirely different. And his own fault. He'd brought that on himself by being too desperate to belong.

But he did belong. He belonged to this town, and the town had proven that today by having his back.

A collective groan came from inside. Zach placed a hand against the stained glass. He wasn't in the mood to be on his own today. Wanted to be part of a crowd. Taking a deep breath, he stepped into the pub.

"Okay, okay, okay," Annie herself said from the small

stage set up against the right wall, holding a sheet of paper. "Here's an easier one for you: On a standard keyboard, what letter is found between X and V?"

Conversation ensued as each team discussed the answer.

It smelled like beer and french fries, and Zach's stomach growled. It was hot in the pub. He unwound his scarf and slipped out of his jacket, hanging both up on the coat rack next to the door. He got several nods hello, even more waves, and a couple of teams made up of older citizens tried to entice him to join their group.

"Zach!" Over on the other side of the room, Mika was waving his arms. "Hey, you found us."

He'd—what?

Zach made his way over to Mika where he sat with Dev, Clark, and Holland, with beers all around and a basket of onion rings in the center of the table. Holland and Clark had their heads bent together, the answer sheet between them. Holland turned at Mika's shout, and his grin awoke something soft in Zach's veins that had him almost tripping over his own feet. Holland snagged Zach's wrist and plopped Zach onto his lap.

"Hi." Holland kissed the corner of Zach's mouth.

Zach's foolish heart pitter-pattered. "Hi."

"How'd you find us?"

Zach ran a hand through the hair at the back of Holland's head. "Luck."

"Yeah? Here." Holland reached for a fifth, untouched beer. "Ordered this for you in advance."

They'd been expecting him? That must've been what the missed phone calls were about. An invitation to join Holland and his friends for trivia night. The knowledge that they actually wanted to hang out with him washed over him like the satisfaction of a well-organized calendar.

Zach stole the pen out of Holland's hands and marked a C down on the answer sheet, right underneath the last answer, *scarab dung beetle*. What the hell had the question been?

Dev peered down at Zach's answer. "God, that's so obvious now that I see it written."

"What was question four again?" Mika pointed at an empty spot on the answer sheet. "Maybe Zach'll know it."

"The name of the hotel the bachelor party stayed at in *The Hangover*," Clark said.

Zach didn't hesitate. "Caesars Palace."

"Ohhhhhh!" The entire table whooped, and Zach got a high five from Dev and Mika.

"Next question!" Annie yelled over the noise of the crowd. "Lateral epicondylitis is a condition commonly known by what name?"

Midway through the questions, Annie called a halt for refreshment refills and bathroom breaks. Zach had claimed his own chair a few questions ago, and he sat back now, pleasantly full of onion rings and beer.

He ran a hand over Holland's back. "What made you guys decide to come here tonight?"

"Needed to take a load off." Holland angled his chair toward Zach and leaned his elbows on his knees. "We spent all day working. Thought we'd have some fun before we start all over again tomorrow. Thank you, by the way." He kissed the back of Zach's hand, eyes so soft Zach felt it all the way down to his toes. "We wouldn't be as far along as we are now without all of the help you found me."

"So it went okay?"

"It was great. Turned out some of the wood was salvageable. Mr. Columbus spent all morning cutting me new pieces to spec, and a couple of people went into Portland to get some fabric for me. There's not much I can do about the glass at this point, but I've still got all of the paint, so I should be able to finish it in time for the judging on Saturday. Mika's crew finished Santa's float today."

"*Mika's* crew?"

"The self-appointed leader."

Zach laughed. "Of course."

"I think you were right about him needing to keep busy." Holland eyed Mika, who sat on the other side of the table, sipping a beer and laughing with Dev and Clark.

Clark picked up the answer sheet. "How many of these do you think we have right so far?"

"This one." Mika stole the sheet away and added an asterisk next to a number. "This one, for sure. And these two."

"And these," Dev piped in, pointing at three other numbers.

"Maybe that one," Holland said.

Dev smirked at him. "You really think Molly Malone sold flowers on the streets of Dublin?"

"Why not? Anybody else got a better answer?"

"We're in an Irish pub," Clark pointed out. "You'd think one of these photographs of Ireland on the wall would hold the answer."

"Speaking of Irish pubs," Mika pulled out a menu seemingly from nowhere. "I'm starving. I need something more than these onion rings. Wait." He squinted. "This menu's different."

Dev rolled his eyes. "Yeah. Last time you were home was over five years ago. They've updated the menu since then."

"The fuck is okra?"

"Isn't it cheese?" said Clark, munching on an onion ring.

"I think it's the slimy vegetable," Holland said.

"Which one?" Zach asked in all seriousness. "There are many slimy vegetables. Shall I name them for you?"

"I really think it's cheese," Clark muttered.

Dev smirked at Clark. "You're thinking of Oka."

"Spinach," Zach said.

"Maybe I'll get the salmon instead."

"Asparagus."

"Bok choi," Holland piped in.

"Ooh, good one."

Play resumed before Mika made a decision. And when it was all over and the answers revealed, it turned out Molly Malone hadn't, in fact, been selling flowers.

"I told you!" Dev was saying as they exited the pub.

"Hey, you didn't give up any better answers," Holland said.

A parked car beeped up ahead and Clark opened the driver's side door. "Anybody want a lift?"

Zach leaned into Holland. "Want to take a walk?"

"Yeah." Holland wrapped an arm around him. "We'll see you guys tomorrow," he called over his shoulder to Mika, Dev, and Clark as they piled into Clark's car.

Tucked into Holland's side, Zach didn't feel the cold as they walked to the park in companionable silence. It was quiet but for the sound of conversation as people exited Annie's, a car started up, their footprints crunched in the snow. It was so peaceful that Zach didn't understand how more people didn't take advantage of how soothing it was to walk in the dark.

They came up to the gazebo and Zach stopped to stare at something next to it. "Hey, it's our bench!" Right there under the willow tree. He swiped the snow off and took a seat, his jeans doing nothing to stop his butt from freezing against the cold wood.

Holland sat against him, an arm against the back of the bench. The giant Christmas tree in the middle of the park glittered and shone under the indigo night sky and silver stars.

"Oh my god." Zach sat up straight, hand to his forehead.

"What's wrong?"

Slumping against Holland, Zach let out a tired laugh. "A week until Christmas Eve and I haven't bought a single Christmas present yet. With everything going on, I completely forgot." Although realistically, who did he have to buy for? He and Alana had stopped exchanging gifts in college. His parents wouldn't be here until the new year. So really, the only person he needed something for…was Holland.

"We can go into Portland on Sunday." Holland's deep voice was a rumble in the dark. "Do some last-minute shopping."

"Yeah. Maybe." Or maybe he'd wait until after Christmas when all of the stores had sales.

Holland kissed his temple. "You must be looking forward to seeing your parents. When are they coming up?"

"They're not." And Zach was actually okay with that. "They'll come in January. Flights are cheaper then."

"True. That's usually when I head to Atlanta to see my folks, and my sister and her family."

Silence descended, a comfortable one. Zach gazed out at the park and imagined what it would look like come Saturday evening for the Christmas fair. Little huts set up for vendors to sell food and products. Warming stations. A band playing Christmas music from inside the gazebo. The elementary school choir performing half a dozen songs for the crowd. Hundreds of townsfolk shopping and chatting. Laughing children. Barking dogs.

And Zach's secret project.

Holland shifted. Crossed one leg over the other. Uncrossed them. Rubbed his jaw. "So…" He cleared his throat. "You're, uh, celebrating Christmas with Alana, then?"

"No." Zach tilted his head up toward him, a question on his face. "She's going skiing with friends, remember?"

"Right, right." Holland coughed. "In that case, would you like to, uh, spend Christmas with Dev and me?"

Was he blushing? It was too dark to tell for sure, but Zach would've sworn Holland's cheeks were ruddier than normal.

Zach kissed him softly. "I'd love to."

"Yeah?" Holland's grin was sweet.

"Yeah."

"'Kay." He did a little wiggle on the bench. Like a mini victory dance. It was ridiculously cute.

Zach bit his lip to hide a smile and snuggled into Holland.

Holland hugged him close. "Should we go by your place, get you a new suit for tomorrow's interview, then go home? You can practice your presentation there."

Home. To Holland's. When was the last time Zach had thought of his own apartment as *home*?

"Yeah." He kissed Holland's throat. "Let's go home."

# CHAPTER FIFTEEN

*3 days until the parade*

WAITING FOR THE PHONE TO RING WAS AGONY.

Zach had killed his interview yesterday. Killed. It. Like Princess Leia killing Jabba the Hutt. Okay, that was maybe not the best analogy, but still. Killed it.

And yet he still hadn't heard anything from the interviewers. Granted, it'd only been one day, but he was *sure* he'd gotten the job. So sure that he almost handed in his resignation to Alana right then and there.

Except there was really no resigning from the family business, so there was that.

The good news was that since he'd placed want ads in local colleges a week and a half ago, Alana had had an onslaught of new applications, and had even held interviews late last week. And then *hired* someone. Two someones, in fact.

It was a goddamn miracle.

Remarkably, he wasn't on sandwich duty at the café today. Instead, he manned the front while Alana showed her two new hires the ropes in the kitchen. It was that lull between breakfast and lunch where stragglers trickled in every once in a while for a midmorning coffee or snack break, but in a few minutes, the lunch crowd would make an appearance. There was currently only one person seated at a table, headphones on and head bent over a laptop.

Zach cleaned spills off the table that held milk, cream, and sugars, and refilled what needed to be refilled. He watered the plant in the corner. Restocked the paper cups and plastic lids. Wiped crumbs off tables. Swept the floor. Swung his hips along to Mariah Carey's "All I Want For Christmas Is You."

And still, the phone didn't ring.

He sighed and slipped his phone back into the front pocket of his apron.

The interviewers had been impressed with him yesterday. He'd surprised them by choosing a lobster festival as a fundraiser instead of going the gala route, which apparently was pretty common. Then he'd surprised them again by demonstrating that not only had he brought costs down compared to last year, but he'd done his research and identified prospects in neighboring towns who had a high giving capacity.

"How did you get this information?" one of the interviewers had asked.

"I have a friend who works for a non-profit in Portland," Zach said. "She pulled a report for me using some fancy software."

The report didn't identify individuals because that'd be an invasion of privacy since Zach didn't work for the organization, but he got a list of zip codes where households had the potential to give more than two hundred and fifty dollars a year.

"I mean…" Zach cleared this throat. "Trying to raise money is great and everything, but what's the point if you can't get the right people to attend your event?"

Yeah. Impressed. He was the *boss*.

Ew, what was wrong with him? He couldn't believe he'd just had that thought.

The door swooshed open and Holland walked in, bringing the wind with him. Some of the ornaments on the Christmas tree next to the window swayed precariously on their branches but thankfully stayed put. The cold front had moved on and hopefully wouldn't return until after the parade. He didn't want his spectators freezing as they watched.

Zach grinned at Holland. So big and so strong. Zach just wanted to curl up into him and stay there forever.

"Hey." Holland pulled off his beanie and stuffed it in his pocket.

The twenty-something at the table paused her furious typing to gawk at Holland, only to glance away in disappointment when Holland reeled Zach in by his apron and kissed him.

"Hi." Zach kissed his jaw. "Is there something else that needs fixing?"

"No. I'm picking up some materials at Marcella's. Thought I'd stop in and say hi on my way."

Zach leaned into him, twining his arms around Holland's waist. "Materials for the dollhouse?"

Had to be. Santa's float was officially complete, and Holland had everything he needed for Christmas Lane thanks to the furious commitment of the townspeople who'd volunteered to help fix his damaged float.

"Mm-hmm." Holland pulled Zach close and ran his cheek over Zach's temple. "When this is over, can we spend a week lying on the couch watching movies?"

"Definitely. But, maybe also snowboarding?"

Holland huffed a quiet laugh. "Sure."

There was just so much *snow*, and Zach wanted to be on it. Instead, he was stuck in Tiny's Panini. All the time. Doing the same thing day in and day out. Like the movie *Scrooged*. But worse.

And still, the phone didn't ring.

The archivists from the historical society, a group of older women who practically lived and breathed the word *archive*, came in for their daily lunch break, forcing Zach to step back from Holland with a grunt of dissatisfaction.

Holland put his hat back on. "Meet you at our bench later? We can take a walk before we go home."

"Yeah."

He was gone a second later and Zach briefly poked his head into the kitchen to give Alana the heads up that orders were going to start coming through, then took care of the historical society ladies. The lunch rush hit full swing after that, and Alana never came to relieve him, which was nice. No gross hands for him today, but he'd probably smell extra strongly of coffee. Worth it not to have to make the food.

It was chaotic for the better part of an hour and a half as customers came and went, and Zach had to beg patience from them since the food was taking a little longer than usual on account of the new people being . . . well, new.

"You mean Alana finally hired someone?" Frank Wilson, the owner of The General Store, said.

Zach held his fingers up in the peace sign. "Two someones."

"Well, I'll be damned," someone at the back of the line muttered.

"Can I have a cookie while I wait?" Frank asked.

Alana wouldn't be happy, but if free cookies helped appease an impatient, hungry crowd, then by all means. "Yes."

Zach removed the tray of chocolate chip cookies from the display case. "Of course. On the house. As a thank you for waiting."

The mayor's assistant patted his hand. "You've always been a sweet boy, Zach."

His phone vibrated in his pocket then, and he had a mini panic attack. A line full of customers. A tray full of cookies. More customers waiting for their meals. A restaurant that was three-quarters full, and a handful of tables that needed to be cleared and cleaned.

Screw it.

He handed the tray to Doug. "Pass these around." Kicked open the kitchen door as he pulled out his phone. "Alana, I need you to take over."

"What?"

"Take over!"

"But I can't take orders *and* train Dolores and Chris on how to prepare the food."

Zach swiped the phone on. "Hello?"

"Seriously? You need me to take over so you can take a phone call?"

"Is this Zach Greenfeld?"

"This is he."

Alana threw her hands up. "Unbelievable. This better be the most important phone call of your life."

That remained to be seen.

"Zach, this is Ken Bartlett. How are you?"

Zach gulped. Ken Bartlett was the director of events he'd be working for if he got the job. Tall, bald guy with a belly who'd taken an immediate liking to Zach over their shared love of organization. "Good, thank you, sir. How are you?"

"Good, good. Listen, Zach." Something squeaked. Mr.

Bartlett shifting in his chair, maybe. "We were highly impressed with your presentation yesterday, with the level of research and dedication that went into something that, frankly, the Gold Stone hotels will never use."

Yes, Zach had known that. It was an interview test only. Which was why he'd given all of his materials to Mrs. Shoemacker to pass on to Mr. Barry when he returned.

Zach straightened taller at the compliment. "Thank you, sir."

"We all think you'd be a perfect fit for the role," Mr. Bartlett went on, "and I'd like to officially offer you the job."

Zach grinned so wide his face hurt. He resisted a fist pump. "Thank you! Thank you so much."

"I'm going to send you an email with an official offer letter that'll detail the role, the pay, benefits, vacation allowances, all that stuff. If everything looks good, sign it and send it back to me. But if you have any questions about the offer at all, let me know and we can talk through it."

He hung up in a daze, staring down at his phone, replaying Ken Bartlett's words back to himself. He'd gotten the job.

He'd gotten the job! His stomach flipped over on itself, like that feeling when an elevator shot up too fast. He opened his mouth to tell Alana, but…

Everyone was staring at him.

His mouth went dry.

It was so silent they could hear the sound of the dishwasher working in the kitchen.

"What was that about?" Alana asked.

He wet his dry throat and said, "I got the job." There was a little bit of awe in his voice.

"The one in Florida?"

"It's not in—"

But she didn't let him finish. She screeched and tackled him in a bear hug. "Oh my god, I'm so happy for you."

"Florida?" someone muttered. "Why would anyone want to live there?"

"Perpetual summer," someone else said.

"Disney World!"

"The ocean."

"*We* have an ocean."

"Well, at least his parents live there, so he'll have some family nearby."

"I can't believe it," Zach whispered. He pulled out of Alana's hug and yanked on his hair. "I have to tell Holland."

"Whoa there, lover boy." Alana stopped his forward march and gestured at their customers.

Right. Work, first. Then he'd find Holland and tell him the good news.

"Did I miss anything?"

Holland sorted through the materials spread over the counter at Marcella's Tools & More. Wood glue—he'd already gone through the tube Zach had given him. An economy-sized roll of masking tape. Sandpaper. A new utility knife since he'd worn the shit out of his old one. Tapewire. Rubber gloves. Liquid nails. And a shit ton of wood.

"I think that's everything."

Marcella bagged everything up for him. "Good. Sorry it took so long to find. Ed was supposed to put it all in one place for you."

"No problem."

Not like he was in a rush. He only needed to have the

dollhouse complete by Sunday, and Saturday was a total right off because of the parade.

Nope. No rush at all.

"Here you go." Marcella handed the bag over. "I'll have Ed take the wood out to your truck."

"I appreciate it."

"How's your float coming along?" Marcella was one of the judges. "I heard you had a mishap earlier this week."

Holland smiled tightly. "Nothing that couldn't be fixed. Plus, I had help."

The float wouldn't be as perfect as it was originally. He couldn't get some of the materials for the awnings in the same color as before, some of the buildings wouldn't have glass windows, and he didn't have time to rebuild the gazebo in the park so he'd had to order one online and have it shipped express to arrive on time…but it'd still be something he could be proud of.

And that wouldn't have been possible without the help of the town, and especially Clark, Dev, and Mika, who'd spent every spare second they could in headquarters helping him.

Speaking of Mika…

Holland found him staring at a display of hammers near the back of the store. That was it. Just staring. Lost in his own thoughts.

Holland touched his shoulder gently. "Mika."

"Huh?" Mika shook his head. His eyes cleared. "Got everything you need?"

"Yeah. Everything okay?"

Mika's smile was sheepish. "Yeah. Just thinking. Time to go?"

"Yeah. Thanks again for helping out. That's a lot of wood to carry in."

"No sweat."

They were making their way through the aisles when the bell over the door tinkled, admitting in a new customer.

"Hey, Marcella. Did you hear the latest?"

Jennifer. Alana's best friend. The town gossip. Seriously, couldn't she mind her own business?

He was about to say something to that effect when she said, "Zach got a job in Florida."

Holland stopped midstep. Zach got a job *where*?

"Did he?" Marcella's voice. "I wonder if he applied for a job there because that's where his parents live."

"Florida?" Mika mumbled behind him. He said *Florida* like one might say *flying cockroach*. "That doesn't make any sense."

It made *no* sense. Zach had interviewed for a job in *Portland*. Hadn't they talked a few weeks ago about how neither of them ever wanted to live in Florida?

What had changed? Had Zach gotten the job he'd interviewed for, but they were placing him in Florida instead? Had he applied for a different job entirely and hadn't told Holland about it?

Florida.

It was Mika all over again. His boyfriend thousands of miles away.

As though Holland had conjured him, Zach appeared in front of him. Face flushed, no coat, Tiny's Panini's apron around his waist. His smile was so radiant, it reached right into Holland and shook his heart. "Hi!"

*Congratulations*, he should've said.

*I'm so happy for you*, went through his head.

But, "I think we need to take a break," came out of his mouth instead.

Silence.

Then, "What?" from Mika.

"What?" from Zach.

"What?" from Holland.

"Are you okay?" Mika asked him.

"I'm…"

Zach lost his smile and glanced around nervously, wringing his hands. "A break from what?"

Holland couldn't stop seeing it. That image on Facebook, of Mika and some other guy. That was the way Mika had chosen to break up with him. By posting an image of himself kissing someone else. And it had gutted him. Completely blindsided him and left him gasping for breath.

That wouldn't be how Zach broke up with him. No, Zach would never cheat on anybody. He'd move away with every intention of maintaining a long-distance relationship. But then he'd meet someone new. Someone young and cool and as completely into day planners as he was. Someone *there* and *available* and not miles and miles away. And he'd call Holland and let him down gently. Let him know that what they'd had was special, but he was moving on.

Holland had been in love with Mika. But he was *in love* with Zach.

And if Zach left him…he wouldn't have anything left.

He took a step back, bumping into Mika. "I…need some time to think." To figure out how to do this. *If* he could do this. He owed it to both of them to figure it out.

Zach's expression shifted, mouth flattening. He wrapped his arms around himself. "Think about what?"

"About…things."

"I don't understand," he whispered brokenly. He blinked down at the floor, and when he looked back up at Holland, his eyes were glassy. "Did I do something wrong?"

"No!" Holland rubbed his hands over his face, into his

hair, and pulled hard enough to hurt. "God, no. You're..." Perfect. So, so perfect. Everything Holland could ever need or want wrapped up in a beautiful package made just for him. "I need a couple of days, okay?"

Zach held his arms out to his sides. He looked so utterly, completely lost. "For what?" His tiny whisper was a plea. For answers. For an explanation.

God, Holland had done that. He almost back-pedaled. Almost told Zach he was kidding. Overreacting. But...

What if he wasn't? Simply the thought of another long-distance relationship made goose bumps crawl over his skin.

"I..." How did he even begin to explain?

Zach lifted his gaze up to the ceiling. He opened his mouth. Closed it again. With one last desperate glance at Holland, he turned and left.

But not before Holland saw his face collapse.

Holland wasn't faring too well himself. His throat ached from swallowing back tears. His heart had been shredded by claws. His soul was screaming at him.

What had he done?

And would it be worth it?

"What the hell did you do?"

"Jesus!" He'd forgotten Mika was there.

And oh, Mika was *pissed*. "What the hell did you just do to that sweet man?"

"I—"

Mika slapped the back of his head.

"Ow."

"Did you learn *nothing* from our relationship?"

Holland rubbed the ache on his head, but it was nothing compared to the ache in his chest. Zach's face when he'd left... That was something he'd never forget.

"What do you mean?"

"One of the reasons we ended up breaking up is because we didn't talk to each other. Not really, not after I left. Not before either. The key to a good relationship is communication." Mika rolled his eyes. "Even I know that now, and I haven't had a serious relationship since you."

Holland closed his eyes. "I don't know if I can do another long-distance relationship."

Mika was silent for so long that Holland thought he'd walked away, but then, "You're an idiot."

"I'm being cautious," Holland countered through gritted teeth. "The last time I was in one, my boyfriend cheated on me."

Mika sucked in a sharp breath, eyes wide and hurt.

"Fuck." Holland sighed. "I'm sorry. That was callous." They'd cleared the air. He had no business bringing that up.

"Zach is not moving to Florida," Mika said, picking up their conversation as if Holland hadn't been a class-A asshole.

"How do you know that?"

"Because I know. Just like you should know. Trust me, as long as you're together, he's not going anywhere."

*As long as you're together.* Oh god. Had he pushed Zach away, like he'd pushed Mika away five years ago?

What was wrong with him that he kept pushing people away when the going got tough?

"But Jennifer said—"

"Who cares what Jennifer said?" So much fierceness in Mika's voice. "What did Zach say?"

Holland exhaled a long, sad breath, shoulders dropping. "Nothing." Because Holland hadn't given him the chance.

"Nothing," Mika repeated, softer now. He knew his

words were hitting home. "Maybe Jennifer's right. Maybe he is going to Florida. But I guarantee you, he's not moving there. It's probably just for training or something equally temporary."

Maybe.

Maybe Holland had fucked things up royally. He needed to find out what was going on, right from the source. Zach had been so happy when he'd shown up. The sun and the moon and the stars combined in his eyes. And Holland had shit all over that. Because he was terrified down to the bone of being left behind again.

He gave Mika his keys and left him to deal with the supplies, then ran up the street to Tiny's.

No Zach.

If he was in his apartment above the café, he didn't answer.

He wasn't in headquarters.

He wasn't at the park.

His car was in the shop, which meant he couldn't have gone far.

So where was he?

# CHAPTER SIXTEEN

*1 day until the parade*

TWO DAYS LATER AND HOLLAND STILL DIDN'T KNOW. Zach hadn't shown up at headquarters, yet the snacks and coffee continued to arrive on schedule. Some of his clothes, three pairs of Converse, toiletries, and his calligraphy set were still at Holland's, so he hadn't been there either. He wasn't at the café. He wasn't answering his phone.

The vibe in headquarters had turned frantic over the last couple of days as people rushed to finish their floats. Holland had officially completed the repairs on Christmas Lane yesterday, taking his time, lingering over the smallest details.

But no matter how long he took, Zach still didn't show up.

In a hopeful attempt at catching Zach here, he'd moved his work-in-progress dollhouse and all of his materials out of his workshop at home and into headquarters. Zach had to show up sometime. The parade was tomorrow.

He'd never felt Zach's absence more acutely than he had the past two days. There was no Zach to smile at him, that adorable dimple in his left cheek making Holland want to kiss it. No Zach to talk to. No Zach to laugh with. No Zach bringing him vanilla tea when his mug ran empty, as if Zach *knew* Holland was in need of a fix. No Zach sitting studiously behind Mr. Barry's desk. No Zach consulting the calendars on the wall or jotting notes in his day planner. No Zach on the phone confirming and re-confirming details with vendors and volunteers. No Zach swatting Holland's hand away when he tried to peek into the *secret* tab of his binder. No Zach leaning into Holland's touch, as though he was starved for human contact.

No Zach.

And it was as though someone had snuffed out the only candle in his life, plunging his world into darkness and cold.

What was wrong with him that he'd pushed Zach away so effortlessly? Why hadn't he stopped to think? To ask Zach if what Jennifer said was true? To talk about it with Zach instead of freaking out? To congratulate him and tell him he was proud of him and happy for him—all of which was true—instead of acting like a colossal douchebag who couldn't communicate?

He was a quitter. That's what it was. He'd quit teaching. The bar. Keeping Bud's books. Hell, he'd quit Mika. And now he'd quit Zach.

Mika was right—he was an idiot.

"Thought I might find you here." Mika sat on the tarp next to him. "Even though we finished your float already."

The only good thing to come out of Holland's estrangement from Zach was that he'd been able to focus on his work, and he'd completed his dollhouse in record time.

But it also meant that now he had no reason to linger in headquarters, which meant he was sitting on a wood shaving-covered tarp on the floor with his ex-boyfriend, tools spread out before him, staring at his dollhouse. Leaving him with nothing much to do. He could start on the new commissions he'd received, but he wasn't in the mood. And Christmas shopping was out since he'd ordered everything online and had it shipped to his sister's and parents in Atlanta weeks ago.

"What are you doing?" Mika asked.

Holland groaned. "Literally nothing, except wondering where Zach is."

"Still no word from him?"

Holland lay back, stared at the ceiling, and didn't bother answering.

Mika had been right about something else too—he really hadn't learned anything from their relationship. Hadn't told Mika that he didn't want him to move to LA. That he was worried their relationship might suffer. About the stress of managing the bar and how much he hated it and how much it was making him hate life in general.

Well. He'd always known Zach was the more mature of the two of them.

"Look." Mika shifted on the tarp. "I'm just going to throw this out there, okay? Say Zach *is* moving to Florida."

Holland sucked in a sharp breath and rubbed his hand over his chest.

"What's keeping you here?"

He froze. Sat up straight. "What?"

Mika shrugged. "What's keeping you here? Why can't you—"

"Move to Florida?"

"Yeah." Mika smiled softly. "Move to Florida."

"To be with Zach."

Holland wasn't just an idiot. He was an idiot without a head on his shoulders. Why hadn't he thought of that? Just because he didn't *want* to live in Florida, didn't mean he *wouldn't.* For the right reasons.

Zach was the right reason.

His heart was beating too fast and he couldn't breathe properly. Now that the solution had presented itself, he couldn't wait to tell Zach.

But Zach was nowhere to be found.

And he wasn't answering his phone.

So Holland sent one last desperate text.

Meet me at our bench tomorrow during the fair. Please.

# CHAPTER SEVENTEEN

*Parade day*

ONCE, WHEN ZACH WAS SEVEN OR EIGHT, HE'D TAKEN the diamond-level ski slopes on his snowboard before he was ready. And it was *exhilarating*. Flying through the air. The wind in his hair. Heart racing and racing as he sped downward from the top of the world, cackling with glee.

But then he'd lost control. He'd been going too fast and panicked, overcorrected…then tumbled, head over heels, for a few feet before coming to a standstill on his side.

He'd come out of it with a broken wrist.

That was sort of how he felt now. Like he'd been flying through the past few weeks, sitting on top of the world, floating on joy and sunshine. Only to have it come crashing down when he least expected, engulfing him in pain.

Rolling over onto his stomach, he hid his face in his pillow. His apartment was depressing compared to Holland's house. And not just because Holland's shower was amazing. Holland's house was cozy and warm, and it felt like a home. Especially compared to Zach's apartment, which was more of a temporary place of residence.

He needed to get up, to get ready. It was a big day today,

and he should've been at it already. But he lacked the motivation. And the cojones to show his face at headquarters.

He'd successfully avoided it the past couple of days, instead choosing to work from the kitchen in his parents' house. It was comforting to be in the familiar space he'd grown up in, even if he had to listen to Alana's pointed questions à la the "Why are you moping?" variety.

But it was parade day, and thus, there was no avoiding headquarters today.

Which was where Holland would be. Holland. Who'd broken up with him.

Or told him he needed a break. Whatever. It amounted to the same thing.

They were the Ross and Rachel of Lighthouse Bay.

What had he done? What had happened between "When this is over, let's watch movies all day" to "We need to take a break?" It'd been half an hour, at most, between conversations. How could thirty minutes be so life changing?

And Holland had done it in front of Mika of all people. Was that what happened? Some switch had been flipped and Holland had suddenly realized that it was Mika he wanted to be with?

Was it their age difference? It hadn't been a problem before, but maybe Holland had realized he needed someone more mature. More independent. More settled.

Was Zach back to being a sidetrack?

Whatever the reason, why hadn't Holland explained? Maybe that was what his constant texts and phone calls had been about the last couple of days. The ones Zach hadn't answered because he was terrified of what Holland had to say. Each call and text made his stomach cramp with dread.

At least Mika had been the only person in the store at

the time. Jennifer had been leaving as he'd come in, and he could only imagine the gossip had she overheard their conversation.

He sniffled and brought the bed covers up to his chin. He'd finally found somewhere he belonged, and Holland had ripped it away without a second thought. Just like he'd ripped Zach's heart out, leaving him cold and alone. They were supposed to spend Christmas together and now...

*What did I do?*

The alarm on his phone went off again.

Okay. Enough. He'd procrastinated enough. Time to get up. Face Holland. There'd be no avoiding him today, not with everything that needed to happen with the float judging and getting all of the floats organized in order and the vendors setting up at the park. He and his volunteers had set up all of the little huts in the park yesterday, and his secret project had worked out exactly like he'd anticipated.

Although now that he and Holland were on a break—whatever that meant—his secret project just made him feel empty and sad.

Zach swiped his phone on and checked for any messages or social media notifications that had come in overnight. He got rid of the social media stuff, responded to a text about the secret project, sent his sister a reminder about the coffee, tea, and hot chocolate stand outside the café for the duration of the parade...

Then stared at the final text Holland had sent him.

Meet me at our bench tomorrow during the fair. Please.

That he still called it "our bench" was somewhat uplifting, but it could've been a slip. Zach didn't let it get his hopes up.

Flopping onto his back, he closed his eyes and took a deep breath. Another. Swallowed the knot at the back of

234 | AMY AISLIN

his throat. It'd been there for the past couple of days, keeping him on the edge of tears every second of every day. Holland's face was painted on the backs of his eyelids, the way he'd looked when he'd told Zach they needed to take a break because he needed to think. As though the words had surprised him. Like he'd been equally shocked at what was coming out of his mouth as Zach was.

What did that *mean*?

Guess he'd find out tonight. Because there was no way he could ignore Holland's last text. Meet me at our bench tomorrow during the fair. Please.

Ok, he sent back.

And got ready to face the day.

Ok.

Holland stared at the text. That was it. Two letters. But it was something. An acknowledgment. It was better than the nothing he'd been getting so far.

Parade headquarters was chaos. People were making final touches to their floats, yelling that they needed this tool or that piece of material. The high school band practiced in an out-of-the-way spot. Baton twirlers twirled batons. Volunteer teenagers were dressed as clowns and zoo animals. Kids were dressed as elves. Some of them would walk the parade route, handing out red reindeer noses, Lighthouse Bay-branded knit hats donated by the sporting goods store, and candy canes; others would sit on floats.

Then, three hours before go time, trucks were driven in via the bay doors, and volunteers hooked floats up to them. Then the trucks drove back out, floats trailing behind them, and the volunteer truck drivers lined up on the side streets. There were so many floats that the parade line went farther than Holland could see.

Zach was everywhere at once. Making sure the truck drivers had everything they needed. That the builders were ready for their floats to be judged. That the floats were lined up in the correct order. Reminding the drivers that they needed to wait thirty seconds after the float ahead of them departed before moving, and not to go above five miles per hour. Double checking all the floats to ensure everything was secure and wouldn't fall off onto the street during the parade.

He disappeared for a little while, and Holland learned from Mr. Columbus that he'd gone to inspect the parade route to make sure the road was closed off, the police were keeping everyone off the streets, and that road debris wouldn't cause an accident.

When he came back, it was time for the judging. He handed the judges, including the mayor dressed as Santa, their score sheets attached to clipboards. Once the results were in, he'd seal them in an envelope and hand it off to Mrs. Shoemacker for tallying.

Holland stood next to his float with Clark, both of them decked out in heavy winter gear. There were people *everywhere*, and Holland didn't know how Zach kept everybody's roles straight. And mingling with the volunteers were pedestrians on their walk to scope out a decent spot on Main from which to watch the parade.

Chaos.

And yet Zach handled it as though he'd been born to it.

Holland couldn't help but notice that Zach was still wearing his gloves. That had to be a sign that Zach hadn't given up on him, right? That Holland hadn't messed up too badly?

Or maybe they were the only pair he had.

At least he'd agreed to meet Holland later at the fair. Pacing to try and keep warm, Holland wished he could go back in time and re-do their entire conversation at Marcella's.

He had a plan for tonight. One that would show Zach just how sorry he was and how much Zach meant to him. But he was so anxious he hadn't been able to eat a single thing today.

"Nervous?" Clark asked.

Man, was he ever. "Yeah."

"It'll be fine, you'll see. Yours is the best float here."

Holland paused his pacing to blink at his best friend, then realized they were talking about two different things. Clark was talking about the judging.

Yet Holland had forgotten all about it, even though the judges were currently evaluating the float ahead of his.

The competition meant nothing compared to how he felt about Zach.

Blowing out a breath, he leaned against the driver's side door of his truck. "Thanks for your help," he said to Clark. "I know you took time off work to help me fix it." He bumped Clark's shoulder. "I appreciate it."

Clark grunted and shifted uncomfortably. "There isn't much I wouldn't do for my friends."

"I know."

The judges made their way over, clipboards at the ready, breath fanning out in front of them as they *ooh*ed and *ah*ed over his version of Christmas Lane.

"Great job, son." The mayor squeezed Holland's shoulder. "Impressive work."

"Is that clock in the clock tower actually functional?" Marcella said.

"It *is*," Michaela breathed.

Zach wouldn't even look at him.

He stood apart from the judges with his own clipboard. Underneath the clip was what looked like a checklist, his pocket day planner, and a mini notepad. A pen was tied to the top of the clip by a string. He shifted from one foot to the other, eyes bouncing everywhere, from the floats, to the snow on the ground, to the rooftops, to his own boots.

Clark rolled his eyes and shoved Holland over to him.

Butterflies the size of baseballs danced a jig in his belly. Clearing his throat, Holland said, "Hey." And resisted the urge, the *ache*, to reach out and pull Zach into his arms, apologize for being the dumbass he was, and keep him forever.

Zach sucked in a breath and jerked back a step. "Hi." His shoulders were up to his ears and his nose was bright red.

"I've missed you around headquarters the past couple of days."

Zach finally looked at him, the expression on his face an odd mixture of disbelief and hope. The disbelief Holland understood—he'd gone from I-need-space-to-think to I-missed-you in the span of three days. The hope…

The hope was delicious. Uplifting. It meant Holland still stood a chance.

The judges lingered on Holland's float, looking at it from every angle, pointing out details, pencils scratching against score sheets, but Holland ignored them.

Zach's hope.

It was everything.

Shoulders straightening, Holland said, "Congratulations on the parade, Zach. It's a hit already, and it hasn't even started yet."

"I…" Zach frowned. "I didn't do anything. Mr. Barry did most of it."

"Most of the organizing and volunteer recruiting, maybe. But you rallied everyone together. Treated them like their contribution was meaningful. Fed them. By being as thorough and detail-oriented as you were, you made them feel included. And that's important."

Zach flushed. "I didn't do anything Mr. Barry wouldn't have done."

"Are you kidding?" Holland scoffed. "Mr. Barry wouldn't have done any of that. He ran the show from his desk in town hall and only showed up once a week to check on progress."

"But he has a desk at headquarters."

"Rarely used."

"Holland." The mayor waddled over, Santa stomach wobbling in front of him, long fake beard curling wildly. "Congratulations, son. Regardless of whether you win the competition or not, just know that this is a fantastic piece of work. I knew I chose well when I hired you to build my pergola."

The praise warmed Holland, but the delighted grin Zach shot him was a million times better. It was the sun reflecting off a patch of snow, lighting him up and blinding him in the best way possible. "Thank you, Mr. Mayor," he said. But he couldn't take his eyes off Zach.

"We're heading to the next one, Zach. Coming along?"

"Right," Zach said. He shook himself and followed after the mayor.

"Zach." Holland reached out and gently grasped his wrist. "I'll see you at our bench later?"

Zach bit his lip. Nodded.

Yes. Hope was extremely powerful.

It was over.

The parade had gone off without a hitch. Zach had watched it all from the staging area on Whippoorwill Street, where he and another volunteer gave the drivers, clowns, elves, animals, baton twirlers, and high school band their cue to depart. The parade took a circular route around town, ending back at headquarters. By the time Zach made it there after Santa's float got underway, half of the drivers had made it back with their floats and they all pulled in to headquarters and parked in neat rows, unhooked their floats, and then drove off. Zach had a ten-dollar gift card to the café for every volunteer, and the surprise on everyone's face when he handed them out was gratifying.

They'd done something special for him. It was only fair that he showed them his appreciation. It wasn't much, a ten-dollar gift card. And yet he was told that it wasn't about the dollar amount, but about the sincerity of the gesture.

"You made this parade special, Zach." Mrs. Columbus rubbed his arm through his winter coat.

"I didn't do anything." Why couldn't anybody understand that? Mr. Barry had done ninety-nine percent of the work. Zach had simply come in at the end and ensured everything ran smoothly.

"Oh, Zach." Mrs. Columbus hugged him. "You were great. I wish you were running this again next year."

He did too. But Mr. Barry would be back eventually, and Zach had his own job to start after the new year. The contract Ken Bartlett had sent was printed and sitting on his kitchen counter in his apartment, signed and ready to send back. He just hadn't had time to get to the post office to use the scan-to-email function on the photocopier.

He stood by the doors and handed out gift cards as people left for the fair on the other end of town. It had been a beautiful day—sunny, a few clouds, the barest hint of wind. Cold but tolerable. The sun was currently setting behind headquarters, throwing shades of tangerine, coral, and violet across the sky, a riot of hues that blended, reminding Zach of the colors in a kaleidoscope.

A good omen?

He'd like to think so.

Had Holland actually missed him? It hadn't sounded like a line. Holland hadn't said *I've missed you around headquarters the past couple of days* like one said *I missed the bread roll with my lasagna.* He'd said it like…

Like…

*I miss you.*

Simple. Heartfelt. Real.

Zach had missed him too. So much so that he'd lain awake at night, curled on his side, imagining Holland's phantom arms wrapping around him from behind.

He swallowed hard as Holland's Christmas Lane float pulled into the warehouse and parked. Holland hopped out of the driver's seat, Clark out of the passenger's. Together, they unhooked the float. Chatted for a few minutes while Zach handed out gift cards absently to anyone who passed him. He probably handed too many to one person, but it was hard to pay attention when Holland was right *there*. Holland didn't appear to be listening to whatever Clark was saying. Instead, his head swiveled, eyes bouncing from one end of the warehouse to the other. And then he did a full 360 before he spotted…

Zach.

And grinned at him.

Joy burst inside him, a bubble exploding, sending brilliant optimism through his veins, making him lightheaded, and he couldn't help but smile back.

"Yoo-hoo! Zach!" Mrs. Shoemacker's boots click-clacked against the floor and she carried not one tote bag today, but two. "Do you have a moment?"

"Um…" He searched frantically for someone to take over for him, but it was madness. People were everywhere, talking, laughing, comparing notes, telling stories, changing out of costumes and into their own clothes.

Holland appeared at his side and held out a hand. "Do you want me to give those out?"

Zach bit his lip to contain his grin, and that optimism from earlier just *cemented* into certainty. Because that look in Holland's eyes? The way they centered on Zach, and Zach alone, despite the activity around them?

He handed the gift cards to Holland. Their hands brushed. Lingered. Tingles shot up Zach's arm and he shivered. It felt like they hadn't touched in years, and this one brief contact hummed in his soul.

Holland nodded at Mrs. Shoemacker, who stood off to the side against the wall. "Go. I've got this."

"Thanks."

"Zach," Mrs. Shoemacker said when he walked up. "I've heard that you've accepted a job in Florida."

Zach sighed. "It's in Portland."

"Ah. Well, either way." She waved a hand. "It appears I'm too late."

"For what?"

"Mr. Barry has decided to stay in Detroit. His mother is getting on in years, and he'll be staying there to take care of her. Which means I'm short a town event planner."

Zach held his breath.

"I've been so impressed with your work that I was going to offer you the position, but it seems you've already accepted a different one."

"No!" Heads turned at his shout. He lowered his voice and tried to gather his thoughts. "I mean, yes. No, I mean no, I haven't accepted. It was offered, but I haven't officially accepted yet."

Mrs. Shoemacker smiled and clapped her hands together once. "Wonderful! I'm not too late. Can you hold off on accepting it until Monday? Come into my office before lunch. We'll talk."

Monday was Christmas Eve, and Zach had to open the café since Alana was leaving on her ski trip tomorrow. But for this? He'd make it work.

His good mood slipped a notch when he headed back to the door. Clark stood in Holland's place, giving out gift cards to the last of the volunteers. The warehouse was empty of people. All the floats were parked. Mr. Mayor, still dressed as Santa, was the last to leave, with a wave over his shoulder at Clark and Zach.

"Where's Holland?"

Clark handed him the remaining gift cards. "He headed to the fair. Said he had something he needed to do."

"Oh." Zach heaved a sigh. He'd wanted to walk over with Holland.

"Want a ride?" Clark asked.

The fair was beautiful. Better than he could have ever dreamed of. The walking path was lined with wooden stalls all the way up to the Christmas tree. Some sold hot drinks, others offered pastries and popcorn, and still others sold everything from clothes, to Christmas ornaments, pet supplies, outdoor gear, and handmade tchotchkes. Affixed to the roof of each hut was a string of white fairy lights and green garlands. In the center of the park, the Christmas tree rose tall and beautiful, lights cascading color onto the snow. Bright white, ocean blue, ruby red, pine green. Additional lights had been set up around the park for extra visibility. In the gazebo, a band played festive, upbeat Christmas music.

Zach hit Tiny's Panini's hut first, where Alana, Mika, and Zari sold hot drinks. "Al, can I have five apple ciders?"

"Gimme a sec." She handed a hot chocolate to a kid, then started on his ciders. "Nice job with the parade."

"I didn't do much," he said absently, searching the crowd for a certain someone.

"Hey, do me a favor and let me know your moving date as soon as you know it. That way I can plan for your absence at the café."

"Moving date?"

She slotted two apple ciders into a cardboard tray. "To Florida. Which part are you moving to, anyway?"

Back to this again. "I'm not moving to Florida. The job's in Portland."

"Oh." She stopped pouring for a second to blink at him. "So you're not moving?"

"Nope."

"Did I know that?"

Oh, he wasn't even going there. "Just give me my apple ciders."

He took them to the gazebo, which was lit in white lights and green garlands. His foot tapped along to "Santa Claus Is Coming To Town," and he waited for the band to

244 | AMY AISLIN

finish before climbing up the stairs and handing out the drinks.

On the path next to the gazebo, a sign with an arrow pointed deeper into the park. *More festivities this way!* Descending the gazebo's stairs, he sat on Holland's bench, the sound of laughter and shouts of surprise reaching his ears. Someone—multiple someones, it seemed—had followed the sign and discovered his secret project. Hopefully they got a kick out of it.

Full night had fallen. Stars flickered in the ebony night sky, and the full moon seemed to smile down at the town. Conversation. Laughter. The scent of hot chocolate and sugar cookies. Kids running in the snow. Teenagers with dogs. Mrs. Doohip's elementary school choir singing "The Holly and the Ivy" to the band's music.

All of it joined together and made his blood sing.

He might've spent most of his life feeling like he didn't belong, but without a doubt, he belonged here in this town. Whether he and Holland worked out as a couple or not, it didn't change the fact that this was home. And the people here would always welcome him.

Zach toyed with the small wrapped gift in his lap. The dancing hippos wearing Santa hats were almost mocking as he waited for Holland to show up. They hadn't agreed on a time, but Holland would never leave him out in the cold for long, which meant he'd probably be here any second.

Should he give Holland the gift? He ran a thumbnail underneath a loose bit of tape, expectation and trepidation somersaulting in his stomach. It was an extremely personal present and would give Holland a look into his innermost self that Zach hadn't ever shown anybody before. This wasn't simply a small trinket with which to woo Holland— it was Zach himself.

"The Holly and The Ivy" came to an end. The choir and the band paused for a moment. Probably taking a second to appreciate the applause from the crowd.

Then a voice started to sing "Have Yourself A Merry Little Christmas." A deep voice. Smooth. Slightly off-key. The band came in after the first line, then the choir joined in, harmonizing perfectly with the lead singer and the music.

Zach stood stiffly, hands clenched around his wrapped gift. Surely his ears must be deceiving him. But no. As he turned slowly toward the gazebo, there stood Holland, on the top step, crooning into a microphone. His eyes never left Zach's.

Zach was breathless. Weightless. His heart soared into the stars. His nose burned, and he pressed his lips together to stem the flow of tears that wanted to escape.

Holland sang to him. It was as though no one else existed. His voice cracked a couple of times, but he never faltered, never hesitated. He held Zach's gaze, and everything he was feeling was right there for Zach to see. It was like the last few days had never happened.

Was there anything more beautiful than listening to someone sing just for you? Being the only person in someone's orbit was exhilarating. Zach felt like he was free falling.

The song ended, Holland's voice trailing off into raucous applause, shrill whistles, and demands for an encore. Holland's grin was endearingly embarrassed. Handing the microphone to the guitarist, he descended the steps of the gazebo.

And headed right for Zach.

Like no one else existed.

He stopped a foot away. "Hey."

"Hi," Zach whispered past his heart, lodged securely in

his throat.

"What do you have there?"

He glanced down and found himself clutching Holland's gift to his chest. "Oh, um…" He glanced around wildly. No one was paying them any attention, the crowd too focused once again on the band, but still. This wasn't something he wanted to give Holland surrounded by an audience.

"Can we walk?" Holland asked.

Relief that Holland understood thundered through him.

They chose the path that led to Zach's secret project, but that was fine. It was the second part of his gift to Holland.

On the far side of the gazebo, Holland led him off the path. Tucked up against the gazebo wall, next to a series of snow-covered bushes, they were out of sight of prying eyes, yet they could see each other by the light of the gazebo's Christmas lights.

"Listen," Holland said. Then, "Wait, where are your gloves?"

"My gloves?"

He'd had them during the parade. Crap. Had he lost Holland's gloves? He vaguely remembered taking them off at headquarters to hand out gift cards. Hopefully they were still there.

Holland tugged his own gloves off. "Here." And slipped them over Zach's hands, making sure Zach's fingers ended up in the correct slots.

Zach swallowed hard. "You know, the first time you did this… I think that's when I fell in love with you."

Holland's hands jerked in Zach's. "Zach." His voice was choked.

"You made me feel like I was worth something."

"Zach, you *are* worth something." Holland's hands, still

warm, cupped Zach's face. "You're worth everything."

Zach sniffled tears back. "Then why did you go away?"

Holland rested their foreheads together. "I got scared."

"Why? What did I do?"

"Nothing." His thumbs ran along Zach's cheeks. "Nothing at all. I'm so sorry I made you feel like it was your fault. Word about your new job in Florida got to me and I freaked out. It was like Mika all over again. But worse."

Zach pulled back to frown at him. "My job where?"

"I want to come with you," Holland said, ignoring Zach's question entirely.

When Zach continued to frown at him, Holland kissed him lightly. It sent tingles up Zach's spine, especially after days of no contact from Holland. But it didn't eliminate the confusion. "Come with me where?"

"To Florida."

"Why are we going to Florida?" The light went on as soon as the words left his mouth. Seriously? He hadn't realized word about his new job had traveled so fast. He should've figured it out after Mrs. Shoemacker mentioned it earlier. Groaning, he buried his face in his hands. "Sometimes I hate this town." He looked up at Holland. "My new job is in Portland. Not Florida. Didn't we talk about this, like, weeks ago?" Although, now everything was starting to make sense. The reason why Holland had pulled away and needed time to think. He'd mentioned weeks ago that he didn't think he could ever do a long-distance relationship again. It must've scared him to think that he'd unknowingly entered into a second one.

Holland grimaced. "Yeah, but I thought maybe you applied for something else you didn't tell me about, or maybe your new boss wanted you in Florida instead."

Anger sparked. Weak, but there. Zach narrowed his

eyes. "And you didn't think to ask me about it?"

"Not at first." Holland sighed and took Zach's hands in his. "At first, I panicked, because I thought I was losing you. But then Mika talked sense into me, and—"

"Mika?"

Holland's chuckle was fond. "Yeah. Mika. I tried tracking you down over the past few days, but—"

"I ignored you," Zach finished for him with a wince.

"It's okay. I deserved it." Holland's smile was wan. "I really am sorry, Zach. For pushing you away. For not talking to you about what I was feeling. I panicked and ran. And I'm sorry."

His words were so soft, so sincere, so full of emotion, a few of Zach's tears escaped. "I'm sorry too. For not answering your calls and texts. I was scared too. That you were calling to tell me it was over."

Holland hauled Zach into his arms, and Zach went without question, burying his cold nose in Holland's neck.

"If I have anything to say about it," Holland rumbled, "this won't be over for a long time. If ever. I love you, Zach."

*Click.* The sound of everything falling into place echoed in Zach's head. Overwhelmed and overjoyed, he smiled at Holland through his tears.

"What's that smile for?"

"I'm happy." He kissed the corner of Holland's mouth. "Really happy."

Holland's eyes flared, and he leaned forward. Zach met him halfway. Their mouths met for a soft, quiet kiss. One that filled every part of Zach's soul and shot him into the sky on a trail of stars.

An electric screech echoed around them, then, "Yoo-hoo! Hello! Can anybody hear me?"

A series of yesses.

"Lovely," said Mrs. Shoemacker. "Gather around, everybody. It's time to announce the winner of the annual Lighthouse Bay Christmas Parade Float Competition."

Zach pulled a resisting Holland along behind him.

"Zach, I don't need—"

But Zach was already pushing his way through to the front of the crowd. "You don't need what?"

"Never mind," Holland said with a quiet chuckle.

Mrs. Shoemacker stood on the top stair of the gazebo, microphone in hand. The band had dispersed, giving her the stage. She gave a quick speech, thanking everyone for their participation in the parade and the fair. And when she called Zach out specifically, he flushed so hard he felt it right down to his toes.

"Now, I'd like to introduce our judges." Mrs. Shoemacker waved them onto the stage.

"Oh my god," Zach groaned. "Get on with it."

Holland nudged him with his shoulder. "Patience."

Zach grumbled while Mrs. Shoemacker introduced the judges. As if everybody didn't know everybody else in this town.

Then, finally, "Without further ado, the winner of this year's competition is…" She handed an envelope to the mayor.

The mayor, still dressed as Santa, took a moment to wave and "Ho ho ho" at some of the kids, before he took his time opening the envelope, then ambled, slowly, up to the microphone stand.

"I'm dying," Zach said quietly. "I'm literally dying while I stand here waiting to find out who the winner is."

Chuckling, Holland swung an arm around his shoulders. "Literally, huh?"

"Good evening, everyone!" The Mayor's deep voice

boomed through the park. "Thank you for coming. Is everyone enjoying the fair?"

A loud cheer rose through the crowd.

"I want to thank our volunteers for setting up the fair last night, and…"

"Oh my god." Zach stared at the sky as the mayor droned on. "Why?"

"What's wrong with you?" Holland asked with a quiet laugh. "You usually have more patience than this."

"I mean, obviously you won. Why can't he just get on with it? He's just repeating everything Mrs. Shoemacker just said."

"And without further delay," Mr. Mayor said, "the winner of this year's competition is…"

"I swear, if he doesn't get to it for real this time, I'm going to bean him with my clipboard," Zach muttered.

Holland turned a laugh into a cough.

The mayor removed a sheet of paper from the envelope. "Holland Stone! For his depiction of Christmas Lane. Holland, come on up here."

Holland had trouble coming on up there given that Zach had enthusiastically plastered himself to Holland's front in a bear hug as he jumped up and down and screeched in Holland's ear. But he made it eventually. Zach hovered off to the side and grinned wildly when calls of "Speech! Speech!" came from the assembled audience.

Holland shook the mayor's hand and accepted a check. The mayor gestured at a handful of people who stood next to the gazebo, some with giant cameras hanging around their necks. Photographers and journalists from the newspapers that would feature Holland and his float.

Holland strode up to the microphone. He cleared his throat. "Uh, hi."

The crowd cheered.

Holland's smile was endearingly shy. "I don't really do speeches, but uh…" He glanced around. Found Zach. Held his hand out to him.

Confused about what Holland was doing, anxious about standing in front of a crowd, Zach nevertheless went. There wasn't much he wouldn't do for Holland.

"Can I also get Mika, Dev, and Clark up here?" Holland said. "I also need Mr. and Mrs. Columbus. Travis O'Flynn. Liam Bryn. Louise Shen." He kept calling people up, and before long a small crowd of people stood behind them, looking just as bewildered as Zach.

Until Zach realized who all of these people were.

"Ladies and gentlemen." Holland spoke directly to the photographers and journalists. "These are the volunteers who helped me with my float. I couldn't have done it without them."

The pleased surprise on everyone's faces brought tears to Zach's eyes. Dev, Clark, and Mika were shaking their heads at Holland, fond smiles on their faces.

"Mr. Mayor." Holland handed him the check. "We'll need that split into about…" He did a quick headcount. "Twenty-seven?"

"That's less than forty dollars each."

Holland shrugged. "Forty dollars is forty dollars."

He got bombarded then, by the journalists, the photographers, the judges, the volunteers who'd helped him rebuild his float. Zach extricated himself from the melee, letting Holland have his moment, watching from a few feet away, marveling at how Holland—beautiful, generous, stable, supportive Holland—had chosen *him* out of everyone he could have.

It took a few minutes, but the crowd finally dispersed

and Holland zeroed in on him. He jerked his head to the side and Zach followed him down the stairs and around the side of the gazebo.

Where Zach pounced on him again. "I'm so happy for you. And what you did…" Too emotional to continue, he held on to Holland and kissed his neck.

"It was only right." Holland's voice rumbled. "This wouldn't have happened without them. Without you. Thank you."

Zach kissed him silly and held on as tight as he could.

Pulling back, Holland kissed Zach's cheek and said, "Want to walk around your fair?"

"It's not my—"

"Zach." Holland kissed him again with a light laugh. "Shut up. Let's walk."

"Wait." Zach held out the gift he was somehow still holding after all that. "I want to give you this first."

The smile that graced Holland's lips was amused. "What's this?"

Zach shuffled on his feet and shrugged. "Just a little something."

"Uh-huh. Then why are you nervous?"

"'M not. Just open it."

Holland did. And threw Zach a quizzical glance. "A day planner? For this year?"

"This is only part one of your gift," Zach hurried to add.

"Okay," Holland said slowly. He turned the day planner around so that Zach could see the cover where the year was written on it. "But it's for this year. Which only has a week and a half left."

"Yeah, no. That's 'cause, uh…" Zach cleared his throat. "This was my day planner. The one I've been using all year." He took it from Holland and flipped through it. "You can ignore most of it, really. It's just appointments and dead-lines and stuff, but this…" He handed it back to Holland, open to December.

And waited.

God, this was *agony*.

"Zach." Barely a whisper from Holland. "Zach, I…"

What part was he at? Zach tried to see but couldn't read his own handwriting upside down.

"This is…" Holland swallowed audibly. "I…"

Zach bit his lip. Blurted, "Is it okay?"

A wet laugh. "Are you kidding?" Holland's index finger circled a date from a couple of Saturdays ago.

Zach knew what it said in the box for that particular day: *The day you made me feel like I belonged.* It was the day he'd had dinner at Holland's with Mika, Dev, and Clark, and he'd felt so included that he'd never wanted to leave. The little day planner's month of December was filled with little notes like that. For Holland. It was always meant for Holland.

*You loaned me your gloves and made me feel safe.*

*Mika came home, and I thought we were over before we began.*

*The day you called it "our" bench.*

*You found me in the snowstorm, like you knew I needed you. Which I did. And do.*

*Your float got ruined and I feel like it's all my fault, even though, intellectually, I know it isn't. I'm sorry.*

*Every time you say my name, it's like I won a million dollars.*

On and on. One for each day of the month starting the day Holland loaned him his gloves.

"Zach," Holland breathed, eyes glassy. His hands shook. "I could never give you anything this special."

"You already did." Zach tapped the left side of Holland's chest. "You gave me this. It's all I've wanted for a long time now."

Holland blew out a broken breath and blinked up at the sky for a second. Then he laughed and kissed Zach's lips. "You're perfect."

Zach scoffed. "Hardly."

Holland closed the day planner gently, almost reverently, and tucked it into the inside pocket of his jacket. Then, as if he couldn't resist, he kissed Zach again. "Thank you."

"You're welcome."

They left their secluded nest next to the gazebo and walked along the path hand in hand. Had anything in Zach's life ever felt more right, more real, than this right here? Walking along a moonlit path in their hometown, white Christmas lights strung around every other tree as the band started a swing rendition of "We Wish You A Merry Christmas." And when it started to snow, Zach paused to grin up at the heavens.

"Hey!" he said as he suddenly remembered. "Want to know what happened today?"

"Something other than your awesome parade and fair?"

"They're not my—"

Holland bumped their shoulders. "Zach."

Zach rolled his eyes. "Whatever. Anyway. Mrs. Shoemacker offered me Mr. Barry's job!"

"She— What?"

"I know." Zach cackled with glee before telling Holland about his conversation with the head of the Lighthouse Bay BIA. "We're going to meet on Monday to talk about it, but… I really want this job, Holland."

"I know you do." Smile wide, Holland brought him in for a hug, right there in the middle of the path.

"Congratulations! You'll be so awesome at it. I'm so happy for you." So happy, in fact, that he picked Zach up and twirled them around, making Zach laugh his head off.

"Next year, the mayor's not allowed in front of a microphone," Zach said, making Holland laugh loudly.

A few minutes later, they crossed over the bridge and onto the other side of the park. Holland sent Zach a questioning look as a couple of people walked past them going in the other direction. "Why do people keep passing us with ice skates?"

"Um…"

"Holy shit!"

Ahead of them was an outdoor ice rink.

"Surprise?" Zach said.

Holland laughed and raced forward, tugging Zach along behind him. "Where did this come from?"

"It was my secret project."

"*This* is what you've been working on?" They stopped on the edge of the ice. Several skaters waved at them.

"Yeah. The volunteer firefighters helped me with it."

"Why, though?" Holland squeezed his hand. "And why not tell me about it?"

"Because this is the second part of your gift. And I wanted it to be a surprise. When we talked about the ice rink the town used to have, you sounded sad that it's something we don't do anymore, so…" Zach shrugged.

"Zach… God, I don't know what to say." He swung an arm around Zach's shoulders. Zach leaned against him. "But you don't like outdoor rinks."

"True. But that was when I was little and everyone would run over me." Zach rested his forehead against Holland's temple. "I don't think you'll let that happen to me."

Holland's arm tightened. "Damn right."

Zach sucked in a breath. "Holland?"

"Mm-hmm?"

"Would you really have moved to Florida with me?"

Holland pulled away to stare into Zach's eyes. "In a heartbeat."

Zach grinned and kissed him lightly. "Merry Christmas, Holland."

"Merry Christmas, Zach."

# ACKNOWLEDGMENTS

First and foremost, thank you to my beta readers Jill, Julia, and Beth for your feedback, to Clare at Meroda UK Editing for helping me whip this baby into shape, and to Posy and Kiki for copyedits and proofreading. Thank you to Jay for the beautiful cover I can't stop looking at, to Tara for the character artwork of Holland and Zach that I love to pieces (which you can find here, along with more bonus content: amyaislin.com/bonus-content/christmas-lane), to Stacey for the lovely interior formatting, and to Judith at A Novel Take PR for making all of my subscription box dreams come true!

# ABOUT THE AUTHOR

Amy started writing on a rainy day in fourth grade when her class was forced to stay inside for recess. Tales of adventures with her classmates quickly morphed into tales of adventures with the characters in her head. Based in the suburbs of Toronto, Amy is a marketer/fundraiser at a large environmental non-profit in Toronto by day, and a writer by night. Book enthusiast, animal lover and (very) amateur photographer, her interests are many and varied, including travelling, astronomy, ecology, and baking. She binge watches too much anime, and loves musical theater, Julie Andrews, the Backstreet Boys, and her hometown of Oakville, Ontario.

Stop by and say hi:

Website:
amyaislin.com

Newsletter
bit.ly/AmyAislinSignUp

Facebook:
www.facebook.com/amy.aislin

Facebook page:
www.facebook.com/AmyAislinAuthor

Facebook group:
www.facebook.com/groups/amyaislin

Twitter:
twitter.com/amy_aislin

Instagram:
www.instagram.com/amyaislin

Pinterest:
www.pinterest.ca/amyaislinauthor

Tumblr:
amyaislin.tumblr.com

Goodreads:
www.goodreads.com/author/show/16693566.Amy_Aislin

QueeRomance Ink:
www.queeromanceink.com/mbm-book-author/amy-aislin

Did you enjoy *Christmas Lane*? Check out Amy Aislin's
other books at amyaislin.com/books.

# TITLES BY
## AMY AISLIN

Made in the USA
Monee, IL
19 September 2023

43035197R00155